Borneo Story

Also by James Albany in Pan Books

Warrior Caste
Mailed Fist
Deacon's Dagger
Close Combat
Marching Fire
Last Bastion

James Albany

Borneo Story

Pan Original
Pan Books London and Sydney

First published 1984 by Pan Books Ltd,
Cavaye Place, London SW10 9PG
9 8 7 6 5 4 3 2 1

ISBN 0 330 28239 5

Photoset by Parker Typesetting Service, Leicester
Printed and bound in Great Britain by
Collins, Glasgow

Do not let go the scent.
Formidable were you from the first;
Hot-foot, hot-foot do you pursue.
If you do not pursue hot-foot,
I will beat you with whips.
If it be a buck, you shall have him for a brother;
If it be a doe, you shall have her for a wife;
If it be my enemy, you shall have his bones.

Hunting-Dog Magic
A Bajau Maruda Charm.

Contents

1 **Marginal man** 9

2 **More teeth in the mouth** 32

3 **Blood hunt** 73

4 **Clouded leopard** 106

5 **Have his bones** 146

1 Marginal man

In the outline of North Borneo no imagination is required to pick out the likeness of a pig. Any old map of the State shows pricked ears, a gaping mouth and lofted snout, the hog's back formed by Sarawak and little Brunei, its chest by Indonesia, known also as Kalimantan. But the head of the beast, in all its glory, is Sabah, East Coast Residency of the former Crown Colony, now an established part of the Federation of Malaysia.

Sabah's nine hundred miles of fretted coastline stretch from the Kudat Peninsula to Cowie Harbour and, cross-border, peter out in stinking swamps which creep away from the big islands of Sebatik and Nunukan Timor. The Sulu Sea shimmers pansy-blue and peaceful offshore while north of the confluence of a hundred rivers that stain the piles of Tawau, the great broad sea-acres of Sibuko or St Lucia Bay gird and protect a chain of tiny islands, home for many a Bajau fisherman and the traditional haunt of gun-runners, pirates and murderers.

Inland from Cowie Harbour lurks the timber town of Kalabakan, remote enough, God knows, and perilously close to the claret-coloured line which artificially divided Sabah from the Indonesian dictatorship of 'Mad Doctor' Sukarno, a gentleman who objected to Federation in any form and wanted to rule Malaysia by himself. Remoter still, attached like a leech to the veins of the Jaumpong River, lies another lumber camp, Balimbuka, out of which the managers of the St Lucia Trading Company float rafts of hardwood to dismember and sell in the markets of the world in small but profitable enterprise. Above the maidenhair of the Jaumpong's Barrier Falls was a place called Gentangan. It no longer exists.

The name didn't mean much in the first place as there was nothing to distinguish the spot from the surrounding tropical wilderness. But at Gentangan, in the early months of 1964, twelve officers and men of 'K' Squadron, Special Air Service, supported by four Gurkhas and a couple of native trackers, established a jungle outpost.

From the *bashas* of Gentangan, four-man patrols were slipped into the green stuff to extract information on the disposition and movements of subversives in the area and thus protect the Iban axemen and Filipino toppers at Balimbuka from surprise attack by Sukarno's guerrillas. Far south of the outpost, however, over the frontier, and, it seemed, out of reach of radio, was the richest single source of military intelligence in Borneo; a scout, a spy, an observer knitted into the very fabric of that primitive land, SAS lance-corporal Barry Greenwood, a subject, in equal measure, of admiration, derision and concern.

Trailing the Armalite by its carrying handle and with the case roped to his shoulders, Barry 'Doc' Greenwood ducked under the shoots of a young bamboo and lowered himself to his belly on a ramp of moss and fern mush.

He had quit the primary jungle an hour ago and the going through the *belukar*, cleared land which had reverted to forest, had been slow. He had left a trail a mile wide but, in the proximity of the river villages, he wasn't too bothered. The Indos weren't magicians. They couldn't separate a white man from a Bajau just by the fall of a leaf or a tear in a banana palm. Footprints were another matter. But half the bleedin' population in this neck of the woods were shod in the same cheap canvas Taiwanese boots as he wore. And he had developed a shuffle which effectively blurred precise identification. If any of the Indo units in the area did happen to have a whizz-kid in their ranks, then it was just hard cheese. Sometimes it was necessary to swop stealth for speed and this was one such occasion.

Lance-corporal Barry Greenwood was no Harley Street physician. 'Doc' was a nickname doled out by the boys in 'K' Squadron after Barry's return from an intensive twelve-week course in Field Medicine at Fort Mapp, near San Francisco, in the good old USA. The nickname was appropriate, however. In the past year young Barry had become expert in certain tropical diseases, to the point where even Doc Tyler, resident MO in South Sabah, had been known to invite his opinion. Greenwood's knowledge had been acquired by practical experience coupled with extensive reading. He thought of himself sometimes like one of those guys in prison on a long stretch who became world authorities on criminal law; because they had time, patience and opportunity. Prisoner of the jungle and of the uniform – what was left of it – young Doc Greenwood had given himself over to a vocation which had initially been wished upon him but which had soon burgeoned into a passion.

It was the passion bit that unsettled his mates. He just couldn't hide it any more. He had been ribbed at first, then quietly reminded that his loyalty was to the 22 SAS, not to a bunch of indigenous natives or even to his personal version of the Hippocratic Oath. There was more to it, of course. There was the fact that he had joined the regiment from a clerking job in the RAMC and had survived training and selection as one sort of soldier but, thanks to his sojourn in Fort Mapp, had been transformed into another.

He should have kept his gob shut about the crowd he got in with in San Francisco, about Barbara Badillo and her brother Tom, and the friends he went back to visit on his furloughs instead of going home to his old man's fish-and-chipper in Scarborough.

It was his application for leave – San Francisco? – that had put the kibosh on his future as a fighting soldier in the SAS, that had brought into question his worth to the regiment.

How could he explain that he plain liked the Californian kids, felt an affinity with them – he was, after all, only twenty-four – though they slagged him rotten about his profession and got angry at his outspoken defence of the ethics of being part of a 'peace-keeping' force, an élite? He swallowed their sweet wine and their poetry, puffed a little grass, made hard love to their chubby blonde birds, and he learned to think a little about God and politics. But in his gut he knew that his efficiency had not been impaired by contact with the American hipster fraternity. Even so, he had this sneaky suspicion that when he wended his way back to Gentagan he would find himself ordered back to Hereford on a Return-to-Unit ticket, which was the worst that could happen to a guy who fought with the world's toughest outfit.

It was to avoid that possible fate that Lance-corporal Barry Greenwood kept himself out of reach and worked like a beaver to supply the kind of information that could only be dredge up by a nut or a hero. He accumulated screeds of data on Indo bases, supply routes and weaponry, doing the work in payment for the freedom to practise his own brand of medicine.

Eleven weeks since he'd last seen a British uniform. Plenty of Indo Tiger flashes had been glimpsed through the leaves, but not a cherry beret or a Winged Dagger in all that time. He had even abandoned the radio. It had gone *phut* on him and he hadn't had the skill needed to repair it, though there were those in the unit who could have got it going again with Elastoplast and a whisker pulled from a civet-cat. He was better without the radio. He had more than enough to carry, what with the Armalite and the bergen and the saxophone case.

Anyhow, without the radio the major at Gentangan couldn't order him in. He could always pretend that the missives he received in reply to his letters, carried by trusted native bearers – David Livingstone lives, man – had gone adrift. So far, though, the letters from Major Dalinart had been not at all chiding, merely asked for more information. They were coded, of course, in the simplest of number/letter codes, which Doc could translate now without the use of a book. Major Dalinart also sent in the supplies he asked for, mainly ether, cotton swabs and streptomycin, plus some other esoteric items which took a shade longer to reach him. Major Dalinart never enquired about the radio or invited him home, though he soon found out that his postmen were quizzed on his whereabouts and state of health.

'What did you tell them, my friends?' he would ask, speaking in a Bajau Maruda dialect which, oddly, bore a strong resemblance to high court Malay.

'Tell everyone you are "one hundred percentage" A-okay, boss.'

'And when they asked where I was?'

'Tell everyone you are safe with the Maruda.'

'Great stuff, man.' The Doc would clap a fraternal hand on

the Bajau runner's shoulder to confirm his pleasure in their kinship as deceivers of soldiers everywhere.

Lance-corporal Greenwood was careful never to send one of his girls back to base. He wasn't sure that would go down too well, though he had the best-looking bunch of runners in South East Asia at his disposal; dainty, doe-eyed native girls who thought he was Mr Wonderful and would do anything for him. But he didn't go hog-wild or take mean advantage of his status among the peoples of the river delta. He treated the girls with respect and affection. He was not the first white man – *orang puti* – that the village-dwellers had encountered, not by a long chalk. He wasn't even some big, bear-sized monster. In fact, he had shed so much weight in the last six months, existing on a low calorie diet, that he was pretty puny compared to some of the bucks of the Bajau Maruda.

Unlike the Simporna Bajaus, the folk of the swamp fringes were not Mohammedans. They had settled in the area thirty years ago under the influence of a hellfire Welsh Baptist missionary. The effectiveness of Dai Bach's teaching had not been lasting, and any Christian belief that remained was tainted with local superstition. In appearance and behaviour, though, the sub-tribe of the Maruda were true-blue Bajaus, blood kin to the sea-gypsies of the coast, excellent swimmers and handlers of small craft, splendid horsemen – and lazy as sin. The men were well muscled and handsome, with bright, alert eyes and close-cropped hair. The women were small-boned, honey-coloured, graceful and good-humoured but with that tiny streak of slyness in them which was the special mark of the Bajau. Perfect material for an SAS man to mould into a network of spies.

Another factor that inhibited the Doc from indulging his sexual appetites in variety was Mouse – birthname Nakalikki – who was not only possessive but had become so valuable that he didn't wish to run the risk of insulting her by playing around. Even when she wasn't dogging his tracks or clinging to his hand like a child she seemed to be with him. Spirit of the jungle, like Rima, so sensual and so trusting that he had an illogical awe of her and was bound by emotions that he did not care to define. Sometimes, when she sang the long *pantun* in a high nasal drone, he wondered if she had him under a spell. Spell or not, she was his Girl Friday, guide and interpreter, cook as well as lover, and could do a great barrack-room lawyer routine when it came to bargaining for food and information with the pot-bellied elders – *mattoa* – of the *ba'anans*.

It was one such pot-bellied elder who had sent the message that brought Greenwood and the Mouse out of cover in the freckled hills above the basin of the Seven Rivers that roughly defined the territory of the Bajau Maruda. The tribe didn't own the land, of course, merely settled it, clinging precariously to mud shoals and cultivating wet rice in the *paddi* where swamps seeped in from the sea twelve or fourteen miles distant. Greenwood and the Mouse had been 'working', laid up in a leaf-screen shelter above one of the few 'bridle-paths' that wended across the comparatively dry ground.

In the course of the last month the Indos had been hauling some fairly impressive hardware along the jungle path, including a couple of pack howitzers. Stripped down and wrapped in oiled burlap to prevent rusting, the guns were toted piecemeal by a gang of grim and sweating Indonesian marines, the muzzles dragged on buffalo sleds. The buffalos were recalcitrant and gave the Indos one heck of a time, being more trouble than they were probably worth. It had taken a whole day for the caravan to wend past Greenwood's observation post and across the low ridge between the Tabuli and Mamisi rivers which, with a lift in the contour, were pretty vigorous here.

Howitzers, plus GPMGs and mortars, seemed heavy stuff for a border post. There were also a couple of platoons of IBT regulars who weren't doing any carrying, except for field packs. They went through like a dose of salts. Greenwood was intrigued. He was puzzled as to where the IBTs could be taking the weapons. He studied his maps, reminding himself that he was far into Indonesia, in the enemy's back yard. All he could suppose was that the caravan would turn west and head up the valley of the Ruasi. If the Indo high command believed, rightly or wrongly, that British forces were pushing hard along the frontier between Sarawak, Sabah and Kalimantan, then they might be preparing a welcome east of Labang. But ferrying supplies inland from the east coast was one heck of a haul.

Greenwood had sent Mouse down to one of the villages to find Leiman, a Javanese who had become Greenwood's Number One runner and spoke excellent English. Mouse was back in two days with Leiman in tow.

Leiman was small, middle-aged, energetic, with a broad nose and a shark-tooth necklace which hung round his neck over his crucifix. He wore an Arrow cheesecloth shirt and Fred Perry tennis shorts, relics of his days as a kitchen boy in the Two Brothers Inn at Denpasar on the beautiful Isle of Bali. He listened to Greenwood's harangue, scanned the coded letter which the lance-corporal had composed and asked, 'How much?'

'Tell the major, two dollars.'

'Three days, five dollars.'

'Get knotted!'

'Five dollars.' Leiman grinned wickedly. He loved putting one over on the young soldier who was embarrassed by talk of money. 'Five dollars, I tell you where they go, the Indo Tigers.'

'You've got your five.' Greenwood retrieved the letter and scribbled in pencil across the foot of the third page; the agreed fee for safe delivery which Major Dalinart would shell out without a murmur. 'Where are they going, man?'

'Tangkan.'

'No swallow,' said Greenwood.

'It is the truth, *tuan*.'

'How do you know?'

'I have ears to hear, *tuan*. Leiman is never telling lies.'

The Javanese might be a con-artist but he was not given to passing duff information. So far. Yet Tangkan was on the upper Jaumpong, practically on the edge of the St Lucia Trading Company's timber concession. Pack howitzers had a range of six miles if they could get elevation over the trees, which was doubtful. If Leiman was right, old Jock McCartney, long-time manager of the Balimbuka timber town, would find some extra bunkers on his rough-and-ready three-hole golf course.

'Not telling lies,' said Leiman again. 'Guns stop in jungle. Some soldiers go to dig pits at Tangkan.'

'I believe you,' said Greenwood.

He licked the pencil and scribbled furiously on the yellowing, dampish paper, pads of which lined the saxophone case and were almost as precious as medicine.

'Do you think I should slog over there and take a look, Leiman?'

The Javanese shook his head. 'Stay here. Let major do it with a aeroplane.'

If the bleedin' IBT *were* digging big fortifications at Tangkan then the boys in the outpost at Gentangan would be closer than he was, better placed to shimmy over and make a recce. Maybe they knew about it already. Maybe not, though, since you could just about test an atom bomb in deep jungle without detection.

Leiman rolled away into the forest as casually as an old *boulevardier*, the letter tucked into the pocket of his tennis shorts.

Greenwood spent the rest of that afternoon brooding, reclining against a log in the hide over the bridle-path which was so quiet now, so unoccupied, that you could almost see the *belukar* consuming it. Mouse cuddled against him like a cat, perplexed by his silence and his lack of interest in *humpi-humpi*.

The following morning, pissed off with his vigil, Greenwood baled out to make a series of 'house calls' in not-too-distant river communes. He was back in the hide, however, within four days. He examined the bridle-path, found no fresh tracks and settled once more, with Mouse, into the leaf-covered *basha* in the trees.

The following afternoon a team of eight coolies and four IBT soldiers trudged up th track in teeming rain, carrying supplies. Dutifully, Greenwood made note of the number and the nature of the stores, as best as he could. So far, nobody had come back by this route; one-way traffice only.

Two days later, late in the evening, Leiman reappeared. The Javanese gave a pre-arranged bird-call signal so that Greenwood wouldn't put a bullet through his kneecap, then slipped into the *basha* where, crouched over a tiny Metabrix cooker, the Mouse was warming rice and a beef cube in a pan of rain water and Doc Greenwood was dusting his feet with an anti-fungicide powder; a sweet domestic scene in Tarzan territory.

Leiman handed over a neatly-wrapped package of medical supplies and a brown manilla envelope which contained Major Dalinart's reply to Greenwood's intelligence.

The letter said: *Leave this end to us. Can you find out where they are coming from*?

Holy Moses, Greenwood thought, aren't they ever satisfied?

Little tracks and paths linked and crossed all across the delta. The region south of the Tabuli river was infested with Indo soldiers. It might be wise to ignore the major's order. Greenwood couldn't see what use the info would be to the SAS unless they planned a counter-attack on the port of entry for the big armaments. And pack howitzers weren't *that* big, after all. Perhaps the major wanted him to find out the reason for the movement of troops and weapons. The reason lay along the Tabuli river, where he had as yet no contacts.

By dawn's early light, what there was of it seeping through blue-black rain clouds, Lance-corporal Greenwood and his native helpers closed up the observation post, scattering the *basha* and carefully eliminating all traces of their presence.

Still with Leiman and Mouse in tow, Greenwood headed down into Seven Rivers country, making for the Bajau Maruda village of Mandelaut, which was an abasement of the phrase *sama mandelaut*, which meant 'sea people'. The bunch who lived at Mandelaut were anything but sea people, though they called themselves by that august name because it sounded better than 'swamp creatures', which is what they were. At Mandelaut, though, the Doc was known and would be made welcome. And Mandelaut was only a hop-step from the Tabuli down whose greeny-brown waters, sooner or later, he and the Mouse must venture.

Mandelaut was thirty miles over the claret, across the Indonesian border. The Tabuli river was six or seven miles further south again. Even in the pilehouses of Mandelaut the Doc did not feel too secure, though the people were entirely trustworthy and wouldn't shop him to the enemy.

One time, however, he had been caught at Mandelaut by a

through-troop of Indo Border Terrorists – IBTs – who had stopped to barter for sago, fruit and dried fish, and had stayed overnight. Doc had lain under the floor of the community's only land-built dwelling, the granary, along with rats and shrews and fleas, learning about the ecosystem and the origins of epidemic fevers right at the root, you might say. Mouse had hung around with the village women, keeping her eyes and ears open. But the troop hadn't been anything more exciting than a roving patrol which had lost its way. At that stage in the confrontation – read 'war' – Sukarno's policy didn't include much terrorism, if any. Soldiers didn't rampage through the villages, raping, looting and burning. They were an army, much like any other army, trained and bored, obedient, often scared and usually full of complaints. The Indo troops left Mandelaut without discovering Greenwood. Even so, the incident had brought home to the Doc just how far he was from aid. Gentangan might be the far side of the moon, instead of the far side of the border, just thirty-five miles away.

Borneo was like that. Foot-slogging through jungle and swamp was a slow business. Ten miles in any given day was good going, even for an experienced runner like Leiman. You could speed down the rivers, of course, in a canoe or on a raft, but that wasn't to be recommended. The rivers were too exposed; you could be picked off by riflemen hidden on the banks, and never know what hit you.

But the Doc had work to do at Mandelaut, for sickness and disease were rife there like everywhere else in the soddin' jungle; spruce, trachoma, yaws, jigger rash and assorted fevers, hookworm, chronic ulcers and, now and again, cases of malignant tertian malaria, the most serious form, which was a bitch to treat due to the complications that could arise during primary attack or stages of relapse. In addition there were all the other ills that natives were just as prone to as less-exposed mortals; fractures and belly-ache, the discomforts of pregnancy, accidental wounds and injuries, plus the odd snake-bite. Doc Greenwood treated them all as best he could. When his medical skill would not rise to the occasion or he ran out of proper drugs, he did what he could with morphine or bismuth or chloroquine and steered clear of that patient for some time until the guy or girl either died or recovered. Not awfully honourable for a medic but practical in a situation over which he had little control and in an environment where the goodwill of the native population was essential to his survival.

Lance-corporal Greenwood shrugged nobody off and never openly admitted inadequacy. To do so would have tarnished his image. When he 'lost' a patient – and he lost quite a few – the Bajau Maruda did not hold it against him. They were a cheerful bunch of fatalists and regarded life itself as one huge gamble. In fact, some of the men had the nasty habit of wagering on the outcome of the White Doktor's treatments. They would hang around the door of the hut where the patient lay, like punters at a corner bookie's, waiting for the results to come through. They would bet on anything, the Bajau Maruda. The first enterprising Britisher to open a touring bingo show in the hinterland would really clean up.

Doc Greenwood was no gambler, not in that sense. Yet he laid it on the line day and daily, taking risks against odds that no pony-player would consider acceptable. It *was* a gamble. You bet that you wouldn't step into a pit, trip over a booby-wire, walk into crossfire, catch a fatal disease, drown in a river crossing, find an ultra-poisonous krait drowsing in your blankets, run into a bull buffalo on a narrow track or a wild boar in the undergrowth or a croc in the mangrove swamp. It was a far cry from dog-shit on Marine Drive and 'Kiss-Me-Quick' trippers and the odour of frying haddock and the dank, winter haar lying over Scarborough's West Bay day after day until you began to wonder if the world had gone away. On the whole, Barry Greenwood preferred the jungle.

He wondered what Barbara and Tom Badillo would make of it, if their Californian Zen-chants and reverence for the Noble Savage would stand up to reality.

He had one Zen-chant, a catch-phrase really, that he repeated to himself when the going got rough.

'Go with the flow, man,' he would mutter, to ginger up his courage. 'Just go with the flow.'

'The flow' took him and moved him along like a leaf on the river, sometimes fast and sometimes slow. He did what he had to do as soldier, medic and man. He might have gone on doing it until his string ran out if it hadn't been for the message from the tiny, scrofulous river village of Palan, ten miles south on the Tabuli, where he had never been before, further than he really wanted to go.

The message was waiting for him when he arrived at Mandelaut with Leiman and the Mouse. It had been brought in by a family who had gone back again at once. But the message, relayed by one of the house founders of the larger *luma* that made up the *ba'anan* of Mandelaut, was urgent and, said the elder, should be obeyed.

It was clear that the folk of Mandelaut expected Doc to obey it. There was every reason why he should. The children of Palan were sick. Only the White Doktor could save them. So Greenwood completed his 'clinic' at Mandelaut, re-packed the saxophone case and, leaving Leiman behind, let the Mouse lead him into pastures new.

As he slogged through the mud-rooted trees of primary forest that licked at the edges of the swamp, at the back of his mind was the thought that the flow had caught him up again. Back in the camp at Gentangan, Major Dalinart would assume that he was being daring and brave, sticking his neck out to obtain vital information. All he was doing, really, was following the dictates of his own peculiar code, the habits of the healer which deprived him of personal volition and might lure him anywhere, any time.

At length, after a full day's trek, trailing the Armalite and with the oblong saxophone case weighing like the burden of sin on his shoulders, Doc slid on to his belly on the hummock of green ground that overlooked the Tabuli.

The pilehouses of Palan were flat against the jungle like a jerry-built movie set, a façade without substance or depth.

Mouse put a thin arm around him and hugged herself against his thigh.

He glanced at her questioningly.

She was staring at the village. On her smooth, honey-coloured brow was a shadowy frown of concern. Did she feel it too, the weird, pervasive sensation that there was something evil down there?

Not even anything as rational as instinct, just a little quailing of the soul, gripped Doc for a moment. There was nothing to account for it in the panorama of river, trees and huts. The Doc had survived some damned hard knocks, had seen many unpleasant things and death in umpteen guises but he had no knowledge of evil as such, evil as pure as fire.

After a long pause, he nudged the girl and motioned towards the empty canoe that was moored to a post against the north bank, waiting for them.

Mouse slithered forward. Barry Greenwood followed her, unaware that from that instant he was doomed and that life, what was left of it, would never be the same again for the wandering son of a fish-fryer from Harbour Street, Scarborough.

Only the Bajau could have cooked up the deception. Only an old devil like Usop, headman of Palan, could have pulled it off with such lack of scruple.

Usop came down the bamboo steps to greet the White Soldier Doktor. Usop was darker than the average Bajau Maruda, smaller too, though age perhaps had shrunk his bones. Doc wasn't well enough versed in anthropology to read the symbols of the headman's regalia; a loose shirt of flaming scarlet with gold embroidery at breast, throat and cuffs, a spotless snow-white sarong, and a hornbill hat held on with a saffron scarf. Silver dollars ornaments glittered on Usop's cummerbund, and loops of gold wire thickened his throat. In the cummerbund was an unsheathed *kris*, the wavy-bladed dagger used for purposes nice and nasty throughout Malaysia. The little chieftain would have been pretty dignified and grand if it hadn't been for the crutch, a crude implement of green mangrove.

Settling the crutch under his armpit, the headman managed a bow of sorts. Other villagers, mostly old men and young women, bowed too. Nobody smiled. Not one of the nubile river-girls giggled as Barry Greenwood hauled himself out of the canoe and, trying to hoist up the sax case, performed a marvellous pratfall in the mud. Mouse helped him to his feet, dusted him down and took the sax case on her own shoulders, leaving the Doc with the bergen and the rifle. He walked forward along the bamboo quay, very upright.

Bamboo was everywhere. Bamboo and more bleedin' bamboo. On to scaffolds of bamboo, walls and roofs of palm-thatch, grass-thatch and rice-stalk screens were fastened. One big puff of wind and there would be nothing left of Palan; it would blow away like froth. But Greenwood knew this to be a false impression. The structures of the village would yield to tempest and typhoon, bend and bow and whip about, but never break. Flood too, up to a certain limit, would do not more than float the floors of the dwellings. Only fire was a hazard.

Bone-weary after the trek, the Doc wasted as little time as possible on formalities. He introduced himself through Mouse and spoke through her until he got the hang of Usop's patois and tried out Malay upon the chieftain. Greenwood spoke the dialects well. It was clear that Usop's ladies were impressed, even if the headman gave no sign of surprise at the White Doktor's accomplishment.

In the trees that soared above the village, monkeys chattered and insects roared. The river was not as narrow or rough as Greenwood had supposed it would be. It was broad and smooth and the depth to which the villagers had placed their fishing poles suggested that it was not particularly prone to flash floods, like many of the little rivers which were fed from the hills. Was it possible that this was the 'port' through which the IBT brought their guns into the hinterland, ferrying them by fishing-boat from the sea?

The dwellings were typical of a river commune, built from the line of the river into the forest, each with its own platform, each set high on bamboo piles. A haze of smoke hung thick in the moist atmosphere and the oily mud of the walks hinted that there had been rain here too, though the river was so far untroubled.

Usop ushered his guest towards the ramp – bamboo poles, of course – that led up to the huts. There was a smell of cooking meat in the air but Greenwood had no appetite and the savoury odour did not attract him. He was still dogged by an oppressive sense of unease.

'Where are the children who are sick?' he asked, speaking loudly and with authority.

Usop swung his body on the crutch and squinted at the medic. 'We have many sick.'

'Your message said there were children who needed my help.'

'There are children.'

'Where?'

Usop jerked his head. 'There.'

In English, low-toned, Greenwood said one word to Mouse. 'Trap?'

The girl put down the saxophone case and rested on it, her elbows bent like wings. She too looked fatigued and travel-stained. Her plaid sarong was soiled with mud and her hair had come unravelled from its topknot, loosed from the bone combs. Spots of colour glowed on her cheekbones. Greenwood hoped to God she wasn't coming down with a fever, not here, not now.

She scowled at the platform that hung at the door of the *luma*. As if to bait the trap, there *was* a child there, a boy of three or four. He wore a tiny loincloth and a vest made out of cotton. He had the arch, sulky look of all spoiled males. He also looked decidedly healthy.

'What do you think, kiddo?' Greenwood muttered, changing his grip on the Armalite from handle to stock.

'Children. Children. See. See,' put in the headman.

It was an hour before dark. Shadows engulfed the dwellings. The doorway beyond the little boy was deep, deep brown with just the faintest wisp of smoke drifting from it. The monkeys were very excited and a barbet was hammering away at a tree while a hawk owl, wakened by the din, screamed mercilessly.

'Tiger soldiers here also,' said Mouse in a shrill accusing tone.

Usop puffed out his wrinkled cheeks and dipped the hornbill hat in resignation. He lied without conviction. 'No, no, no Tiger soldiers. Not today. No Tiger soldiers.'

But Mouse was not easily persuaded.

Raising her voice, she shouted. 'Tiger soldiers.'

The women broke for cover, chattering. The elders followed them. Four young bucks, in loincloths, appeared as if by magic from under one of the huts. They had each a sharpened fishing spear and a knife. Greenwood dropped the bergen where he stood and hoisted the Armalite into his hands, spreading his legs.

Usop drove his armpit into the crutch and flung up his right hand. He barked out a command which Doc didn't understand and the four young males let their spears fall. White flag time, Doc thought, though he didn't lower the Armalite so much as an inch. Mouse had taken three paces towards the chieftain. She was haranguing him like crazy, giving him the sharp edge of her remarkably sharp little tongue.

Holy Moses! Greenwood thought, if the huts *are* swarming with Indo guerrillas, then poor Mouse will die nagging.

Usop had to bellow to stop the girl's furious speech.

'One soldier. One Tiger soldier. Sick soldier. No children. One soldier. Sick,' Usop confessed at the pitch of his voice. 'Not shoot anybody. Too sick.'

'Where is he?' Doc said.

'In my house.'

'Just one?' Doc held up his index finger.

'To the Lord Jesus, I swear,' said old Usop.

'Okay,' said the Doc. 'Let's go take a look at him.'

He believed the chieftain of Palan. A ruse had been necessary to lure him this far into enemy territory to treat a wounded Indo. Treating the enemy wasn't his bag, though he had patched up an occasional prisoner before the poor bastard was shipped out to the internment camp in Brunei for interrogation and trial. If he had been asked to brave the jungle to attend a Tiger soldier, he would, out of duty and common sense, have refused. But now he was here . . .

'White Doktor is good,' said Usop, swinging on to his crutch once more as the woman and the elders returned.

'White Doctor is a bleedin' idiot,' said Barry Greenwood.

He was a shade put out when Mouse agreed with him.

The moment Greenwood clapped eyes on the soldier he knew that the man posed no threat. No doubt he was a regular IBT. The boots, never mind the uniform, were a dead giveaway, with soles of ribbed black rubber and diamond-shaped ankle protectors. His tape-puttees had been untied. His trouser leg had been torn to accommodate a swollen thigh. He still wore a bush shirt, neatly buttoned, and an old-fashioned webbing belt. Behind the bed, propped against the wall, were a jungle cap, a steel helmet and a standard M.14 rifle. The weapon was larger than anything used by Allied troops and, in theory, easier to keep clean.

Mouse planted the saxophone case on the floor and sprung the twist-turn padlocks. She lifted the lid and took out a pencil torch. The supply of batteries were kept in an oilskin pouch. She unrolled a couple and deftly fitted them into the barrel of the torch. She had worked so often with the Doc that she performed the tasks out of habit. She handed him the pencil torch with a little slap, like a theatre-nurse.

Usop and the women gathered by the doorway. This was no long-house, though its almost square interior gave shelter to probably four or five families. Greenwood paid no heed to his surroundings. If there were other IBTs in the rafters or hidden by the rattan screens he didn't want to know. He had been taken over by his obsession, by medical curiosity. His concentration was as narrow and intense as the beam of the pencil torch.

Above the bed – really just a mat and a folded-mat pillow – dangled an *anchak*. Woven out of strips of dried leaf and suspended on vines, the sacrificial tray would contain grains of rice and a piece of rotting fish, a chicken's foot, perhaps. He, Doc Greenwood, hadn't been the first medical practitioner to minister to the ailing terrorist. A *pawang*, a witch-doctor or medicine-man, had done his funny number already. The mumbo jumbo was usually harmless. Greenwood had even heard of a few cases where the old 'mental magic' seemed to be beneficial.

'How long has he been here?' Greenwood asked, speaking Malay.

One of the women answered. 'He was left three nights ago.'

'Who left him?'

The woman was not so young as the others and her breasts were uncovered. She had begun to show wrinkles about her eyes which, in this country where females aged with appalling rapidity, put her at twenty-five or six.

'His people,' she said.

'Who are his people?'

'Soldiers.'

'Tiger soldiers?'

'It is so.'

Doc Greenwood still hadn't touched his patient. He sat back on his heels contemplating the Indo soldier. It looked almost as if he was praying. In fact, he was systematically absorbing every shred of visible evidence. The soldier lay on his back, absolutely motionless, though conscious. His dark, slitted eyes never left Greenwood's face. Globules of sweat beaded his hairline, his shirt dark with it.

Doc Greenwood held the torch in finger and thumb, switching it on and off absently.

He said, 'How many Tiger soldiers came this way with him?'

There was no guile in the villagers.

Usop replied, 'Twenty soldiers.'

'How did they come? By the river, in boats?'

'No. On feet.' Usop again.

'Where are they now?'

'Towards the mountains.'

'Up river?'

Usop grunted. There were only two directions as far as the tribe was concerned – towards the sea and towards the mountains. It was quite possible that Usop had never laid eyes on either sea or mountains. Whatever – the Indos were moving men, possibly arms, further up river. He would go take a swatch tomorrow. He wondered if it would be worth the risk of borrowing a canoe. He had done it before, stripping, putting on a loincloth, covering the Armalite and the medical case with leaves. At a distance, he could pass muster as a Murut or a Kelabit, especially with Mouse in the bow, her breasts bare like a figurehead. Already he had gathered enough information to interest the boss. He would fill blanks on the maps with tracks and crossing-points and all the other useful details that might one day be needed if and when policy carried the war into Indonesia.

'Did they stay here? Did they take food?'

'No, they did not take food.'

'Are they coming back for this man?'

'They say he will die. It is better if he die at his home place.'

Doc glanced round. 'His home place? Is he from this village?'

'He is the son of my brother's son. He was born in Palan.'

Family ties were strong in Borneo. Choice, though, was a basic aspect of the social system. The guy lying on the mat in sweat and pain might have elected to travel, to seek other associations, but he was linked to this God-forsaken spot in the jungle by ties as strong as steel. God knows what sort of luck had brought him back here, to die here. Only the guy wasn't going to die. Whatever was wrong with him – and Greenwood hadn't quite decided yet – it didn't appear to be fatal.

'Open your mouth,' Doc said, speaking Malay.

The patient would have none of it. He was apprehensive, which was also a sign that confirmed Doc's theory. Doc repeated the order. Still the Tiger soldier would have none of it. He quailed when Greenwood put out his hand and tried to clasp his jaw. Perhaps it was fear of the enemy and not a condition of the disease that made the guy afraid.

When the patient did open his mouth, it was to snarl weakly, 'Go away. Go away. I am dying. Leave me to die.'

'He says that he is dying,' put in Usop.

'He is not dying,' said Mouse.

'Hold him, kiddo,' Doc said.

The girl was too quick for the sick Indo. She had him by the shoulders before he could change position. She locked a slender forearm about his throat and pinched his nose. Not exactly recommended procedure for nurses. But effective.

The Indo opened his mouth.

Doc shone the torch into the cavity. The guy's breath smelled of rotten fish. But there were no spots on the back of his throat or on his palate. His tongue was like dried red leather, indicating a mild general toxaemia. Doc didn't bother to take a temperature. Free sweating was obvious. He asked the Indo where the pain was. The soldier waved one hand in the direction of his abdomen and thighs. With a razor-sharp penknife Greenwood slit the trouser leg over the swollen thigh still more. The patient jerked.

Usop and the spectators gasped, imagining perhaps that the White Doktor had cut flesh. Doc ignored the audience. He peeled away the sodden clothing, making another cut across the fly. The soldier wore dirty grey underpants which smelled worse than his breath. Most of the Bajau Maruda tribes were very clean, bathed a lot, but the Indo trooper had probably been on the jungle trail for weeks.

'Water. Boiling hot water,' said Greenwood.

Lest the command be misunderstood, Mouse translated it. Usop waved to one of the crowd in the doorway.

Glancing up, Greenwood saw that five or six kids had weaselled into the dwelling and stood in a mute half-circle by the far wall, watching him, round-eyed. He realised that there was no epidemic here, no sick kids. He had been hauled into enemy territory solely to treat this trooper. Hell's Bells! What sort of army was Sukarno running when there wasn't a medic experienced enough to diagnose and deal with a straightforward tropical myositis? Big deal medical treatment was unnecessary. A shot of any antibiotic plus hot fomentations and bed-rest would cure the complaint. Doc wondered if the guy had been dumped or had deserted.

Though sure of his ground, Greenwood conducted a standard diagnostic survey. Gently he probed the affected parts with his fingertips. Light pressure made the Indo flinch and cry out. Local pain was obviously severe. Greenwood held the torch in his mouth and directed it at the limb.

Diffuse swelling, tender in the extreme, a tense woody feel. Yep, he had it now. The lesions were in the anterior muscles of the thigh, the abscess deep in the group of three muscles around the femur. The lesions had probably been developing for weeks before the guy got worried about the pain. Latterly, though, deterioration would be rapid. There might be some pus formation but not enough to tempt Greenwood to use the knife. Surgical intervention was something that should be avoided in the treatment of tropical abscesses. There was no established cause for myositis. Most likely the guy had acquired it through secondary infection, from an untreated wound or after a bout of malaria.

'Mouse, let him go.'

The girl released her grip on the soldier, who sank, groaning, to the bed and covered his face with his arms.

'I die. I die. I die.'

'Oh, no, you won't, Sunny Jim.'

Hanging on to the crutch, Usop peered with interest at the White Doktor.

'He will die?' the chieftain asked.

'He will live for ever,' said Lance-corporal Greenwood confidently.

Doc did all that was necessary to aid the ailing Tiger. He broke an ampoule of Penicillin G and administered it by local injection. Slow release and a relatively low concentration were just right for the condition. He dished out tablets of Streptotriad, a polycrest of sulphonamides and streptomycin, with strict instructions that only one per day was to be given. He bathed the limb in hot water, dressed and splinted it. He checked that the Indo had a beaker of fresh water to hand, and that the women who would be looking after him knew what they were doing. All that worried him, as a medic, was possible adverse reaction to one of the drugs. He had a horror of sending some poor hypersensitive native into fatal anaphylactic shock. The Big White Soldier Doktor's credibility would hit the deck like cow flop if that ever happened. Even the Bajau weren't *that* stoical.

Treatment complete, Usop saw to it that the hospitality of Palan was extended to his guest. The villagers didn't consider Doc an enemy, opposed to the Sukarno regime. They didn't even think of themselves as Indonesians. This far up country natives had no political awareness, in spite of having fostered a soldier boy. They were no different from the Bajau tribes across the border in Sabah, though they 'belonged', if that was the word, to a different nation and owed allegiance to a different master.

Evidence of 'civilization' was everywhere in Borneo. Palan was no exception. There were tinned soups, beef stock cubes and big quart bottles of Handbury's Lemon Extract which the natives of Malaysia loved. The convenience foods were used mostly to flavour plain boiled rice and to mix with tea. Usop's friendliness, the familiar sight of Lemon Extract containers and the taste of Campbell's Oxtail didn't erase Greenwood's anxiety, however. He could not settle. He did not feel 'right' in this community. Maybe he was tired. Sweet Jesus, he had every right to be tired. Let's face it, he was knackered.

Doc could hardly keep his eye open as he ate supper, the usual mess of rice and fish flakes and fruit. The bleedin' fruit wasn't so fresh either.

Family gathering. Old ladies, young girls and suckling babes. When he squinted at them all he could see were problems, minor illnesses which would yield to the treatments he could easily administer. He let Mouse do most of the talking while he dutifully fed his face and drank tea. He refused the local brew, which would not only knock him out but would leave him with a head like a balloon in the morning.

Tomorrow he must be sharp. He had a couple of early-morning decisions to make. He must choose between going up river in a borrowed canoe or retreating cross-country to Mandelaut, from where he could dispatch a reliable postman like Leiman back to Gentangan with the info he had already collected. Maybe it was even time to drift back to base in person, take a chance on being slapped with a Return-to-Unit ticket.

On the other hand he was well into Kalimantan. If Usop would provide him with a canoe and a couple of paddlers, he could nose down the Tabuli, see for himself where the Indos were loading, what sort of bases they had and how many men were ready to push into the jungle along the border. Naturally he would prefer to hang around Palan for three or four days, organise a series of clinics, nurse his soldier patient through possible crises, even take a look at Usop's mysteriously crippled leg.

He could imagine a headline in the *Jungle News – Miracle Cure Makes Native Chief Walk Again*. The silliness of it amused him. Momentarily.

Crapola! He was too bleedin' weary to concentrate.

Mouse on one side and the Armalite on the other, the sax

case for a headboard, Doc Greenwood reclined on a rattan mat under a tent of mosquito netting and tried to stop fretting long enough to fall asleep.

Mouse had stroked and fondled him, and tried to rouse his interest in love-making. She had no sense of propriety, that girl. Doc had never felt right making hay in public. Usop's clan was spread out only yards away. Firmly, he had rejected the girl's advances and, disgruntled, she had turned her back on him and had fallen asleep instantly.

For Doc, however, there was no quick nod-off. His feet itched inside his canvas boots. His gut was queasy. The sting of the strong lemon tea was still in his mouth. He lay on his back watching insects bounce against the net, listening to the dunning of the river and the din of the trees and the denizens that dwelled therein.

Nature's great lullaby: the Borneo Cradle Song: Rockabye Barry.

Up river? Down river?

Fly away home?

Lance-corporal Greenwood closed his eyes.

Seconds later, or so it seemed, the first 20mm cannon shell ripped through the village and exploded forty yards from the *luma*. The second shell was closer. The gable wall of Usop's house collapsed on the blast wave. The slaughter of the innocents had begun.

Marginal man had finally written himself right off the page.

2 More teeth in the mouth

The long bar in Kuching's Aurora Hotel had seen its share of rough stuff. Sailors on shore leave from the frigates that patrolled the China Sea made a beeline for the watering-hole. Scots engineers and English prospectors, to say nothing of commercial gentlemen of all nationalities, found haven there. Even introverted colonial wayfarers waxed eloquent about the Aurora and some could show knuckles scarred in violent arguments behind its genial three-storey façade.

For many, many years there had been nowhere else to 'put up' in Kuching, except government rest houses, which were not to everybody's taste. Of late, however, Kuching, capital of Sarawak and centre of the White Rajah dynasty, had spread outwards. Marked intensification of building in the municipality had been matched by rapid growth of its boundary settlements, including a spanking new industrial estate at Padungan.

It was a far cry from the *atap* village of half a century ago. Here were Malay *kampongs*, Dyak longhouse communities, Kayans, Melanans, Muruts, a few Indians, and legions of Chinese. In the wake of the Brunei revolt and the outbreak of 'confrontation' with Indonesian guerrillas, there were also many odd bods in uniform; officers and ratings from the RN's 846 Squadron, Irish Hussars, Yorkshire Light Infantry, Gurkhas, Commandos, Border Scouts and, though hardly visible, an occasional bird of passage from the Special Air Service.

British Forces were not, thank God, all in the long bar all of the time. There were periods when the Aurora had the somnolence of a chapel, with fans stirring the listless air and flies too drowsy to drone.

During one such period of quietude Major Jeffrey Alexander Deacon entered the Aurora. Still carrying his valise, he wandered unchecked into the long bar where, by appointment, he was met by Major Tim Dalinart.

Deacon and Dalinart were both veterans. They had begun

their careers by waging war against the Nazis and had continued to put their skills as Special Force soldiers against Communists and dictators alike. Deacon had flown from Singapore to the airfield at Sematan. He had been whisked from there to Kuching by Land Rover.

The years of comparative peace – read 'inactivity' – had been hard on SAS officers. A little of their cutting edge had been diminished. Returned from a deep probe in the jungle, Dalinart looked ill and aged. He had lost the boyish softness which had been his outward mark ever since Deacon had known him. Humidity, low rations and inevitable tension had whittled at the major. This, Deacon thought, was how Tim would look when he was seventy, the true inner core of the man. Nothing in Dalinart's manner, however, suggested senility or hinted that he had been sapped by the efforts of a long patrol. On the contrary, he was as crisp, energetic and as affable as ever.

'Deacon. Good to see you.' Dalinart raised his glass and rattled the ice cubes which bobbed in gin. 'Lord, don't you look fit.'

'Fit enough,' said Deacon. 'How about you?'

'Pale but interesting, what?'

Deacon laid his valise on the floor and seated himself at the table. There was no barman in the long room, no servants; only Dalinart, a bottle of Beefeater, a plastic ice bowl, a dish of sliced limes and a large jug of tonic water.

Dalinart lifted the bottle. 'I assume you're ready for a bracer?'

'Absolutely.'

Deacon shifted in the chair with a certain care. He was a seasoned traveller by land, sea and air, and suffered hardly at all from trips that would have bludgeoned a man half his age. But his knees did tend to stiffen and an old injury caused a nagging pain in his spine when he idled too long. His near-white hair was neatly trimmed. He did not affect the careless, ragamuffin style which had been the fashion for certain SAS officers during the fifties. In any case, though discretion was always a watchword, the Deke was not here in secret. He found it helpful to adopt the disguise of a standard regimental officer, show a trace of spit and polish. As a home-based, high-ranking 'instructor', he knew he was obliged to be smart, even in a regiment which tended to be a shade neglectful of soldierly niceties.

Dalinart had bathed and shaved and changed out of his filthy jungle togs. He wore a bush-style jacket over an Aertex shirt with a cigarette tin poking out of one pocket and a conglomeration of sun-glasses, pens and papers fattening the other. 'Panda' circles patched both eyes. Around his steel watchstrap flared an angry red rash. A piece of him still seemed to be stuck in the jungle, like the sting of a hornet.

Dalinart fashioned a gin and tonic. He passed it to Deacon.

'Well, we're back in business, it seems,' he said.

'How in God's name was General Walker persuaded to bring us in?'

'Sweet talk and common sense,' said Dalinart. 'Usually he can't see past his damned Gurkhas. But on this occasion he had to admit that our chaps were ideal for the job.'

'What exactly is the job?'

'To assist the Border Scouts in gathering intelligence about Indonesian movements forth and back across the border.'

'What are we really doing?'

'"K" Squadron,' said Dalinart, 'is chancing its arm.'

'Where?'

'Far from the madding crowd. On the east coast.'

'What do you have in mind for me?'

Dalinart leaned across the table, pushing ice-bowl and lime-dish to one side. 'I want to drop you into the jungle from a Westland helicopter.'

'Why?'

'To find somebody.'

'Who?'

'One of our lads, a medic named Greenwood.'

'Is he lost?'

'I've a notion where he might be.'

'Why drag me out from England . . .?'

'I didn't drag you out just for that,' said Dalinart. 'I requested your presence because we're desperately short of officers with jungle experience. Those we do have can't be spared from base duties and, at this particular time, I require somebody I can trust to work the point.'

'Smells of fish,' said Deacon.

'I agree,' said Dalinart, unabashed.

'Greenwood's important,' said Deacon; statement not question.

'Very. Apart from the fact that he's been out long enough.'

'How long?'

'Pushing four months.'

'Who's with him?'

'A native girl. Full stop.'

'How do you know he's still functioning?'

'He was last week. Five days ago, to be precise. He keeps in touch by native runners. Postmen.'

'In that case,' said Deacon, 'why don't you use a postman to order him in?'

'He's strayed a mite too far into the Mad Doctor's territory.'

'Into Kalimantan, do you mean?'

'Yes.'

'How far is too far?'

'Forty miles.'

'Good God!' said Deacon. 'Now *that* isn't in line with present policy. Gentle probes, low-profile stuff, isn't that the official state of the art?'

'Yes. But it's changing.'

'Who's changing it? Runaways like Greenwood?'

'The General.'

'Walker?'

'You know what a lion he is,' said Dalinart. 'As Commander of the British Forces in North Borneo, he isn't content with a strictly defensive policy. He'd like to alter the function of the Security groups to one of offence. He regards mobility as the key; not getting bogged down in static positions. Hold what's been gained with heavy artillery and push forward to block the main crossing points used by the Indos.'

'How do *you* know what's on the general's mind?'

'It's fairly common knowledge,' said Dalinart. 'He can wax quite rhetorical, the old boy. Declares that he wants to own the jungle, dominate it by night and day, week in and week out.'

'A tallish order,' said Deacon.

'Ah, but the general believes it can be done.'

'How?'

'More teeth in the mouth and less length of tail.'

'How close are we to General Walker's dream?' Deacon asked.

'Well, Sukarno keeps switching from military to political pressure like a damned yacht tacking into the wind. Sukarno's no genius, believe me. His thinking's very woolly. His tactics are based on theories which stem from the Indo Defence Minister, Abdul Nasution.'

'I've read translations of some of Nasution's writings,' said Deacon. 'He's fundamentally a Maoist. Prolonged struggle. Hit-and-run attacks followed by consolidation of the guerrilla army. Isolation of the enemy. And so on. The flaw in that particular theory is the attitude of the population. The population *must* be won over to the cause of revolution. That isn't happening here in Borneo any more than it did in Malay.'

'Failure is inevitable,' said Tim Dalinart. 'On that score, Mad Doctor Sukarno won't succeed. But he might, just might, shake the unity of the Federation, cause it to fall apart. It hasn't quite jelled yet, being so new.'

Deacon drank from the glass.

He said, 'What sort of news has come in from Greenwood? Has it to do with build-up of forces?'

'Yes, it is a build-up,' Dalinart admitted. 'Over in Sabah. The guerrillas have had a shot at disrupting the timber trade before. It's difficult terrain. The swamps, islands and navigable rivers aren't well charted. Even our maps disagree in important respects.'

'Local eyes and ears?'

'So far the SAS have helped to string up early warning systems all along the borders. Including Sabah.'

'Without thrusting into attack situations?'

'We've erased a fair number of Indo terrorists,' said Dalinart. 'There's no embargo on shooting back.'

'What about the Communists?'

'Glad you brought that up. You don't much care for Commies, as I recall.'

Deacon trickled fresh gin into his glass and drank it at a swallow, as if the mere mention of Communists had created a bad taste in his mouth. He had waged what amounted to a personal war against one Communist overlord in Malaya. He detested all that Communism stood for.

Dalinart said, 'For the most part, the Indo guerrillas are "volunteers", trained and led by Sukarno's regular army officers. The dog-soldiers aren't low grade. Many have experience in fighting of this sort. Others have been culled from the criminal element, smugglers and the like. They've shown a degree of initiative and are used to living in the jungle. Specialist regular units stiffen the guerrilla squadrons. The mob that we encounter most is the Border Terrorists, the IBT. The Commies are another matter.'

'The CCO,' said Deacon. 'Clandestine Communist Organisation.'

'That's it,' said Tim Dalinart. 'They are much more highly trained than we gave them credit for. Even Sukarno didn't realise just how well organised the CCO happened to be.'

'It's backed by China, I assume?'

'Naturally,' said Dalinart. 'The CCO is an opportunist organisation. Its grand design is to let the Mad Doctor make all the running then to move in and snatch an ultimate victory.'

Deacon realised that Dalinart was not being long-winded or evasive. The situation in North Borneo *was* complicated, in that peculiarly oriental way. Motives and final objectives remained obscure. To the layman, far away in England, the battle for Malaysia might appear simple, even minor, but subversive forces waited in the wings.

Deacon's first thought on being summoned from England was that Tim wanted him to act as Squadron Commander. The fact that he was being briefed for a penetration mission suggested that the 'bosses' above Tim Dalinart were concerned about something brewing on the east coast. He decided to nudge Tim back to immediate practicalities.

'Apart from a wandering medic, what else am I looking for across the Indo border?'

Dalinart paused. When he spoke it was with unusual gravity. 'We've picked up a rumour that the IBT are setting up for a raid on the timber towns on the Jaumpong river. Specifically on the St Lucia Trading Company station at Balimbuka.'

'Surely raids – even big ones – are common?'

'Muck common,' said Dalinart. 'But so far they've all been hit-and-run. This time, however, the IBT have given signs that they intend to have and to hold.'

'For what purpose?'

'That,' said Dalinart, 'is for you to find out.'

'Unless Greenwood already knows.'

'Precisely.'

'Tell me, where exactly *is* Greenwood?'

Dalinart pushed back his chair and got to his feet.

He said, 'Time to study a map. And meet an expert. Let's go upstairs.'

'What's upstairs?' said Deacon. 'An Ops Room?'

'More or less,' the major answered and, snitching the bottle of Beefeater, led the way out of the long bar.

Weird though he was, Barry Greenwood had been trained by SAS instructors and there was no finer course for bringing a man to that peak of mental and physical fitness which resulted in instant reaction to crises. Debilitated by months in the jungle, by weight loss and minor fevers and perhaps a touch too much sexual play, Lance-corporal Greenwood would not have matched up to an instructor-sergeant's notion of how fit and fast a trooper should be. Even so, within three seconds of the cannon shell's first whistle, Doc was sprinting up the floor of the stilted house, with the Armalite dug into his armpit and the saxophone case dragging in his left hand. Mouse was right behind him, slender fingers hooked into his belt, for it was dark within the hut.

Greenwood and the girl weren't the only ones on the move, though they were the only inhabitants of Usop's *luma* who seemed to have found direction. The rest of the family, plus hunting dogs, chickens, a litter of pigs and several large rats, were caught up in a whirlwind of panic. Doc knew where he was going, though. If the shells had come from anywhere this side of nightmare, it had to be the river. Even the Indos wouldn't haul a 20mm gun into the greenery when the river lay on the doorstep.

Greenwood still assumed that he was the target; an excusable conceit. This, after all, was not some close-to-the-border hamlet. Palan was unmistakably within the boundaries of Indonesia. Usop's clan, though they might be blissfully indifferent to the honour, were ruled from the top by Sukarno's government. It did not occur to Greenwood that the village might be under attack from British or Malaysian forces. Malaysian brigadiers were under strict orders not to mount counter-terrorist attacks across the border; which was why the SAS did it in secret. But the SAS would never shell a native village. Never.

Lance-corporal Greenwood imagined that he had been 'reported' by a loyalist in Usop's community and that the village was being pasted in a ham-fisted attempt to flush him out; which was why he dove for the jungle behind the huts. Away from the Tabuli. Conveniently, the wall at the rear of the hut had been flattened. He could make out a square of lighter darkness washed with smoke and dust, through which he plunged. The walkway had been blown asunder. Jagged ends of bamboo stuck up like spears.

When Doc stopped, the girl ran into him, almost pushing him over the edge. Across the corner of the village, east to west, rustled a pink flare.

The jungle palms appeared totally unreal beneath its illumination. He heard the boom of the gun again, the chatter of MGs. He flung the girl in front of him and let her jump, eight or ten feet out of the smoke over the collapsed scaffold. She was yelling. Not scared but excited. He laid down the Armalite, took the sax case in his arms and heaved it towards her. She caught it awkwardly, toppled back and sat down in the mud with the case hugged against her breasts.

Greenwood, with the rifle, jumped.

And Usop's *luma* and the men, women and children therein, including the patient, vanished in a demon-king puff of smoke.

Doc was on his knees in the mud when the explosion demolished the hut. The blast wave passed harmlessly over him, spreading into the forest. Doc didn't loiter. He glanced round, saw flames clawing upwards from the collapsed heap and instantly got to his feet. Dragging Mouse by the arm, he sprinted up a steep, slippery ramp on to a crouch of high ground that banked the shoal on which Palan was built. He veered sharply left – seaward, Usop would have called it – and smashed on down into a patch of wet rice paddi that the tribe cultivated. Knee-deep in mush, Mouse toiling behind him, Doc ploughed back towards the river and, through the lattice of palms that fringed the paddi, caught his first sight of the attackers.

Under the falling pink rain of a second flare, he saw the boat clearly. Skilfully it was being held against the current in a curve of the Tabuli thirty yards below the village reach; a gunboat, similar to those used by Malaysian police and customs. Doc was under no illusions that this was an official vessel on official business. Thirty feet long, a bit beamish for a river venturer, the gunboat had a sloping-roofed cockpit on the aft deck and a cannon mounted in the prow. Bolted to the aft rail were a pair of light machine-guns. Two guys operated the cannon, one guy on each of the MGs. Standing upright on the roof of the cockpit was the Chink.

The Chink was a joke, posing in a manner that robbed him of menace. He was huge, tusk-yellow, with smooth, glistening arms. He wore a quilted combat vest, wide open, denim shorts. Knotted about his brow was a kerchief of crimson silk, the ends sticking out like pigtails.

As the flare faded, the cannon boomed once more and one machine-gun pumped a long burst of fire across the shoal.

Doc pushed Mouse into the paddi.

'Stay. Don't move.'

Kneeling, she looked up at him. He detected fear in her eyes now.

The girl said something; a Malay word he couldn't interpret.

It probably meant 'pirates'.

Doc had heard that pirates were active among the islands of the Sulu Sea. But he had never quite managed to relate them to the conflict in which he was engaged, to bring them out of the realm of fantasy. Plenty of tales circulated in Tawau about their exploits, including the ransoming of hostages and the capture, for a fleeting period, of Kalibakan. In his imagination, however, Doc had visualised black beards and baggy trousers, top-heavy, wallowing junks with painted sails. Not a bleedin' alloy-hulled gunboat powered by 200 hp marine engines and a captain in Levi shorts.

Doc crouched and pushed forward, lifting his feet high in the wet mush. Bright light had gone but seemed to leave an after-trace – smoke, maybe, or the first filter of daylight – against which the palms were visible and the outline of the boat against the forest wall.

One more flare, Sunny Jim, and I'm going to shoot your balls off, Greenwood thought. *Just give me one flash and you'll be yelling in high falsetto.*

In the back of his mind the Doc could hear Barbara Badillo's insistent American drawl berating him for succumbing to violent urges. What would the buxom Barbara do? Offer the Chink a flower and tell him that all men were brothers? This was no dressed-up clown swaggering down Stockton Street. Some brother who went around shooting up innocent savages.

The gunboat, one of the Star class, Doc reckoned, blundered forward, props thrashing the muddy water, and held to the middle of the stream. Its draught couldn't have been much more than three feet. Presumably the Tabuli was warted with mud-banks and rock ridges like most other rivers in Borneo.

Doc reached the undergrowth that sprouted from the brow of a little hillock above the river. He glanced at the paddi field behind him. He could see nothing of Mouse. He hoped to the Good Lord that she wasn't dogging him and had the sense to keep out of sight.

Fire had eaten into the *atap* roofs of the village dwellings and radiated upward in harsh yellow sheets, with a noise like somebody crushing tissue paper, amplified a thousand times. He could hear the piercing note of a woman's screams and curt, brutal bursts from automatic weapons. The pirates had guys on shore. At least they weren't looking for him, specifically. Not if they were pirates. They would be after loot. God, what sort of loot could they hope to find in a dump like Palan? A few chickens, buckets of rice, a pig or two. They could have bought that sort of provender for less than the cost of the fuel the gunboat had burned. Doc couldn't see anybody on shore, neither villager nor pirate. Even the gunboat was running past him. He could dig Mouse out of the paddi, slide off into the undergrowth and nobody would be any the wiser.

Flames crawled upwards, crackling, and feather-headed trees turned black against the glow. A buffalo trampled out of the brush and charged across the edge of the rice field, panting and grunting. Domestic beast, maybe, which had torn its tether in panic or bulled down the gate of its feed-pen. Who could blame it?

All right, all right, Barry Greenwood thought; *you don't have to make a final decision right now. Get the bastard in your sights, that's all. You don't have to pull the trigger.*

Horse-sense told him that there was nothing one guy, even an SAS trooper, could do to halt the rape of Palan. Sukarno or no Sukarno, confrontation or no confrontation, the pirates would ply their filthy trade. It was a hazard as endemic to the river peoples as hepatitis or yellow jack.

Greenwood mounted the rut that ran to the crown of the hillock. Below to his right was the bamboo sluice through which water flushed into the paddi field when the river rose. Every landscape feature had clear definition now, garnered from clambering flames. The river was dappled black and angry red, swirled with yellow. The medic could see perfectly. He was on the path that field-workers used, a track worn into the subsoil. It provided cover and an ideal firing position. He could see the gunboat holding steady in the current. But he could not see the village, only the line of fishing poles advancing into the water. He wondered why the natives hadn't made a break for it, going for their canoes.

Settling the Armalite comfortably, he pressed his knees into the banking. Even an inferior marksman could hardly miss at this range. Doc was no slouch with a rifle, though he didn't practise much and remained unimpressed by the tales of legendary sniping feats which circulated in the barracks and round the bars. Right now, though, he wished he'd more affinity with the weapon, could point it out as if it was part of his body, which, so he'd heard, was what real hot-shots could do.

The guys manning the cannon had stepped away from it. Hanging on the prow-rail, laughing and pointing, they looked like children tickled by a game. The machine-gunners too were resting, gun muzzles raked steeply against the bolt-rods. The big guy – the captain? – was still in position on top of the cockpit roof.

Greenwood felt sure he could pick off at least two of them before they could fix his position and retaliate. He wasn't squeamish about taking life. He'd been in ambush situations before now. But he was reluctant to kill in cold blood. Eighty per cent of his mates would have stiffed him rotten for his hesitation. They would have wasted those pirates immediately. Nobody was going to make an international incident out of the elimination of criminals. No political capital could be cobbled out of it. There was nothing that could be glibly defended in the UN or some solemn conference concerning the stability of the Federation of Malaysia.

Undeniably this was one of those situations when a Special Forces operator should let his rifle do the talking.

Greenwood fished a loaded magazine from his pants pocket and inserted it into the rifle. He pulled the charging handle to the rear and pushed it forward again, muffling it with his left hand. He flicked the selective-fire lever to 'semi'; the gun would now fire when the trigger was pulled. He lowered his head a little and adjusted the rear sight. He threaded rear and fore into line with the deck of the pirate craft and zoned in on the big guy on the roof.

Then he paused, staring.

A quirk of the current brought the rope out of the water. It came up suddenly, surfacing like a monstrous krait, water popping from its fibres like droplets of blood. Doc hadn't seen the attachment point which, with the boat sitting back and props thrashing, was below the water line. But when it came, it led his eye down river and, leaning his chest on the hillock and craning his neck, he saw the raft.

Bamboo, standard, narrow and long, with some sort of buoyancy float slung under it to keep it upright. Oil drums, maybe, or rubber 'ducks' which were common enough along the quays. Without the floats the raft would have been swamped. As it was, it rode a foot below the water line. When the rope jerked, the bow wave washed down its length and the girls' bodies waved like fronds.

Eight, ten of them; young girls. No men. No guards: just the fragile bamboo raft with its cargo of humans tied by the ankles, dredged through the brown, unhealthy waters of the Tabuli. Maybe for miles. They uttered no sound, the girls.Bedraggled, they clung to each other and to the ropes that bound them. Hostages? Prisoners? Slaves? Yeah, slaves for the brothels of the Indo coastal towns, those communities where tribal laws had been obliterated by money and greed.

The tribes of Borneo weren't exactly angelic. Some natives had no more morals than alley cats. But there was still a cherished notion of freedom in their simplicity; Lemon Essence, trannies and basketball boots, all the 'civilised' truck, was only superficial. But *this* wasn't superficial. This was *disgusting*.

Greenwood watched the slave-raft rise through its own bow wave and tilt. The girls slithered like hake in a fish-hold, limbs tangled. The rope fell slack and sank as the gunboat hove to off the tail of the mud-bank.

Doc Greenwood sighted and fired.

The big, tusk-yellow devil on the cockpit roof roared, whipped his hands to his shoulders and fell, with a last-moment spring of the knees, into the river.

'Nice one, Barry,' Lance-corporal Greenwood murmured.

He pulled the trigger again.

The room, on the third floor, faced to the rear of the hotel, into a kitchen garden; no view of speak of. It contained two single cots, one of which had been up-ended against the window, not to cut out daylight but to provide floor space. All in all, the bedroom had the cluttered, improvised air of a *basha*, littered with maps and photographs in lieu of leaf debris.

Seated cross-legged in the midst of the chaos was a stocky little man of approximately Deacon's age. He wore a starched white shirt without a collar, sleeves rolled to the shoulder. Blue duck pants. He was barefoot. Save for a fringe of greying hair over ears and nape, he was completely bald. Screwed into his right eye was a monocle. In his mouth was a black plastic holder from which a handmade cigarette drooped, spilling ash like snow.

When Tim showed Deacon into the room, the man looked up, blinked and grudgingly smiled. He got to his feet with weightless ease, like a swami versed in levitation. He held out his hand.

'I'm Boyd – no hypen – Goddard.'

'Jeff Deacon.'

The hand was dry, the grip firm. In spite of the bald dome, monocle, and cigarette holder there was nothing effete in Boyd No-hyphen Goddard's manner.

The glass, as it turned out, was not an article of dress but a tool. Goddard had been studying an aerial photograph, one of the dozens strewn on the polished wood floor. Along the counterpane of the bed eight of the RAF's best snapshots had been arranged in sequence, a worn map-case, open like a Bible, set on end above them.

Goddard pocketed the eye-glass. He clenched the cigarette holder between his molars and spoke around it, a habit which gave him a tough, gangsterish intonation.

'Major, are you?'

'Yes,' said Deacon.

'I'm a poxy civilian, I'm afraid.'

'Sabah Police Special Branch officers are hardly civilians,' said Dalinart.

'Ah!' said Deacon, 'you're the expert.'

'Try to be, try to be.'

'You'll be working together,' said Dalinart, with a degree of uncertainty.

'Good,' said Deacon.

Jeff Deacon's last experience of close liaison with a Special Branch officer had not been pleasant. But Saunders had been a stiff, selfish martinet without much understanding of the Far East. If his first guess was correct, Boyd No-hyphen Goddard was an old jungle hand with a deep, abiding love of this strange and primitive land.

As if to appease Deacon's curiosity, Goddard explained. 'Dropped in during the war to fight Japs. Liked it. Stayed on.'

Behind that terse outline lay many a tale, Deacon suspected. But he respected reticence, which was much in tune with his own character.

'Believe we're going cross-border rather briskly,' said Goddard.

'Tomorrow, if possible,' Dalinart said.

Deacon squatted by the bed and studied the photographs.

'Have you actually been in this neck of the woods?' he asked.

'Never,' Goddard answered.

'Show me on the map.'

Using the flat-bitten end of his cigarette holder as a pointer, Goddard leaned over Deacon's shoulder and dabbed at the map. 'I've never been far across the Jaumpong.'

Deacon said, 'How large is the lumber camp at Balimbuka?'

'Quite large, actually,' said Goddard. 'Couple of hundred workers plus families and general hangers-on.'

'Chinese?'

'My, my, Major Deacon! You do catch on quick,' said Goddard. 'Uh-huh, a few Chinese. Cooks and victuallers. The cutters are either Ibans or Filipinos. The manager is Jock McCartney, a tough old Scot. Been there for fifteen years. Hardly ever leaves the place, except for a bi-annual trip to Tawau to meet his bosses and catch the markets.'

'Married?'

'No more,' said Goddard. 'His wife walked out about two years ago.'

'Is there an airstrip at the camp?'

'Helicopter pad,' said Goddard.

'Is there much trouble at the St Lucia?' Deacon asked.

'Do you mean Indo trouble or the other sorts?'

'Both. Either.'

'The usual squabbles among the workers. Jock handles them himself. He has fists like knobkerries and a fierce temper. I've only been up there once "officially". Indo trouble's another matter. The St Lucia concession is isolated. A natural target for IBT raiders. After all, disruption of the teakwood trade and the economy of Sabah is part of the

Indos' avowed intent. It would have been odd indeed if Balimbuka had been left alone.'

'Many casualties?'

'Three killed, a dozen or so wounded over the past couple of years. The timber rafts which come down from the holding pools are rather vulnerable. The police provide escorts when we can. Jock applied for and received a number of gun licences. Most of his foremen carry rifles now, and some of his workers have side arms.'

'How do the workers feel about being targets?'

'Enraged. The St Lucia pays excellent wages and the work's steady. The majority of employees are on contract. They're pretty well "westernised". They even have a golf club.'

'You're not serious?'

'Hacked out of the jungle. Three holes. Jock will play anyone for a shilling a hole. He never loses.'

Tim Dalinart had been searching around the room for glasses. He had found only teacups, which he had cleaned with a towel. He poured three generous gins from the bottle and passed one each to Deacon and Goddard.

'Greenwood has been instrumental in protecting Balimbuka,' Dalinart said, casually.

'Greenwood?'

'Hm. He's mapped all known crossing-points across the Seven Rivers basin. We've thwarted several attempted raids after receiving a bush telegraph from the Lance-corporal.'

'Do the Indos know he's in there?' Deacon said.

'Not sure,' said Dalinart. 'The tribesmen – mostly Bajau Maruda – are his friends. The White Doktor, they call him. Medicine Man. He does sterling work among the villages and is repaid by information and practical help. Eyes and ears.'

'Greenwood,' said Boyd Goddard, 'is worth his weight in gold.'

'But he won't come home?' said Deacon.

'No. The business with the radio was very bad,' said Dalinart. 'He claims the radio broke down. I sent in spares but nothing happened. I tried to persuade his Number One Postman – an English-speaking Javanese named Leiman – to lug a brand-new set back to Greenwood. But Leiman went all coy, jabbered about "evil spirits". A load of rubbish. Leiman's a materialist. He has no belief in spirits. He was merely protecting his master from an excess of interference.'

'Where is the forward post?'

'Was, not is,' said Dalinart. 'It was here. At Gentangan. I closed it up three days ago and pulled the chaps out through Balimbuka by chopper.'

'Does Greenwood know you've toddled?'

'No,' said Dalinart. 'I have, however, left a sergeant and a couple of troopers at the St Lucia. When Greenwood decides to leave the jungle and finds Gentangan closed I'm certain he'll have the sense to push on to the lumber camp. It's only an extra day's hike.'

'But his postmen may not know that?'

Dalinart shrugged. 'I simply couldn't risk squatting at Gentangan any longer. By the book, I'd been there far too long as it was.'

'Frankly,' said Deacon, 'Greenwood sounds like a renegade and more trouble than he's worth to the squadron.'

Dalinart shrugged then said, 'The truth is, Jeff, I sent him in even deeper.'

Deacon said, 'I think you'd better explain.'

'According to Greenwood there's a movement of arms across the breadth of the Seven Rivers.' Boyd Goddard pointed with the cigarette holder. 'The rivers rise in the hills here and flow outwards in various directions to the sea, like a hand with seven fingers. According to Greenwood the Indonesians are digging in somewhere above the Jaumpong. With howitzers.'

'Howitzers?' said Deacon. 'Are you sure?'

'Greenwood's message was unequivocal.'

'Did you send out a recce?'

'Naturally. But we found nothing.'

'Where do the howitzers come from, by what route?'

'Along here,' said Goddard. 'You see, there are only certain tracks and paths capable of taking big stuff. Patrols on our side of the border would pick up a direct river shipment.'

Deacon peered at the map again. 'The Indos ferry the stuff up from the sea and haul it inland across the saddle. But why?

Are British Forces in the area or moving into the area?'

'Of course not,' said Dalinart. 'That's what's so puzzling. I can't understand why the Indos would want to dig in above Balimbuka, to create a defensive position. They don't have anything to defend.'

Boyd Goddard said, 'The aerial reconnaissance boys brought in these photographs. Confirmation of Greenwood's reports. You can just make out the buffalo sleds through the trees if you look closely.'

Deacon didn't bother. He had lifted the map case and was studying it with great care. Years of experience in 'impossible' terrain had taught him to read maps with imagination. He had a notion of how difficult the country would be; similar to chunks of Malay.

'You probably didn't find anything because you didn't have enough chaps on the ground.'

'Thousands of acres of rubbish; eight men on foot,' Tim Dalinart agreed. 'Boyd has a theory, however.'

'Do indeed, do indeed,' said Goddard. 'I think the Indos intend to send a squadron up the Jaumpong. It's navigable all the way to the sea. From information received we also know that the Indo Marines have a garrison on the big island of Nunukan Timor. With an artillery battery installed at the head of the river, a task force coming across the border about here, and a co-ordinated thrust up the Jaumpong, Balimbuka would fall for sure.'

'We have patrols and observation posts along the river, of course,' said Dalinart. 'But not enough to hold off a three-pronged attack.'

'Are co-ordinated attacks common?'

'Not on the East Coast.'

'Is there close liaison between the CCO and the IBT?' Deacon asked.

'They are uneasy bedfellows.'

'All right,' said Deacon. 'There must be a base. Goddard, where, in your opinion, would the IBT start from?'

'Probably on the Tabuli river. It's unexplored territory. There are some small, impoverished river villages but we don't even know how navigable it is. However, if you look closely at the map, you'll see that it meanders through swamp. Freshwater swamp. There might be a route for shallow-draught craft, a link between the rivers.'

'Do you think that Greenwood's somewhere on the Tabuli?'

'Possibly. He's pretty bright, Jeff. I'm sure he'll reach the same sort of conclusion as we've done.'

'But you can't *depend* on him coming out with the gen?'

'He may be dead, a prisoner, or just plain lost,' said Dalinart.

'Therefore, you want me to execute a pipe-cleaner search across the upper part of the Seven Rivers basin and down the Tabuli?'

Dalinart pursed his lips. 'It's an unofficial exercise, Jeff. Oh, you'll have backing, and lots of it. But if you're caught by the Indos then we'll claim that you got lost. First observation mission to the border, with Mr Goddard, etcetera, etcetera.'

'The old Mad Major routine?'

'You do it so well, Jeffrey.'

'What do you feel about it, Goddard?' Deacon asked.

'Nervous,' Goddard confessed.

'All right,' said Deacon. 'The problem is, how do you get us out again?'

'Three possibilities. If you must, for some reason, reverse the route, we'll lift you out at a pre-arranged point. Let's assume, however, that you carry on all the way down the Tabuli to the coast.'

'The river comes out in swamp off the northern tip of this small island here,' said Boyd Goddard. 'It's messy country but the SBS, based in Tawau, have promised assistance if needed.'

'And the third possibility?'

'I've found a Westland pilot who's willing to make a run across enemy territory. It's dangerous, of course. Choppers are vulnerable to rifle and mortar fire. He won't hang about and he won't trail up river. But he will make a run across the Tabuli, here, three days after the drop.'

'Three days. Isn't that pushing it?' said Deacon.

'You'll have a signaller with you, and various useful objects, like a SARBE, balloons. . .'

'Very well,' said Deacon. 'When do we leave?'

'Dawn's early light,' said Dalinart. 'I suggest you tuck away a hearty dinner and get a good night's sleep. We'll fly across Borneo to Tawau, transfer to an RN helicopter which will take you up to the St Lucia, refuel and pop you into the jungle on the upper basin in the late afternoon.'

'Who's running the show?'

'I am,' said Dalinart.' From Balimbuka.'

'And the rest of the team?'

'We'll pick them up in Tawau. Both volunteers.'

'Good men?'

'Scruff,' said Dalinart. 'What would you want with good men?'

Deacon grinned. 'I'll bet it's bloody Harper.'

'How ever did you guess?'

'And the other?'

'A grizzled ghost from your past.'

Deacon frowned. Dalinart's phrase conjured several faces to his mind. But most of these men were dead.

'Who, for God's sake?'

'You'll find out tomorrow, old chap.'

The Armalite was fitted with a flash suppressor. The prong-type device didn't hide the spurt of flame at the muzzle but it did reduce it. Bearing this in mind, Doc Greenwood calmly held position on the bank and fired again. He was delighted at the result of his markmanship.

Killing never gave him satisfaction as a rule, though it caused no canker of guilt in his soul either. It came with the badge, was part of the profession. Humanitarianism wasn't another name for suicide, however. He fought for his survival in an honourable cause and in the unshakeable conviction that nobody British would ever ask him to do otherwise. But something in the leering face of the big Chink on the gunboat roof had made killing easy. If the Chink had surfaced, Doc would have had no compunction about picking him off.

There was no sign of the captain, however. Doc assumed that he had killed him or that the crocodiles – if there were any in this section of the river – had grabbed the carcass and hauled it to the bottom. He lined up on the window of the cockpit of the gunboat. He couldn't see through the glass because the fire streaked it red. Safe to assume, though, that there was a guy at the controls and that with that guy knocked off too, the gunboat would go out of kilter and start drifting and the gunners would have to abandon their weapons and stop carving up the inhabitants of Palan to do something about it. Then – Doc fantasised, as he aimed and fired – he would be able to slide into the river, cut the rope that linked the boat to the raft and free the poor, terrified girls.

Greenwood experienced a sudden heightening of awareness. Barbara Badillo, back in San Fran, would have valued the moment, called it transcendent, would have revelled in it, her chubby, grubby face tilted to Heaven, boobs thrust out. She would have regarded it as mystical. To Lance-corporal Greenwood, however, the clarity had more to do with his adrenal glands pumping steroids into his metabolism.

High as a kite, he emptied one magazine into the gunboat. Flakes of blackness filled the frames of the cockpit. The guys on the LMGs roved their weapons in search of him, then, panicking under waspish fire from the riverbank, strafed the jungle wildly.

Doc was annoyed at his inability to score again and went on raking the gunboat with determination. Went on raking the bleedin' gunboat far too long. Sergeant Bryce would have bawled him out for neglect of standard operating procedure. He should have got off half a clip and changed position, gone left or right, up or down, even backwards. To stay put in the circumstances was damned stupid. Proved what a lousy soldier he was, really. His only excuse, if you could call it that, was that he got clean carried away.

Doc didn't even hear the Chink. The guy, big as he was, must have come up out of the river and over the mud like a crocodile. Only the very, very best blokes in the SAS squadrons could have matched the Oriental for speed and silence.

It had dawned on Doc that he must shift position. He had most of the second clip left in the Armalite. The gunboat was still holding to the middle of the river and the raft had walled out behind it again, the girls cowering. If he hoped to set them free then he would have to be nippy about it. He saw himself as a liberator, a knightly crusader. He turned his head, glanced back over the paddi in search of Mouse, since he was responsible for her too. He saw her splashing towards him, arms raised over her head, fingers wagging, the way she did when she was excited.

Bits of charred leaf-debris floated over the paddi-field. The roar of flames from the village had already softened. No gunfire now, no screams. It was as if Usop's clan had been wiped out by the first shells, which couldn't, of course, be the case.

Doc lifted the Armalite to wave back to Mouse, assure her he was okay. He kneed himself away from the mud slope, grinning, then saw Mouse jump, the way a real Borneo mouse jumps, with a high, straight-up leap, all legs, hands bunched into her belly like little paws. She even squealed. First thought that entered Barry's head was that she'd been hit by a bullet from one of the LMGs. But when she struck the wet ground again she was upright and running. Running *away* from him.

Bloody peculiar!

He opened his mouth to shout, 'Mouse.'

Out of the corner of his eye he caught the movement. At the same split second he heard a throaty snarl. He whipped round, head tilted, saw the Chink above him. Painted by reflections from the incandescent trees, skin glistening, the man was poised, half crouched, arms balanced out from his torso. Greenwood took in an inordinate amount of detail; filed teeth, thick, veined throat, slanted eyes blood-red with hatred. A needle-thin, straight-bladed knife was clenched in the Chink's mouth.

Breath sucked into Doc's lungs in horror, then the Chink was in the air. Greenwood has no chance to react. No opportunity to swing the Armalite, grip it like a fending-bar. No time for anything. The Chink was on him. All that bulk hurled from the breast of the hummock bore him to the dirt. Greenwood was jarred by the force, neck bowed and face crushed into the skid of watery mud where the path trod in to the edge of the paddi-field. The bugger hadn't been wounded at all. He had done what any good leader would do; he had taken the initiative. That was the last clear piece of reasoning that

Lance-corporal Greenwood would achieve for some time. The rest of it was feeling and response. And the rest of it didn't last too long.

Gasping like a gaffed fish, Greenwood felt the Armalite being torn from his grasp. Next would be the sharp, cold burning of the knife – and he would be dead. He didn't cry out for his father or Barbara or even for Mouse. Instinct vibrated his vocal chords and a pathetic croak emerged.

'*Major. Major.*'

Then the Chink hoisted him up by crotch and forearm and slammed him down hard into the broth-water by the paddi's edge.

And Lance-corporal Greenwood blacked out.

Dingo and the headhunter got on famously from the first. They had met eight days ago in the transit hut on the Naval Quay at the end of Printer Street and had been hanging round Tawau like a couple of tourists, having a hell of a time, while waiting for somebody to inform them why they had been summoned to the port on Cowie Harbour. They had managed to deduce from conversation that it had something to do with that Olde English Bluestocking, Jeffrey Alexander Deacon, since an acquaintance with the Deke was the only thing the Dyak and Aussie had in common, apart from an unquenchable thirst for bottled beer.

Umgah, the Dyak, had been a tracker for the Deke's outfit in Malaya in 1952/53. Captain Maurice Harper had backed the major in a brief but hairy mission to the mountains of Oman five years ago when he, Dingo, had been but a fluffy, untempered lieutenant. Since then he had bumped into the Deke in Singapore on a couple of occasions but the Deke was not much given to socialising and did not encourage close friendships, and Dingo had retreated, chastened.

Dingo had been in North Borneo for almost eight months. He had put in a stint as a Troop Commander, working out of Bareo, under another young captain from 'A' Squadron which was on its second tour of duty in the country. Guarding the approaches to Brunei, which was still thought to be under threat of internal revolt, didn't grab Dingo where he lived. He wanted to be more 'involved'. That, so far as the policy book for 'A' Squadron was concerned, just wasn't to be condoned. Dingo was relieved to be pulled out and flown over to Sabah on the instruction of Major Tim Dalinart, who had a handful of 'K' Squadron wallahs buried in the swamps and was rumoured to be up to the sort of tricks you don't ask too much about.

Umgah, on the other hand, had been angling for work with the Special Forces for months but had been dismissed, rather disdainfully, as being far too old to have retained his 'jungle sense'. He had long since abandoned the primitive practice of collecting the skulls of his enemies and had built on his association with the British Armed Forces in Malaya by becoming more westernised and versatile. He had even learned to speak comprehensible Americanised English, thanks to the patience of some of the Filipinos with whom he'd worked for a spell on the timber hauls coming out of the Kalabakan. He had been employed too by *Pioneer Industries* in one of their sawmills in the Third Division of Sarawak. It was from this fate that Major Dalinart eventually rescued him. The Major didn't forget the regiment's old friends and had a letter of sorts on file to remind him, a letter typed on a dot-and-carry typewriter by an aged Chinese amanuensis in the bazaar at Bintalu, in which the Dyak begged for re-employment as a tracker. Umgah was to be Deacon's surprise.

The wrinkled, tobacco-brown, bright-eyed old codger might have lost some of his sharpness but his enthusiasm and his natural guile would make up for it. Given a few days on the trail, Dalinart assured himself, Umgah's other qualities would return. Besides, the Dyak spoke fluent Malay and a number of obscure dialects. Only his English was fractured, and Deacon was used to that.

Tawau, which had a resident population of about five thousand, had been founded as a settlement in 1892. It was a pleasant enough spot and pretty damned healthy when you compared it to most of the holes along the coast. The government station had a shady garden and a view across the sea through a lattice of tall coconut palms. There was an excellent, informal hotel at the heart of the harbour district, where Dingo put up in preference to billeting in the Navy's shore base.

Before the war the Japanese had been the dominant commercial influence in Tawau but the Jap colony was long gone and European and American interests had taken over. Grassroots trade, however, was conducted by the usual mélange of Asian races, and the sprawling Sunday market offered a harvest of home industries and some exotic little sideshows.

The kind of local colour that captivated Dingo Harper lay in a sprawl of clapboard bungalows around the gambling-farm down by Alexander Street. There the captain and the Dyak would gravitate of an evening to stroll among the open-fronted booths and low dark doors of the illicit opium-houses. Here were vendors of prawns and fish-cakes and monkey meat, quaint pastry kitchens, coffee-shops, pawnbrokers, and a miniature supermarket stacked with a medley of European goodies in jars, bottles and cans. Here too were bars where ice-cold Koors was sold and tankards of a local brew which would blow your ears off in you weren't careful; also drapers hung with the latest dresses and sarongs and flashy muslin coats, and jewellery stalls and trinket sellers, honeypots for native girls and innocent-looking 'almond-eyes' who would barter their favours with hot-blooded bucks from the fishing fleet or the lumber camps.

Though Dingo was a bachelor and as hot-blooded a bloke as you'd find in South-East Asia, he heeded Umgah's advice and steered clear of the sheilas. He stuck to beer and singing and still managed to make a hell of a week's R & R out of it until the khaki-clad, ultra-smart native police sergeant marched into the hotel at the ungodly hour of ten a.m. one morning and gave the captain a message over the breakfast table.

'It is the wish of Major Dalinart that you report at noon today, sah.' The police sergeant wouldn't sit down. He stood at attention by the table in the dining-room. 'You are to report to the Mission House on Harbour Street.'

'The Mission House?'

'Sah.'

'For what?' said Dingo.

'It is the wish of Major Dalinart that you are accompanied by the hired tracker, sah.'

Dingo made the effort and got to his feet. 'Thank you, Sergeant.'

'At noon today, sah.'

'Yip. I've got it loud and clear.'

So that was it. The party was over, the booze-up brought to a close. Dingo Harper was not disappointed. He hadn't been on a real patrol for years and he craved action with a need which puzzled him. Educated and intelligent though he was, Captain Maurice Harper was nonetheless an Australian male in the prime of life, fit as a flea and stirred by a desire to prove himself. With Deacon involved, and a communications system as confused as a basket of snakes, this was no ordinary jaunt into the jungle. The Deke was up to something, something that reeked of plot, of danger.

The cloudy dregs of his hangover lifted, Dingo finished his breakfast at the double and dived upstairs to shower, shave and pack his few belongings. He would pick up Umgah from the so-called 'boarding house' where the old bloke was kipped out and make it to this Mission House by midday. He would not be late. Mission House sounded appropriate. It would be one of the rented premises that the Special Forces in the province used, since they had no powers of requisition in a mere confrontation. He didn't quite know what he would find there or who would be kitting him out and nudging him on. He didn't much care. It was the first step towards adventure and Dingo, at that stage, loved the prospect of adventure.

He didn't sing in the shower. Being a student of literature, he declaimed a handful of stanzas from Thomas Gray, those he could remember, those whose rhymes seemed to fit his mood.

Alas, regardless of their doom
The little victims play.
No sense have they of ills to come
Nor care beyond today:
Yet see how all around them wait
The ministers of human fate
And black misfortune's baleful train.
Ah show them where in ambush stand
To seize their prey, the murderous band.
Ah, tell them they are men.

Full of pith and spirit, the Aussie recited poetry strictly for his own amusement, unaware of the irony that the words contained.

If Dingo had known what was in store for him over the next few days, he would have kept his trap shut, would have lathered his body in grim silence. But on that Tuesday forenoon Maurice Harper had no reason to be apprehensive. He hadn't even heard of Greenwood, the Tabuli river, or a Chink who called himself Arunja, the sort of sadistic, inhuman bastard that gave piracy a bad name.

Doc opened his eyes. Day had come. He lay motionless. His head pounded. His skull felt soft. Rubbery. Left arm and right leg were paralysed. Though his limbs were still, his body moved. Had he *become* the leaf? Zen-leaf? Going with the flow? Blood vibrated in his spine and buttocks. His middle ear was stuffed with hay. It rustled when his head rolled. He blinked, clearing sweat and catarrhal agglutination from his eyes. Overhead was a long, pale-blue sinew. Tentatively he tried to breathe. Head pounded worse. His nostrils were clotted with mucus. He gagged. Coughed. He raised his neck. Tried to spit. Messed his stubbled chin. His head pounded, pounded. He lay still. Eyes closed. Sea-green shadows flitted over his lids. Daylight. Motion. Odour of mist. With an effort of will Doc opened his eyes once more. Concussion. Disorientation. Passing off. Breathe. Breathe. Passing off. Motor activity intact. Left arm? Right leg? *Shackled*. Skull thudding. Nape taut. Pale blue sinew torn by dark emerald flesh. Holy Jesus! Hurting. Eyes closed. Eyes forced open. Riverine trees. Trees and the morning sky.

'Drink,' Doc said.

Throat was scraped. Dry. Rusty.

'Water,' Doc said.

Focus the eyes. Double vision? Nope. Okay. Mild concussion. Passing off.

'Please, water,' Doc said.

Blood vibrating. Steady thudding. Props. *Engines*. On the gunboat. On the deck. Shackled, left leg and right arm. Twisted. Immobilised.

'Water,' Doc shouted.

Shadow stole over him. Neck taut, he strained.

Smooth, hairless columns, tusk-yellow, pasted with a tiny leaf on the calf, a strand of grass on the inner thigh, muddy. Cut-down Levis. Shorts. Denim pressing the thighs. Tight. Bulging. Superb musculature, shaped like sculpture. Quads like you wouldn't believe. A giant towering over him, legs spread. Pelvis and torso and chest. Naked. A towel draped, boxer-fashion, over the shoulders.

'Water. Please?' said Doc.

The big Chinese laughed. Chin vanished. Belly ribbing as he threw back his head. Returning into view. Hands clasping thighs. Stooping. Grinning. Filed teeth. Whites of the eyes tinted pink. Towel flecked with red. Two filaments of coagulated blood hung over each clavicle. Lips and mouth were brownish red, like those of a pomegranate eater.

'You want water?' asked the giant in soothing English.

'Yeah. Please.'

'Sure,' said the giant.

He lifted away.

Doc waited for the shadow to slide from him. Waited. Waited. He cocked his head impatiently. Saw fingers fumble at the Levis' flies. Saw the shorts squeezed down.

Doc muttered, 'Ah, bloody hell, man.'

And the Chinese was saying, 'You want water, I give you water, English.'

The penis was short but thick. Glands like a viper's head. Almost hairless. Scrotum wrinkled. Tight. Held in both hands. Flaunted, the Chink laughing while he did it.

Doc closed his eyes. Hot, stinging spray over his chest, dashing against his cheeks and mouth. He spat. Cringing. Saw in his mind's eye the girls on the raft. Not just vulnerable but degraded. That was it. Degraded. Open his eyes. Saw the slow, deliberate shaking of the shaft. Every last drop. Heard the sigh of pleasure that went with it. The Chink hoisted up his shorts again.

In the sun that fell on the river the stink of the urine was strong. It dried on Doc's skin astringently. He lay for a while after the Chink had gone. Still cringing. Filled with an impotent disgust. One man did not do this to another. This wasn't enmity or hostility or self-survival.

Chains, steel links. Stout manila rope woven into the links. Ropes knotted about his left wrist. Chain locked to the stanchion of the LMG. He was on the aft deck. Ankle ropes led to a chain too, stretched.

The gunboat ploughed on. Engines with an unbroken beat. Going downstream. To the sea. Deep enough draught for it, especially with a shallow beam. Tabuli *was* a navigable river. Transport artery. Below the bend of the village of Palan. Had they taken girls from Palan to tether to the raft? Least they hadn't nabbed Mouse. Mouse was out of it. Grafted on the image of the small-boned native girl was the memory of that short, brutally thick penis. Greenwood tried to hang slack against the chains. Breathe. Breathe. Breathe. Find your own centre. Keep still inside, man. Zen-nonsense. Float yourself out of fear. But Barbara Badillo's teachings seemed childish, too bloody childish to comfort him.

Consolation was that Mouse had wisely scarpered. Didn't have Mouse to worry about. Maybe she would find Leiman, trek back to Gentangan, to the major. Bring help. Bring retribution. He didn't think he'd mind retribution right now. Teach that bleedin' Chink a little respect.

The clink of a ladle on a metal pail wakened Doc from sick reveries. The plopping slosh of water by his ear. Shifting awkwardly he managed to turn his head.

Mouse, solemn as a prayer, knelt by him on the deck.

'Bloody hell!' Greenwood groaned.

By her side was the big Chink. The towel was still around his shoulders. He had the saxophone case in his hands. Both hands. He thumbed open the lid and showed Doc the contents, tilting the case downward like a street trader displaying his shoddy wares.

'She says that is your belongings. Is she telling the truth?' said the Chinese.

Doc paused. He was tempted to be stubborn, defiant. He wondered how the pirates had found the bleedin' medical kit, since he'd left it in the paddi along with Mouse. Still an' all, if they'd got one, there was no reason they couldn't have located the other at the same time.

'Yeah, it's mine,' Doc said.

'You are a healer?' The Chink was serious.

'Sort of.'

'This girl says you are great doctor.'

'What's your problem, man?' said Greenwood. 'Clap? Or swine fever?'

If the big guy dug the insult he gave no sign of umbrage. He wasn't laughing like a maniac any longer, though. He towered over Mouse, who had a pail and an iron ladle between her knees and whose anxious eyes scanned Greenwood's face.

The Chink brought out the knife. He kept it in a sheath at the back of his shoulder. He brought it out with a swift, sweeping action and Doc, in spite of his bravado, hissed in fear as the man knelt and the blade came forward. Forearm muscles flexed and he ripped the rope from Doc's wrist with three tugs of the knife. Thankfully Doc flipped over on to his side. He felt as if he'd been in the rack for days, not hours. He stretched his aching arms, rolled his tender neck then, propped on his elbows, sat up.

'You.' The Chink nudged Mouse with his toe. 'Give him water.'

Mouse held the ladle, supporting it with both hands.

Doc drank. The water was sweet and fresh, not out of the Tabuli. He gasped in relief. Mouse refilled the ladle. He drank again. She wetted her hands and bathed his face. The fine supple stroking of her fingers made Doc want to cry. Holy Jesus, that would be the last straw.

The Chink smiled. Didn't show the filed teeth. Meant to be friendly.

'See. I treat you well. I treat all prisoners well.'

Doc bit off a question about the girls on the raft.

'I give you good food. Dry clothes.'

'Fine,' said Doc Greenwood.

The Chink leaned forward. 'You do me favour?'

'Let's talk about that,' said Doc. 'Listen, I want you to understand, this is *my* lady. Got that, man? *My* lady. Belongs to *me*. She's my nurse.'

The Chinese nodded.

Doc said, 'Do me favour; do *her* favour. Maybe I do *you* favour. Okay?'

'Okay,' said the pirate. 'I keep the medicines safe for you.'

'You'd better.'

'My name is Arunja.'

'My name's Doc.'

'That is no name.'

'It's *my* name.'

'You have no IDs. All soldiers should have IDs.'

'I don't need IDs. All I need is that case. You just call me Doc. Okay?'

'Okay,' said the big Chinese meekly.

The good old medical mystique was working again.

Even before he talked with Mouse and clued himself in a little, Doc had grasped the salient points of the situation as it now stood. Arunja had taken him prisoner, hadn't slaughtered him on the spot, because Arunja intended to keep him in one piece and to ransom his back to the British. Perhaps trade him for a box of grenades. Keep him as a hostage. Whatever, he was of more value alive than dead. But the contents of the saxophone case, the ampoules and the jars, the hypodermics and the ether bag and the stethoscope, not to mention the wallet of shiny surgical instruments, had impressed Arunja no bleedin' end. Doctors were the whole cheese in backward communities. White Doktor. Heap Big Medicine. *Pawangs* in the super class. The favour would be a medical one. Whatever it was, Doc would do it. He would dole out remedies to a sick platoon or stitch up some trusted lieutenant's busted leg. Anything to keep sweet with the big yellow bastard. Just to survive. But he wouldn't be pissed on again.

He looked at the girl. Mutely she offered him him the water ladle.

Doc said, 'You in one piece?' She didn't understand. He said, 'Are you unharmed?'

'Yes.'

'How did they catch you?'

She said nothing. He twigged at once. The stupid cow had given herself up. She'd hauled the sax case out of the mud and sprinted after the bleedin' pirates. It wasn't so daft, right enough, in terms of saving his neck. But it was foolhardy. He felt both annoyed with her and grateful too. This wasn't even loyalty; it was a kind of blind faithfulness. Love, maybe. Only he didn't want to dwell on that possibility right now.

He touched her lank, untidy hair with his hand.

'Mouse,' he said. 'You're crazy.'

She nuzzled against him. He heard the men snigger, looked up, round.

There were fewer than he had expected; only eight on deck. They didn't look like Arunja, like pure-bred Chinks. They looked more like Filipinos, though a couple sported bootlace moustaches and one even had a thin, black beard, more like fungus than hair. They were less gaudy than their captain, dressed in bits and pieces of army gear, some of it – like the GI steel helmet – of American origin. Doc didn't leap to the conclusion that the Yanks were supplying the Borneo pirates with equipment. Any decent officer could pick up the stuff anywhere in South-East Asia. Jerkins and jungle hats and Bowie knives, even the handsome, rubberised, ankle-high jungle boots could be purchased in the bazaars. But the weapons gave a more specific picture. They were Russian. You didn't have to be an arms expert to recognise an AK-47 assault rifle or a Mosin Nagant carbine. Both types of weapon had been in common use in Korea. But these weren't scarred and scratched old shooters. They appeared to be almost factory fresh.

The pirates were gathered by the sides of the cockpit, lounging. Some were eating fruit. When Doc put his arm protectively round Mouse they jeered again and made obscene gestures.

Doc gave than the V sign, and kept his arm about the girl.

'What happened to the villagers?' he whispered.

'Some killed. The rest ran away.'

'What did the pirates do? What did they take? Girls?'

'Food. Only food.'

Doc stared at the raft, which was still being dragged along behind the gunboat. The girls had flattened themselves on it, hanging on to the binding ropes, their breasts lifted above the fluctuating bow wave.

'What about them?'

Mouse told him what they were. She used an English expression; not even English, Anglo-Saxon. Doc needed no further explanation. Mouse, realist and stoic, was probably right. The girls were fresh meat for the boys back in base camp.

Greenwood was quiet now, surveying the river. It had broadened. The surface had that smooth, oily, snaking appearance which told him that the channel was deep. On the banks the forest came down in steps to the very edge of the water, into mangrove and swamp-type shrubs. The jungle, usually, was full of noise; monkey chatter, insect hum, the alarm calls of invisible birds.

The little Star gunboat passed several hamlets. Like Palan, they had been razed to the ground. Villagers could be glimpsed loitering disconsolately among the trees by the slick back stumps of their dwellings. Like ghosts, though, they melted into the forest when the boat appeared. Recovered from his concussion, Greenwood was alert now. He observed that the racks where fish were hung to dry were empty, that there were no pigs in the mud wallows and no chickens on the scratchings. The Tabuli tribes had been robbed of their food sources. Somebody was feeding a bleedin' army or stockpiling provender. A dozen pirates hadn't munched their way through twenty miles of jungles.

Greenwood sat up again. He made no secret of his interest in his surroundings. The pirates paid him no heed. Up ahead he noticed that the sky had widened. The forest must be thinning out into typical swamp. Tidal swamp, maybe. Above the open country, flocks of voluble, predatory birds were stacked in territorial layers. He could identify hawk eagles and kites high on top of the heap. Doc squeezed the Mouse's hand. But she frowned, giving no answer to his unspoken question.

Arunja appeared from the cockpit. He was naked from the waist now, having shed the towel. Across the crown of his shoulders was a livid weal. Greenwood snorted. So he had hit the bastard after all. Half an inch higher and the bullet from the Armalite would have broken the pirate's neck like a stalk of straw. An inch, and it would have blown out his brains. And the whole lousy scenario would have been different.

The big Chinese seemed to suffer no discomfort at all from the superficial wound, and strode into the bow to survey the river ahead. The rest of the pirates had sidled aft to catcall to the girls on the raft. Doc couldn't make out what they were saying but he could well imagine the sort of promises that the roughnecks would be making. Then the pirates moved to the port-side rail and there was a degree of excitement among them, as if they were returning from an epic voyage and not just a dandle up the Tabuli.

Wheeling, Arunja boomed, 'We are close now. Soon I will give you breakfast, English. See. We are near to my place. Ukiti.'

Home sweet bloody home: pride in the Chinaman's voice made that explicit. No tall masted brigantine for this lot; they must have set up camp in the jungle.

Greenwood watched, salting details away in his memory as the boat edged shoreward.

There was nothing to be seen on the river bank, not even a streamlet feeding into the mother river. The Star appeared to be heading into a line of *nipah* palms and a tangle of mangroves. Then, jerking the raft behind it, the boat spurted forward and thrust its metal bows into a fringe of oatmeal-coloured *lalang* which screened some sort of channel.

Doc Greenwood's eyes widened as a lagoon unfolded to view.

The camp at Ukiti was no temporary collection of leaf *bashas*. It was a lakeside paradise completely veiled by trees. Permanent huts, a couple of trim-looking stilted bungalows, a cookhouse with a disperser smokestack jutting from its roof. And, astonishingly, a ship. A ship large enough to make the little gunboat seem like a toy. A ninety-foot-long Vosper fast-strike torpedo-craft, armed like a floating fortress.

'Sweet Jesus!' Greenwood exclaimed.

What he was looking at wasn't a pirates' hide-out but a whole damned garrison ready to wage war.

Survival would no longer be enough.

Now he was committed to escape, to carry the news back to Major Dalinart before somebody got gobbled up.

Tim Dalinart was surprised at the lack of enthusiasm shown by the Deke on his meeting with his old Malayan buddy, Umgah the Dyak. To the best of Dalinart's knowledge the men had parted company a decade ago on the friendliest of terms and he did not imagine that the Deke had changed quite so much in the intervening period. What Major Dalinart did not know, because Major Deacon did not bother to explain, was that Umgah the Dyak had a mortal fear of flying.

It was with solemnity that Deacon shook the Dyak's hand. Not the whisper of a smile crossed the major's lips.

Drawing Dalinart to one side, Deacon said, 'Is this my surprise?'

'I thought you'd be pleased.'

'Does he know we're going in by chopper?'

'He knows nothing of the operation. No more does Harper.'

'Is there time to find another native?'

'What's wrong with the one we've got?'

'Is there time?'

'No,' said Dalinart, firmly and rather crossly. 'There isn't time.'

'All right,' said Deacon. 'Where's the medical kit?'

'Medical kit? What do you want with a medical kit?'

'Never mind. Just find it for me, please.'

'It's there. In that bergen.'

Deacon hoisted up the sack and up-ended it carefully, spilling the contents on to the trestle-table in the centre of the Mission House's main room. He found the cloth-wrapped, oilskin-wrapped wallet that contained standard up-country medicines, together with dressings, bandages and plasters. There were two ampoules of morphine solution and a hypodermic, the disposable variety.

Carefully Deacon filled the hypo and returned to the Dyak with the needle on show.

'Sorry, Umgah. Regulations say you must have a vaccination.'

'Shoots?' said the Dyak.

'Yes, shoots.'

The Dyak rolled up the sleeve of his new bush shirt and offered his arm. Deacon inserted the needle into a vein and depressed the plunger. With luck Umgah would fall asleep and would hardly be aware that he had been bundled into a helicopter and was high, high over the jungles and swamps. Sedated, his fear would be under control.

Goddard and Harper watched with interest as Deacon soothed the native, cajoling him, relaxing him before the Wessex landed on the pad behind the Mission. You couldn't have guessed that the major had been up since four a.m. and had already spent the best part of seven hours in a transport craft, dog-legging across the island of Borneo from west to east.

How much of this toughness was the product of will, how much of stamina, Dingo Harper had never been certain. He found Major Deacon an enigma, but put the puzzle down to the fact that the bloke was one of the 'old school' of warriors. It would never have occurred to Dingo simply to stick a jag into the native's arm.

The four-man team was on its way within the hour. Kitting-up had been done in the Mission House's empty rooms and departure made from the packed-earth pad only fifty yards behind the building. Unless the CCO or one of its cells had eyes specifically on the nondescript old building, then nobody in Tawau was aware that a very special group had arrived in the town, much less taken off again. There were advantages in being so far from the headquarters of operational units. Much of the red tape, what there was of it, just disappeared. Tim Dalinart, backed by the Special Branch police chief, had had no problems in persuading the Royal Navy to help out, though most of SAS 'flying' was undertaken by the Air Force.

As the Wessex rose up above the bustling town, however, the last shreds of 'organisation' seemed to drop away. Dingo felt as light as a skylark, in spite of his emergency 'chute and overlay of equipment. The Dyak, heavy-lidded and passive, sat in the troop hatch by Major Deacon's side, one thin arm about the officer's shoulders, crooning some tribal chant in time to the thunderous pulses of the turboshaft.

After ten minutes, the Dyak fell asleep.

Pilot and co-pilot were seasoned flyers and, as this was no contour-hugging reconnaissance mission, they took the chopper up into the thinner air above the thermals that rose in the afternoon sunlight and made fast time across the rugged country, soon picking up the silver scribble of the Jaumpong.

It was coming on towards evening when the Wessex alighted on the St Lucia Trading Company's pad at Balimbuka. There was nothing in the sight of an RN chopper to arouse the interest or curiosity of the timber workers. Only Tim Dalinart left the helicopter, however. He would be based here, a guest of Jock McCartney, during the course of the operation, would be in close attendance on the radio operator in the 'shack' in the camp's main compound. Drummed fuel was hand-pumped to top up the Wessex's tanks and the helicopter took off again within twenty minutes of first touching down.

The pilot had been given a broad instruction as to map reference but issued a free hand in finding a suitable drop point. Both Deacon and Harper had made jumps into the trees several times in the past. But it was not a recommended hobby for military gentlemen and would be, in any case, quite unnecessary. 'Holes' in the jungle could be found. You just had to be careful that they hadn't been deliberately set out to lure a chopper into an ambush. Natural clearings had certain distinctive characteristics which the RN pilot had learned to read.

Lengthening shadows and the gathering of thunderheads across the mountains to the north-west made the jungle even more dense. It seemed to the men in the helicopter to have taken on the quality of paint, not brushed over a surface but deep, like a lead-based pigment in a pot, bubbled and thick and clinging. The Wessex flew low now, just clear of the tree-tops, swinging and dipping as the foothills ribbed up from the forest-infested plain. The sky was enamel, lowering and molten across the distant mountains. The rivers below had the fiery glow of raw lava, as if they were cracks in the surface of the earth.

The co-pilot came down from the forward cockpit. He was

cheerful, unphased by the gathering gloom and the apparently impenetrable quality of the jungle. He wore a pale blue quilted anorak over his uniform and a pair of expensive leather ski-gloves. He looked, even to the youthful Harper, too boyish and wholesome to be competent.

'Righto, chaps. All ready?'

'Have you found a spot?' Goddard asked.

'Any moment now. We're in the zone. Shan't take long. You'll see.'

Deacon said, 'We have a minor problem.'

The co-pilot glanced at the sleeping Dyak. 'Drunk, sir, is he?'

'Sedated. He's a nervous flyer. Can we net him down?'

'No problem, sir. No problem at all.'

The co-pilot slammed open the hatch. Warm, rather foetid air rushed into the cabin, the ozonic whiff of rot and growth that is the breath of most tropical forests. Umgah stirred, snuffled, opened his eyes, smiled at the rush of wind on his face, and began to croon the soft, gabbling song again.

'Jesus!' said Dingo, and chuckled.

The co-pilot ran out cable from the winch, checked a T-coupling and two steel links. There was a secondary motor, button operated. He fired it to test it, then, leaving it running, unpacked a stout nylon net from a fuselage locker.

'Done this before, gents?' he asked.

'I haven't,' said Goddard.

'I see,' said the co-pilot. 'Not frightened, though, are you, sir?'

'Not in the least,' Goddard lied.

The cable looked frail, the stand-bar incredibly narrow. Goddard wasn't at all sure that he wouldn't prefer to be lowered down in the net like the Dyak, and to hell with dignity.

'Be all right, sir?'

'Perfectly.'

The chopper spun round, hovering, then slithered towards the trees. It wasn't primary forest, and underbrush formed a mat for mixed softwoods and palmates.

'Oh-oh! Budgies,' said the co-pilot.

Swiftlets darted below the belly of the aircraft, hundreds of tiny dart-winged birds, their flight-paths flattened by sudden down-draught. The birds reminded the men in the Wessex that there was teeming life below. But it wasn't the creatures of the forest that gave them a brief, ill-defined pang of anxiety. It was the realisation that, by chance, the chopper might have been marked by an Indo patrol, that IBTs might be hurrying towards the area to pluck the chopper out of the sky with a hail of bullets or, more probably, to pick them off as they stepped down from the winch-bar.

'Davie-lad?'

'Aye-aye, skipper.'

'On the spur.'

'Aye-aye, skipper.'

The Wessex rose levelled in the air and seemed to sink, like a lift in a shaft, with hardly so much as a jerk, settling smoothly and deliberately into the massy trees. Then Deacon saw the 'spur', a rounded knob of grass, bleached and tinted rose-red. The trees enhanced the little 'hole', made it seem more exposed and broader than it was, built out with contorted roots and prostrate stems. The jungle took form from it.

'That's it, skipper.'

The helicopter continued its descent, down into the inverted funnel, oak and other giants closed around the rotors. The pilot dipped the Wessex like a fly into the centre of a spider's web, and hung it there.

Carrying his pack and weapon, Deacon went first, stepping from the hatch on to the winch-bar. There was little or no sway on the cable on a lower of twenty feet. The co-pilot let him down carefully. Deacon was too seasoned to leap to the ground; a twisted ankle might result. Around the major, leaves and tall grasses lashed angrily in the wind from the chopper's blades. Dust billowed from the rocky knob across a little swale. Deacon stepped from the far to the earth and laid his bergen to one side. He did not, however, release the gun while he steered Goddard to join him.

Letting out a sigh of relief, Goddard touched down. He winked at Deacon. 'Beats jumping, I suppose.'

Next came the net with the Dyak inside. The effects of the morphine had worn off slightly and the old tracker was unhappy inside the soft cage of nylon mesh. Wide awake, curled up, it took several minutes to untangle him. His pack and the short spear, without which he would not travel, were lowered separately, followed, finally, by Dingo Harper, relaxed on the bar.

The cable snaked upwards and vanished into the hatch and the co-pilot, leaning out, gave them a thumbs-up. Deacon replied with a clenched fist. The Wessex rose straight, creating a brief storm of wind, then tacked to the north and, within seconds, was out of sight.

Deacon drew the men down where they were, holding the Dyak by the arm. But Umgah needed no assistance or instruction now. Though he remained dazed by the effects of the drug, instinct rescued him from stupidity. By dawn, when the real slog would start, the old boy would have recovered.

Night was seeping fast through the trees. Monkey quarrels and the roost-twitter of diurnal birds were giving way to owl-hoots and the bark of nocturnal predators and stealthy rustlings which lay below the sibilance of the trees and plash of streamlets. They were, Deacon reckoned, in the first fold of the foothills, just below the series of 'saddles' that joined three rivers, Mamisi, Ruasi and the Tabuli. He had an urge to push on, to travel as far as possible into the heart of the basin-jungle. But it would have been dangerous. He was not adjusted yet to jungle country. Besides, he would need to be fresh for tomorrow's arduous hike.

Taking the lead, he pulled the team away from the drop point and, in ten minutes of twilight, found a narrow boar-track that curled into a patch of giant marrow fern. Without consulting Umgah, he skirted away from the fern and into the trees. The undergrowth was not particularly dense. He'd encountered worse in Malaya many a time. He led on for fifteen minutes, to clear the area of the drop zone thoroughly, then slung his bergen against the base of a tree.

'Umgah,' Deacon whispered. 'How does it smell to you?'

The Dyak knelt on the ground and made sniffing sounds for a moment. 'Okey, bass. *Rasak* trey. No arnts. No itchy gum.'

Goddard grunted.

Basak was one of several species known as Borneo cedar,

though it didn't have the distinctive smell of cedar. More important, it did not attract colonies of white ants, being impervious to their predations. The trees to avoid at all costs were the *kayu tai*, which gave off a dreadful stench when damp, and the common *rangas*, which exuded a tar-like sap that caused an intense itching rash. The *rasak* was broad-boled and dry and would provide a temporary shelter against rain that might fall in the night. There would be no *basha*, only a camp on the ground, without fire or light. They were twenty-three-or-four miles into Indonesia, behind the line of patrol activity. Even so, Deacon played it by the book.

In silence they ate cold chicken, washed down with mouthfuls of a light wine, a bottle of which Goddard had thoughtfully stowed in his pack. It would be their last 'civilised' meal, their last luxury. In the morning the chicken bones and wine bottle would be buried in humus and covered with unturned leaves.

It seemed that they had made it undetected into the heart of the Seven Rivers country. All they had to do now was survive snakes, mosquito bites and that swift malaise which could come at you out of the earth like a poisonous vapour, make fifteen miles or so through dense hostile territory, locate the Tabuli river and find a chap called Barry Greenwood.

Deacon was not daunted.

'Dingo. First watch. Rouse me at twenty-two hundred.'

'Right, boss.'

With his head wrapped in a loose bag of cheesecloth mosquito-netting and his body laid on a thin sheet of rubberised cotton, Major Jeffrey Alexander Deacon fell asleep. Fast asleep.

On his right the Dyak slept too. On his left, Goddard lay relaxed, looking up at the infinite sky where tiny, swimming, blue-black patterns were just visible through the *rasak*'s leafy branches; while Dingo Harper, squatting with his arms around his knees, kept himself alert by thinking consciously of girls and poetry and by wondering just when the boss would see fit to tell him what the hell he was doing here in darkest Kalimantan.

3 Blood hunt

The bed was a nice piece of furniture, box-sided, dowelled not nailed, made out of dark mahogany. The mosquito-net frame was of ubiquitous bamboo, split and whipped. The sheets on the bed were of rose-petal silk, clean except where the wound had leaked. The pillow was a real old mess, for some nitwit had plastered the guy's throat with gentian violet. Blood, serum and burn lotion had mapped the feather bolster, staining it beyond redemption. The bed was in the largest room in the long bungalow. The window shutters were roped open. There was even a turgid sort of fan which lagged the air like egg-white and probably used most of the juice eked out by the garrison's spluttering generator. At the foot of the bed, like mourners from a circus family, stood the Chink, the native girl and the skinny, unwashed soldier, Barry Greenwood.

Greenwood's mouth was open and his eyes were round.

'Hey, man, you can't be serious?' he said in disbelief.

'I gave you food. Now I want my favour,' said Arunja.

'It's not a favour you need, it's a bloody miracle.'

'Are you not a doctor?'

'Yeah, sure. But I'm not, repeat not, a surgeon.'

'You carry knives like a surgeon.'

'Listen, I thought you guys, Chinese, had great doctors. Acupuncture, that kind of—'

'Do you tell what is wrong with him?' Arunja interrupted.

'Anybody can tell you that. He's been shot through the neck.'

'He is dying.'

Here we go again, thought Doc Greenwood. This time, though, he did not disagree. It was patently obvious that the little Chinese guy in the neat wooden bed *was* dying.

Doc said, 'How long's he been here? I mean, when was he wounded?'

'Two days ago.'

'How?'

'With a bullet.'

'What sort of bullet?'

'It is not important. A bullet is all same.'

'Wrong,' said Greenwood. 'Bullets aren't all the same. If it was a small calibre handgun—'

'Rifle.'

'Good. Fine. What make of rifle?'

'The bullet comes out.'

Doc hesitated. He had already surmised that the big Chinese might be a savage, but that he wasn't completely stupid.

As the gunboat had crept across the lagoon to the jetty that jutted out into the water, Doc had had ample opportunity to study the layout at Ukiti. The lake was encircled by *tengah* and *bakau* trees, *nipah* and *nibong* palms. Some shrubs were in flower and the air around the camp smelled sweet, not foetid as you would have expected in a pirate's lair. The jungle had been cleared and the camp set out to a pattern. The bungalows were built of the stuff of the forest; well built. The jetties weren't sagging structures of bamboo. They were constructed from ironwood, which didn't grow in this sort of country but was plentiful around the coasts and had probably been ferried up river for the purpose. The tents were quality canvas, ridge and pup. Some of the men that Doc saw wore an unfamiliar grey-green uniform.

But it was the Vosper-type craft that really made him goggle.

He had bummed around enough ports to make some fairly accurate estimates. She would be fast. She would require a crew of around fifteen or twenty, which must include engineers, since she would be powered by complicated diesels. There was a midship funnel, a raffish, streamlined vent, presumably needed to feed air into the engine-room. What's more, she was in spanking trim. She had a name on her bow, painted in Chinese characters.

Mouse had translated. *Clouded Leopard*.

Instead of teeth, though, this particular leopard would have torpedoes. Instead of claws she had four 25mm cannon, plus a turret-mounted machine-gun and a contraption that Doc took to be a mine launcher. She wasn't flying the skull and crossbones. In fact, she carried no flag of identification. He had it in mind, though, that the *Leopard* was Chinese, a product of a

Shanghai shipyard. The name was a dead give-away. Russia and/or the Chinese People's Republic were obviously contract agents for Arunja's travelling battle troupe. Most probably the Chinese. Most probably the CCO in one of its guises. The guile and organising ability of the CCO had caught Special Forces out before. Unless he was way off beam, Doc Greenwood reckoned that the Special Forces were about to be caught out again. Fast strike capability. A gunboat and the *Leopard*. Two hundred trained men, a river navigable all the way into the hills – things were beginning to shape up like a fur-and-feather version of the Normandy Landings.

Greenwood added up facts in his head, not forgetting the heavy artillery that he'd seen man-handled across country by IBT troops. Pirates, Indo Tigers and Commies were beavering away in harmony. Major Dalinart would give his left ball for intelligence on this operation.

Right there and then, as the gunboat puttered to a mooring by the jetty, Lance-corporal Greenwood might have deduced that the target could only be a timber town; Balimbuka or, for a second time, Kalabakan. He might even have gotten to the root of it, worked out that enemy forces intended to secure the length of the Jaumpong, use it as a supplies artery to establish a new frontier.

Would Tawau be next on the hit list? Too bloody ambitious by half? Maybe not, not with the Chinese behind it and British Special Forces spread thin on the ground in the east coast zone. It was a far cry from six-man border crossings and sticking-up shops in tiny rural townships. The guys on the ground at Ukiti seemed to be disciplined. You could see it when the raft-load of nubile native girls floated alongside the jetty. Though the men eyed them hungrily there was no whooping rush to lug the captives away. Like the dead chickens, hog carcasses and sacks of rice and sago, the girls were off-loaded in an orderly manner and marched away by a detail of armed men. By that time Doc and the Mouse had been led away from the lagoon-shore jetties and were being ushered into the bungalow like honoured guests.

Breakfast, the price of cooperation, was substantial. It was served by a young boy, an Indo, in the small back room of the larger of the two bungalows. Fresh fruit and a fish dish, then a plate of Spam slices dipped in egg batter and fried. There was also coffee, a rich, dark, American blend. Doc, who had been pecking at the food without much appetite, found himself restored by the coffee, the first he had tasted in weeks. Coffee had always been his weakness. Real, well-brewed coffee, black as treacle and laced with sugar. He drank four mugs of the stuff. Instantly it shot up his blood sugar level, made him all bright-eyed and alert. Which was just as bloody well, considering that he hadn't had any sleep for fifty hours and had had his brains bounced off the side of a paddi field for good measure.

Mouse and he were left alone to eat the meal. They were not unguarded, of course, and hadn't the slightest chance of manufacturing an escape. Guards patrolled the verandah outside the room and there were sounds of men constantly coming and going beyond the bamboo curtain that served as a door. But it was cool in the room and the food was plentiful. And the coffee gave Doc a lift that transformed him, even made him forget the fact that, sooner or later, he would have to risk his neck to get out of here.

After half an hour, Arunja returned. He had changed into white duck-pants and a dark-blue terrycloth shirt, wore a gold Rolex on his wrist and a shark's tooth on a fine gold chain about his neck, a charm not an ornament. He looked more Californian than ever, Doc thought, but when the pirate asked him if he had enjoyed his breakfast he gave a non-committal reply.

Arunja walked Doc and the Mouse across a square-shaped hallway and into the broad room with the bed in it. He led them softly to the foot of the bed, nodded at the wounded man.

'Now you must heal him.'

After that, Greenwood hadn't much time for gathering information or for hatching an escape plot. He was too busy trying to convince the big guy that the little guy in the bed was beyond redemption, that a mere army-trained medic had no hope of pulling him back from the brink of the grave.

Arunja would have none of it. No excuses. No protests. Wouldn't wear them. Kept the head, though. Didn't make threats. Cajoled rather than bullied. Behind his rationality, however, was inflexibility, a determination that filled Doc with fear. After four or five minutes of argument, Doc made his pitch.

'Listen,' he said, 'and stop me if you don't understand. Okay?'

Arunja's features were flat and expressionless, his eyes impenetrable.

Doc said, 'Neck wounds carry a high mortality rate. Many major vessels, nerves and so forth, lie in the neck. For all I know he may be dying of fluid in the lungs or from blood loss. The bullet may have damaged his spine.'

'The bullet comes out.'

'Yeah, yeah,' said Doc Greenwood. 'But high velocity missiles do immense damage—'

'Im-mense?'

'Lots of damage, big damage. Big hole. Inside the neck. Listen, I've seen what happens. At a place called Fort Mapp, in America. Experiments with dogs and sheep and pigs. Photographs.'

Greenwood checked himself from running on about his education. He had put in one month on wounds. He recalled the 'gelatin block' lessons when the medics had studied the effects of missiles fired into blocks of solid gelatin, which was of much the same density and texture as human flesh. He remembered the expansion of the wound. Small entry and exit holes, with a 'hollow' of destroyed tissue within. It was called 'the cavitation effect', and that described it perfectly. A reasonably small wound, without much bleeding, invariably screened an internal cavity of sickening magnitude. The lessons had progressed from gelatin blocks to animals. The medics had learned how to excise specific types of bullet wounds, to clean and drain and dress them. And which ones to leave strictly alone.

Neck wounds were always a bitch. He recalled Surgeon-Colonel Hamilton Osman, a hefty and laconic gentleman from Georgia, lecturing in the Pathology building on a day of hazy heat, with the acacias hanging limp, and nothing on the hospital lawns except Osman's doberman, one of the live dogs, which lay there in the shade, panting. It had been cool in the demo lab, air-conditioned, but still reeking of ether and formalin and smoke from the cigar that Hamilton Osman puffed while he worked.

'Neck wounds,' the surgeon had told his students, 'fall into two categories. In category one, the patient dies within minutes. In category two, we marvel at his miraculous recovery.'

'Is that it, sir?' Greenwood had asked.

'Yup.'

'Isn't there anything we can do, sir?'

'You can try to check arterial bleeding by applying thumb pressure to the common carotid. In desperate cases you might use Treves' method. Expose the carotid by incision and loop it with catgut. A kind of tourniquet. But, frankly, if it's a bullet in the neck, boys, I suggest you send for the preacher. The only kind of intervention that can pull a neck wound through requires skilled surgery – and back-up. If you're out there in the boonies you ain't gonna have that on call. If you've got four, five cases queued up for attention, put the guy with the neck wound on ice. It ain't the kind of thing a field medic wants to meddle with.'

But whether he liked it or not, whether Colonel Hamilton Osman would approve or not, meddle with a neck wound was something that he, Lance-corporal Greenwood, was going to have to do. Otherwise the big Chink might forget he had hostage value and do more than pee all over him.

The placid little Chinaman in the nice neat bed was obviously a VIP. Greenwood, though he didn't think it through, had an inkling that Arunja had bungled, had allowed a high-brass officer from the CCO or even the Chinese army to get shot. It was on the tip of Doc's tongue to ask for details, circumstances. But suddenly it didn't seem to matter much. It also came home to Doc, with cynical certainty, that Arunja was only going through the motions of having the VIP patched up. Arunja really didn't give a hoot, not in his heart, if he had one. It would be a sop to conscience, maybe, to have a White Doktor make passes over the body, to have a British scapegoat to blame for the VIP's death.

Zen rubbish about going with the flow, man, suddenly

seemed like an irony, of even less philosophic value to a guy in his situation than Doris Day belting out that number from *The Man Who Knew Too Much*.

Que sera, sera: Whatever will be, will be.

Waves of fatigue gathered in Barry Greenwood, starting in his bowels. It wasn't your ordinary sort of weariness, rather a sudden sapping of confidence. He was forced to see himself clearly. Couldn't kid himself along. He was no damned doctor at all. Never had been. He was nothing but a glorified First Aid man, no better than the guys you saw trotting round the track at soccer matches.

He slid a hand under his belt and pressed his knuckles against his diaphragm, breathing, trying to control panic.

'Is it not time for examination?' said Arunja, who hadn't, of course, absorbed a bloody word he'd said.

'Sure, yeah, sure,' said Doc.

He pressed lightly on the trembling pulse at the base of his sternum. Nerves.

'You will heal him, make him well?'

'What if I don't? What if I can't?'

The Chinese crooked a gigantic forearm round Mouse's waist, fanning his hand over her lower belly. He drew the girl against him, chuckling. Mouse had enough savvy not to struggle or protest. On the pirate's wrist the gold Rolex gleamed. Terrorism, murder and extortion obviously paid well. But Arunja wasn't a mercenary, Doc realised. Arunja was a psychopath who needed cover for his sickness.

'I will kill your lady first,' said Arunja, with a smile. 'Slowly. You will watch to see how I succeed.'

Doc said nothing, did nothing.

Arunja's brutal fondling was a deliberate demonstration. Abruptly he released the girl. She stepped away, seeking the comfort of Doc's hand. She clung to him trustingly, staring up into his face.

Arunja said, 'What will you need to do healing?'

Doc swallowed. The pulsation had ceased. His bowels were steady. Panic waned, leaving a kind of resignation. No choices, no options. He had to be in reality what he had fancied himself to be in imagination. Big White Doktor.

'Clean blankets, clean white cotton sheets, boiling water. And a table. The breakfast table will do. Have it brought in here.' There was no trace of apprehension in the lance-corporal's tone. 'I need brushes for scrubbing. And a place to bathe. Her an' me, both. And my gear. The long case.'

The Chinese folded his arms and bowed.

Doc could read smugness in his eyes, an absolute, positive belief that this skinny British gink with his Bajau tart would complete the job of assassinating the VIP.

Already stripping off his filthy vest, Doc felt steady again, steady as a rock.

He murmured, 'The hell I will, man. The hell I will.'

'What you say?'

'Nothing,' answered the medic, and stepped out of his underpants to make himself ready for the bath.

Goddard proved himself to have an instinct for the jungle, honed by hundreds of up-country patrols. Even the Dyak, born and bred in a longhouse, could not quite match the police officer for speed and certainty in route-finding.

Boyd Goddard reminded Dingo of one of the old 'dowsers', water-diviners, that Queensland ranchers hired to find subterranean streams for them. He wore that same 'removed' look, not dreamy or mystical, just distant. And he walked with the same sort of gait, as if he could feel what lay ahead through the soles of his feet. The cigarette-holder in his mouth, plugged with an unlit butt, would twitch occasionally as he pondered a change in direction, then, like an antenna, would turn and point through the undergrowth or separated trunks of the primary forest. Deke relinquished leadership without a qualm. Goddard and the Dyak were, after all, navigators and he was a stranger in this strange land. The Deke's time of command would come soon enough.

Dingo was reconciled to being not much else but a pack-mule at this stage in the operation but, even allowing for the extra weight of the radio in his bergen, he was confident that he could walk any of the others into the deck.

At first the ground was dry but as the team descended from the saddle into the broad, palm-shaped river basin the earth became slippery and the nature of the foliage changed. There were streamlets to wade across, then deep-cut ravines massed with leaves and criss-crossed by fallen timber in a state of wet decay. Goddard led, Umgah behind him, not close. Dingo came next with the Deke at the rear.

The packs were cumbersome. Pockets of moist heat gathered between them and the skin, rivulets of sweat running down the spine. Weapons, one Sterling and two Armalites, were carried in the hands, never slung. Even although the team were well beyond the zone of border activity they had to be prepared for surprise attack or, more likely, for running into a column of Tigers hiking to the border posts. But it was not all pack-and-hack, not by a long shot.

Almost as if he had studied inch-to-the-mile maps – of which, of course, there were none – Goddard had the knack of finding grass patches and those so-called bridle paths, often made by animals, which gave easy passage. They had one unexpected halt when the track fell suddenly into a lush clearing of half-acre size in which grazed a herd of Bantings, big aggressive bulls, handsome and not common in the wild, and their milky-legged cows. Goddard hesitated for a couple of minutes, the Dyak crouched by his side. Then Umgah sniffed what wind there was and directed the team around the clearing on the safe side, disturbing the animals hardly at all.

Through most of that humid day the team trekked. Boy Goddard had privately determined that they would camp on the banks of the Tabuli before nightfall, close enough to post a watch on the river in the hope of sighting Indo activity. Dingo found it odd that they encountered no tribesmen, not even a trace of hunters' encampments. It was as if the forest was not only virgin to British troops but undiscovered by man.

It was mid-afternoon when the rain began. Through the trees the sky remained blue; and yet it rained. Straight, glassy rods of water pierced the leaf cover, drummed into the grass and, disturbingly, made the forest alive with nodding ferns and trembling palm-leaves. The rain soaked Goddard's concentration as it soaked the fabric of his shirt. His instinct disintegrated like the unlit butt in his cigarette-holder. Then, too, there was that nagging worry about the duration of the downpour. If it lasted long enough, streamlets would swell into gushing torrents and creeks would be transformed into bolting horseback-brown floods, and rivers, namely the Tabuli, would become totally impassable. A night of heavy rain in the foothills would be enough to do it. Though the floods would drop just as swiftly, delay would be incurred. Delay this early in the hunt would have a knock-on effect which, in three days, might prove fatal.

Dingo was too uncomfortable to look beyond his next step. Within minutes the ground had become snake-slippery and treacherous. In the bergen was a cape, an oilskin poncho. He wondered when Goddard would call a halt to put on the rainproofs.

Then they came to the innominate creek.

It was never properly identified. But forever after the place was etched in Dingo Harper's mind, each spray of leaves dented by rain, the great banks of vegetation, porous as leprosy scabs and of somewhat the same hue, the soar of cork trees going up to a scribble of washed-blue sky.

Goddard stood, hands on hips, by the drop. Below was a steep cliff of mud and curly growth, the growing stuff fine as a baby-hair. You could see gathering water trickling through it, see how, a half-hour before, there wouldn't have been much down there, forty feet below, except a stand of near-stagnant lettuce-green water. But infiltration from the falling land had filled it already, giving mass and movement to the lentic stream. It gurgled and flowed mysteriously and might well be deep. It ran uncommonly straight for at least three hundred yards to Goddard's left, though to the right – north-west – it vanished into a mass of shrubs.

Umgah scratched his nose with the tip of his spear.

Dingo had no means of knowing what was on the Dyak's mind.

'Shall we cross, Umgah?' Goddard whispered. 'Or had we better follow the bank on this side?'

'Go that wey, *tuan*. River over der.'

'How far?'

'Tew mile, mebbe.'

It was on the tip of Dingo's tongue to mention poncho-drill.

But he didn't wish to intrude. He could have fished the bloody thing out on his own initiative but the Deke had joined them too, now, and there was something going on between the three seniors that slotted the young officer into a subordinate place, something he didn't quite understand.

'Trouble, Deke?'

'No.'

Goddard whispered, 'It's blank. We'll cross here.'

'It'll save time, certainly,' said Deacon. 'If the river rises . . .'

'Yes,' said Goddard. 'I don't much care for rain of this sort, out of a clear sky. Can go on for hours and hours. Odd phenomenon.'

Englishmen discussing the vagaries of weather.

Umgah agreed by nodding his head.

The men shifted to the left, halted again at the base of a fallen log, a cork-like trunk eight or ten feet in diameter which had grown too heavy for its own support and, with roots ripped from the sub-soil, had toppled across the ravine. Moss had continued to grow around it and there were a few feather-light leaves from a species of vine here and there. It was not the only piece of dead-fall. The creek was crossed by three or four such bridges, plus a few tousled trees that had slid bodily into the basin and stood at drunken angles, quietly decaying.

Two miles to the Tabuli, Dingo thought. Thank God, they would be on the river before dark. He hated struggling with chuck-tins and a hammock-sling in the pitch bloody dark. Besides, he wanted to get the bergen off and peel away his shirt. There was something on his back, just below the shoulder-blade, and he was desperate to pick it off, whether it was leech or tic or an innocuous fern spore that had wriggled down his collar. He stood there, like a bloody dumb-bell, with rain running off the bill of his hat, and waited for the other three to sort it out.

The Dyak went first. He was light and carried no pack of any weight. If the log seemed solid then the other three with their heavier burdens would tackle it. Umgah, Dingo noticed, didn't rush the crossing. He went over in twenty little steps, bare feet curved to the shape of the log, and the spear held before his breast like a rope-walker's pole. He went off the end of the log and into the tangle and, after a couple of seconds, put his head out, grinned and waved them on – Dingo, Goddard and Deacon, in that order.

Umgah was not to blame for what happened.

The Indo patrol hadn't passed this way. They had come off a more prominent track to the north. Why they had stopped, why they had been so silent so many miles into their homeland, apparently in no danger at all, was something that couldn't be explained. There was no reason for them being there, unless it was to play out some deadly game that chance had dictated for the express purpose of knocking the shit out of Dingo and souring the whole bastard operation before it had hardly started.

All the time the SAS men stood on the edge of the cliff they must have been under observation, the Indo Tigers belly-down, hearts racing, breath caught in their mouths, fingers on the triggers of their assault rifles. Waiting. At least one trained man among them knew that there was a proper moment to shoot, and that moment would be when the team split and the signaller was balanced on the log.

If Kipling had been with them he might have written up the encounter, not heroically, but with tongue in cheek:

How the Dingo Lost his Radio.

Just so.

Almost on the stroke of noon Greenwood made his first incision into the flesh of an Oriental gentleman whose name was not known to him. He was assisted, if that was the word, by two so-called medics, Filipinos, that Arunja dredged up for him. The slender-necked medics were young and appeared insolently indifferent to the responsibilities which Greenwood allotted them. Doc had no faith in the pair. In fact, in the whole room the only person he could trust was Mouse.

Like Doc, Mouse was dressed in a white cotton sheet, slits cut for the arms, back fastened with cotton stitches. Beneath the improvised surgical gown, the girl, like Doc, was naked. The pair had bathed and Doc had carefully shaved the hair from his forearms, had washed hands and arms with the block of ether soap from the saxophone case in a galvanised tub of warm water that Arunja's servants produced. He had found no suitable gloves. He would be obliged to delve bare-handed into the guy's cavities.

There was light enough in the bungalow, though he had asked Arunja for gauze to fashion some sort of curtain over the windows. No gauze. He compromised by leaving two unglazed windows open but closed those nearest the operating-table. The wooden table had been scrubbed with a latherless 'Chinese' soap and, after humming and hawing for a minute or so, Doc had finally had it padded with clean blankets quilted with a couple of sheets. The stuff had been well laundered and came, Doc suspected, from the MTB, *Clouded Leopard*.

Medically Doc had no help at all from Arunja or his aides, and the pirate turned up no medical supplies, except basic dressings and pots of the foul gentian violet. Doc Greenwood was thrown back on the meagre resources contained in the sax case, resources which hadn't been gathered with a view to performing surgery of this complexity.

In a little pocket in the sax case, though, was one useful item, a dumpy volume entitled *Primer of Anatomy for Surgical Nurses*. He had bought it years ago – when his interest in medicine was merely that of a layman – in a second-hand bookshop in Scarborough. It had cost him a couple of bob but had repaid that outlay a thousand times. Never more so than on that weird morning by the lagoon at Ukiti. For a half-hour, while Arunja's guys got on with preparations, Greenwood sat on the step of the porch and drank coffee and pored over the primer. The plates were explicit but not, alas, in colour. He studied them, though, as if they were prayers in a missal or *The Thought of Chairman Mao.* Last-gasp refresher course in where veins and arteries coiled in relation to muscles groups and bony structures. If only the guy had had a nice clean chest wound or a hole in his belly, he could have made a show of coping. But neck wounds meant high risk of mortality. He had no plasma, no whole blood, no saline. He could have rigged some kind of transfuser but he lacked the ability and the confidence to group-test. If the little guy, past the meridian of life by the look of him, had survived for forty-eight hours, though, he must have stamina and a definite will to live.

At ten to noon, Doc went into the long room in the bungalow. He saw the patient carefully transferred from bed to table. The three side-tables he had asked for – bamboo jobs, of course – were in place, covered with cloths. Four shallow galvanised wash-basins were on hand too. In one, in a mixture of alcohol and water, he washed the instruments he thought he would require. He had a fair kit with him, including three haemostats. Also – thank God – an Edward's vein-seeker. This was an ingenious if old-fashioned piece of equipment which Greenwood had learned to use in a dozen different ways. A large hollow needle was fitted to the seeker, a needle usually used to infuse anaesthetic into bone marrow. But on this occasion he intended to administer minimal doses of Pentothal via the needle by insertion into a prominent vein at the fold of the elbow. With the vein-seeker in place he could juice up the anaesthetic as required, no more, no less than he needed to do what had to be done.

Doc laved and sterilised the patient's skin. The man's hair was black and fine as silk, cropped short. Doc used his own safety razor to enlarge the area around the ear and nape of the neck, to make it shiny bald.

During all this procedure Arunja watched intently, a faint, faint smile upon his lips.

Doc ignored his captor.

It was at this point that Doc began to realise that the patient was no longer comatose. Flicker of the lids, a stirring, so slight and suppressed that Doc could hardly detect it. He hesitated, hand on the man's arm.

'Hey?' said Doc.

How long had the guy been conscious? Maybe he had been conscious all the time, just lying there, supine, kind of floating. The lids flickered. Doc felt again for the pulse. Found it steady, not thready.

'Hey, man?'

The Chinese opened his eyes, black, flat eyes but with something odd in them, too subtle to be false.

The tongue moved on dry lips. With a certain firmness the patient uttered a word. He didn't address it directly to Doc but spoke straight to the ceiling. It wasn't English or any of the Malayan dialects that Doc recognised. Doc glanced at the Mouse. She shook her head. The little guy, flat on his back, still in that state of utter relaxation, repeated the word.

Arunja stepped to the table.

Patient and pirate; their eyes met briefly.

The patient said another word, spreading his lips. The pronunciation was clear and precise, the meaning, to Doc, unclear.

Arunja did not reply, gave nothing away.

The black flat eyes picked up on Doc. The little guy knew exactly what was going on, everything, right to the nub of it, right to the fact that Doc had suspected from the word Go, that the White Doktor wasn't here to save his life by medical skill but to take it through lack of it.

The patient spoke again, to Doc this time. It wasn't that the voice was weak, just that Doc didn't dig the fact that the guy was speaking yet another language. Doc leaned closer, still touching the thin, healthy left arm, ready to draw it out and plonk it on the side-table and stick in the needle of the Edward's vein-seeker.

'Sorry?' Doc said.

'*Bon chance*,' said the patient, and closed his eyes.

French, for God's sake. The half-dead Chinkie VIP was wishing him Good Luck. He would need all the *bon chance* he could get. Both of them would. Doc felt a peculiar rapport with the patient, and a fleeting transference of ultimate responsibility, as if he had been absolved for his temerity. Also, passing intangibly between them, some of the Chinese relaxation, transcendental and mystical. If ever, by some miracle, he got himself back to San Fran, to Barbara Badillo and her gang, he would have a real tale to tell. No shit.

Doc stretched out the patient's arm, held it comfortably down on the side-table and dabbed the skin with a swab of alcohol. He lifted the glass tube of the vein-seeker, loaded with all the Pentothal he possessed, found the vein and inserted the long needle. With his fingertip he tabbed strips of sticky tape he had cut to length and, showing great dexterity even in this simple action, rubbed them smoothly into place across the breadth of the arm, fixing needle and rubber-tube attachment in place. Gently he depressed the plunger, paused, then, as the patient's lids drooped, lowered the vein-seeker to the table.

Doc stepped around the table and took his place on the right side, hands held up and forward like a priest offering benison. Mouse was just behind him now, seated on a rattan stool. Knives and other instruments, all that he had, were laid out neatly. He had instructed Mouse to put them into his hand in order, unless he told her otherwise.

'Okay, kid?'

She laid the scalpel into the palm of his outstretched hand.

Doc worked it into the tips of his fingers.

He studied the contour of the patient's neck, seeing it in relation to the primer's diagramatic drawings, but knowing full well that a gaudy and confusing mess lay beneath the surface.

Without looking up, he said, 'Bugger off, you.'

Arunja grunted, displeased.

Doc said, 'Go on, man, bugger off. Move out. Shove. I don't need you breathing all over him. Right?'

The first infusion of Pentothal would be taking effect. The patient gave every sign of being truly unconscious, no faking. Doc heard Arunja creak away across the floor, out of range. Behind him, one of the Filipino boys sniggered. He would us them to fetch and carry water, if he needed it; for nothing else, though.

'Ready, kid?' he asked the Mouse.

'I am ready.'

The blade in his fingers felt lithe.

Greenwood marked the line of initial incision with the forefinger of his left hand. Pressing lightly into the flesh, he laid the blade to the line and made a bold stroke.

As he had anticipated, there was a tempestuous release of blood.

Artery or vein? He had less than five minutes to locate the sites of the damage and ligate them. After that the patient would die.

Five minutes.

Greenwood drew in a deep breath, held it, and swiftly and surely enlarged the wound.

Three bullets whacked almost simultaneously into the bergen, shattering the radio instantly and, by force of impact, lifting Dingo Harper from the log. The noise behind his head was like somebody kicking a can of screwnails.

Coupled with muffled reports from the assault rifles buried in the leaves, and a sudden scare of macaques that had been browsing in the trees nearby, the din momentarily confused the Australian. But speed of reaction had been instilled in him by long training. He turned the ungainly fall into a para-style jump, gun held in both hands above his head and knees flexed into a half-seat position.

Thirty feet may not seem much but it was fall enough. If the water in the creek had flowed over rocks, Dingo would for sure have suffered injury. As it was, though, it was like leaping into sponge rubber. Oozy mud grabbed at his calves and thighs, sucked him backwards so that he could not keep his head up and the Armalite in shape to fire. Gravy rushed into his mouth and nostrils, making him gag. The bloody bergen was dragging him down. It was snagged by its straps in a tangle of roots or a submerged branch. Dingo had no option but to release the rifle. He thrust it from him, extended his arms and beat upon the water like a butterfly.

Neck jerked backwards, he would drown in the shallow flood if he didn't, somehow, get shot of the anchoring bergen. He fumbled at his webbing belt, found the knife, unsheathed it, and started sawing frantically. He couldn't see a damned thing, of course, since the water slopped over his upturned face. Had a vague image of cavernous trees, black-massed banks of the creek topped by the straight line of the log. Whorls of colour. He reared, breathed, sagged, hacking at the strap. It tore, broke and Dingo cam up on his side. Ramming his right arm down into the slimy depths to find purchase, he went on down, spluttering, since the creek had no base. Deliberately he drove down, paddling knees and feet. He twisted, couldn't see, felt for and found the bergen and hoisted it up, extricated his body from the remaining strap and was, at last, free.

By then Harper had been in the soup for a couple of minutes. He hadn't a bloody clue what was happening around him. If he hadn't gone arse-over-elbow he could have had position and angle immediately, would have realised that he was out of the firing line. Deke was greased lightning when threatened in a routine attack like this one, and a nice, brisk little shooting match was going on upstairs long before Dingo surfaced. Naturally he hadn't any hope of dragging himself out of the creek up near-sheer banks slicked with rain. Squatting, treading water, he raised his head and surveyed the situation.

The current was far too sluggish to drag him away. He hung suspended. He spotted the Armalite only three or four feet from him, resting rather than floating on the surface. Bubbles of gas and a trash of leaf debris had been churned up but he could make out the butt of the weapon and, dog-paddling, reached it in three strokes. He held it aloft, stripped water from it with his right hand, then, still with the weapon raised, paddled against the south wall and started upstream towards the source of the rifle fire at a sort of half-swim, half-walk. He made hardly any noise, just the soft plash of his belly parting the stream. He breathed through his nose. He passed under the log bridge, forged on for another ten yards then paused behind a screen of foliage that sprayed from an uprooted shrub.

Rifles barked intermittently. At least he wasn't a sole survivor. Umgah had got over the bridge, would be all right, probably. The old tracker would know how to melt into cover. Unless he had walked straight on to the Indo guns. But the Dyak wasn't providing that stammering barrage. Must be Goddard or, more likely, the Deke. Up ahead, the creek issued from a narrow corner overhung by emerald leaves and shored by a gable of coppery rock. There was flow there, eddy and coil, even a little slithering fall. Maybe a means of getting himself out of the trough and into the action.

Dingo waded on, low in the water, shimmying his hip to propel himself forward. The rain, he noticed, had intensified, hissing hard now, the creek webbed with it. The downpour washed the dirt from his face. He curled his tongue, stuck it out and tasted sweet rain-water, swallowed it in little sips. The ground under his feet became solid, a shoal or rock shoulder protruding into the liquid. He picked his steps with care, came rapidly out of the creek until he was standing, ankle-deep, by the copper-coloured outcrop. Sense told him that the ambushers had no sight line down the creek bed and might therefore assume that he was a gonner. Communication with the Deke would have been useful. But that was out of the question.

Dingo didn't hang around. Even if the Indos withdrew – and they would be tactically correct to do so – the patrol would have to be hunted down and exterminated if the secrecy of the operation was to be preserved.

Needle-in-haystack time, Dingo, Maurice Harper told himself.

A grenade exploded. A branch fell with a smothered rush. A wisp of smoke drifted across the creek by the screen of emerald leaves.

Dingo pushed on quickly, rounding the rock corner. Ahead, the creek was emphatically narrower, less swampy, the banks not quite so high. He couldn't make out too much beyond the leaf-screen but he aimed for it, hurrying, head tilted back and his gaze anxiously roving the banks, from which direction trouble might stumble on him at any second. Of one thing the battle-hardened captain was reasonably sure – the Tigers hadn't crossed the creek. All to the good. It meant that Deke or somebody had put up a show of resistance.

There was a helluva volume of water in the tunnel-like creek a hundred yards upstream from the bridge. He passed through the umbrella of emerald leaves carefully, with tumbling water pressing up to mid-thigh. A pool under a rock chute was laced with falling rain. Dingo knew now what he would do. Circle behind the enemy positions. If the bastards were lying doggo then he might be able to weave behind them, provided he could wriggle out of the creek. He was about two hundred yards upstream from the log bridge when he found an exit, a low loamy fold in the bank, a kind of earth slide. It was pierced by knuckles of new growth, grotesque bone-like roots and hairy shoots like caterpillars. Dingo swarmed up it.

At the top he paused, pressed himself down. He checked the

Armalite. He had no dry cloth with which to wipe it. Wouldn't have done much good, anyhow, since the rain was teeming. At least the sound of the rain in the forest would help to obliterate any careless noises he might make. Dingo had no fear, no real fear. It wasn't like one of the patient patrols along a path through dry jungle. He had the distinct impression that he was the hunter and not the hunted. Behind him, left and downstream, three snap shots reverberated through the drenched shrubs, bounced in dull echoes from the tree trunks. With aching concentration, Dingo listened for return fire.

Yip, there it was, the bark of a submachine-gun, snarling. The Indos were dug into the bush and he had them flanked.

He adjusted the Armalite, tucking it into his elbow. He took out the sheath-knife again, held it in his fist, and left the creek, heading away from the water, keeping the enemy on his left.

Trees stepped up and down, some unhealthy palms mixed in the softwoods, knitted together by moss and vines and creepers. Dense secondary jungle, *belukar*. It had apparently been cultivated at some period in the past, though by what crazy sub-tribe, Dingo couldn't imagine. This wasn't paradise. This was the armpit of an armpit island.

Dingo changed direction.

The Indos came within range and into view abruptly. They weren't so close to the creek as Dingo had fancied. He had come within an ace of failing to make a wide enough arc to work behind them. Luck was with the Aussie, however. As he parted a stand of wild maize he spotted the bastards. They were slightly below him. Five uniformed Tigers. He noticed at once their nervousness and the fact that none of the kids had a submachine-gun. Must be more of them, at least one other. Shit! In spite of himself, Dingo experienced a squint-over-the-shoulder sort of dread which is the lot of the jungle fighter, the jumpy sensation that somebody is right behind you, stalking you.

If there were a dozen men in the patrol then he was pretty-well cooked. But if there were only five or six – and six was normal for the Indos too – then he had the drop. Gingerly, Dingo lowered himself to one knee. The stalks of the wild crop, like a big tuft of white hair among the green stuff, were soft and sappy. He inched forward, tucked the knife into its sheath again, extracted two mags from the pouches of his webbing belt and laid them by his left hand on the ground. He thumbed the catch, lifted the Armalite and sighted.

The Indos were high with fear and excitement, slung between the feeling that they had done something wonderful and the uncertainty which plays havoc with a guerrilla's satisfaction in a kill. Though the five were young, Dingo had sight of the 'official' uniforms to salve his conscience – if it needed salving. They were soldiers all right. For all he knew, they had murdered Boyd Goddard. Christ, they had tried very hard to murder him, come to think of it.

Dingo fired five single shots without changing position. The range was about forty yards. Nothing disrupted his aim. He got two Tigers in the back, two in the head and the last – who had whipped round in blind terror – in the centre of the chest.

Dingo didn't hang around to count his tally. Almost before the bullet exploded into the body of the fifth Tiger, Dingo was retreating. He pulled back thirty yards from the maize stand and buttonhooked again, following a route with the maize stand as marker. He was now at his most vulnerable. He had no real notion how many guerrilla troops *were* in the area. But he knew for sure there was a machine-gunner, probably a senior NCO, and that he had better not step on the bugger.

There was also the danger, not to be underestimated, that he might unwittingly shoot Deke or Boyd Goddard or be shot by them. The dreaded 'own goal'. He figured that survivors of the SAS team were still across the river but he couldn't be one hundred per cent sure. Ten minutes at least had elapsed since he'd been wafted into the creek. In jungle warfare ten minutes was an eternity. He had just decided that he should find a hide, and settle, when he heard the unmistakable click of a metal clip being fitted to a weapon. Dingo held his breath and carried himself forward on the balls of his feet. For a big man he moved lightly and silently when he had to. But he had no further sound to home in on and the Indo sergeant was hidden in an excellent position to cover the creek crossing.

Dingo didn't see the bloke until it was too late.

He could not have saved himself.

He stepped forward, slithered and skidded down into a bowl of yellowish marsh grass. Suddenly he knew where he was, could see the rise of ground to the creek ahead of him, twenty yards away, the streaked wall of the forest beyond it. The Indo sergeant *had* drawn back. But hadn't retreated.

It was all over in the time it takes to draw one breath.

Instinct caused Dingo Harper to whirl round. The Indo's gun, a submachine-gun, was trained on him. The bastard was standing. You could see virtually nothing of him. He had found himself a screen, a dropping leaf-laden branch that covered him from head to heels. Only when he extended the muzzle of the weapon did Dingo pick him up. And by that time the bloke's finger was coming tight on the trigger. Dingo didn't even have time to swing the Armalite. He was cauvht wide and handsome and waited for the spurt of flame that would bring a spasm of agony and, immediately thereafter, darkness, eternal darkness.

But the Tiger sergeant didn't pull the trigger. He seemed to hover behind the leaves, then came out. Not walking. Falling. He fell face down on top of the gun without a yelp or gasp, in utter amazed silence. Dead before he struck the leaf mass at the verge of the clearing. Out of fear and panic Dingo might have blasted the redoubtable Dyak to kingdom-come, if he hadn't noticed the spear sticking upright from the soldier's back. He jerked the snout of the Armalite towards the sky and the one shot he had snatched from the rifle winged harmlessly away.

Umgah made round eyes at the Australian. He fluttered the fingers of his left hand then straddled the body of the Indo sergeant. He put one naked foot on the sergeant's buttocks and extracted the spear. The tip was neatly painted with bright red blood which began to trickle thinly down the shaft in the rain.

Umgah called out, 'Gettimal, *tuan.* Fetch Mejer Deck, okey?'

Shaken, Dingo did not enquire as to how the old tracker could be certain that all the members of the Indo patrol had been accounted for. When the Dyak shooed him with his hand, Dingo meekly obeyed. He trudged across the grass bowl and climbed the slope into the trees, making a considerable noise.

If the Deke was alive then the Deke would have heard shooting and would be on his guard. Anyhow, the major did not make elementary mistakes. Dingo hauled himself on to a moss crown by contorted tree roots. Below, the creek meandered impassively under the log bridges. Dingo peered through rain and gathering darkness and, naturally, saw no sign of life.

'Boss?' he said, his voice rusty. 'Boss, are you there?'

A shape rose from the ferns, the stocky figure of Boyd Goddard, then the Deke, both unharmed.

'I'm here, Dingo,' said Major Deacon. 'What happened?'

'I lost the bloody radio,' the Aussie answered despondently.

'Careless devil,' Deacon said and, nudging Goddard, made his way across the bridge.

Wound ballistics had never been one of Doc Greenwood's favourite subjects. He had, however, mastered it sufficiently to pass with high recommendation from the Special Surgical Unit attached to Fort Mapp Veterans' Hospital, which was in itself contained within the larger establishment of the United States Army MMS complex: Military, Medical and Surgical. He had seen what bullets could do to human flesh. Hence it came as no surprise to discover what lay within the Chinaman's neck, the characteristic pulping caused by a high velocity missile. Thrombosis and statis had increased in ratio to time elapsed between injury and surgical intervention. The volume of dead tissue was considerable. Plasma had seeped from damaged vessels and pooled with blood from the carotid artery and jugular vein to form a tense internal oedema. In other words, the neck was a right fucking mess.

Swift examination revealed an unexpected and amazing benefit from the wound type, however, and explained quite a lot. The very oedema which should have swamped the Chinese VIP had saved him. Contused matter had blocked spurting blood from damaged vessels and, with a bolus of clotted blood adhering to cotton fibres sucked into the cavity by the explosive passage of the bullet, had coagulated in the sac between the sterno-mastoid and the hem of the trapezius muscle. The sub-clavian artery was depressed by it but, lying deep in the vee of the long oblique incision, it did not appear to be bruised, let alone severed.

Jugular and carotid were active now that the plug had been washed out. Gouts of bloody matter dribbled down the slope of the patient's chest. With a clean rag Mouse wiped them away, darting in and out and impeding Greenwood's examination not at all.

'Swab,' said Greenwood.

She handed him the cotton. He cleansed away the blood from the aperture and, for a moment only, had a perfect sight of the damaged area. He turned the surgical blade and cut across the thick muscle, the sterno-mastoid, making sure that he bisected it completely. Now he had access to the interior of the neck. He swabbed again, tossed the soaking swab away, and pinched the common carotid artery between finger and thumb. It had been, so far, easier than he had anticipated.

'Stat, kiddo,' he said.

She had no idea what he was talking about, really. But she didn't hesitate, placing the haemostat into his hand.

He had to be real careful. Blind, haphazard application of haemostats might prove disastrous. He had only three of the damned things anyway, those useful tools, like butter-curlers. He inserted the stat under the rim of the muscle, dabbed away blood, and stretched the muscle back. Strictly speaking, his 'assistant' should help. But he had no assistant, except the Mouse and he needed her for other things. What he really needed was an extra pair of hands. The whole of the neuro-vascular bundle was exposed, though, and he had stopped obvious bleeding from the artery, at least temporarily.

'Stat.'

Mouse slapped another haemostat into his hand. He released the carotid long enough to clamp the stretcher in place. The wound grinned wet and red.

Doc couldn't understand why the guy wasn't dead. The bullet had passed through the side of the neck but hadn't bored deeply into the infra-structure. The jawbone should have been smashed by impact but wasn't, which indicated that the bullet had been close to the surface. Maybe the Chink had flinched an instant before the missile struck, had cocked his head. There should, in theory, have been splitting of the skin, a long burned wormcast. But there wasn't.

Greenwood let the wound bleed freely for a second while he reached across the guy and injected another portion of Pentothal through the Edward's vein-seeker. He was moving faster and faster. He seemed to have risen above himself, as if he was some kind of robotic machine being ordered about by a detached intelligence. His brain, his thinking mind, was oddly separated from his hands. They had a nimbleness and a dexterity that he hadn't suspected, an intelligence of their own. But he needed the Mouse, couldn't now do without her.

'Hold and swab,' Greenwood told her. 'When I nod my head, swab.'

She understood him, remembering his lesson.

Mouse ducked under him, made herself incredibly small and unobtrusive. She didn't appear to be squeamish or uncertain. She applied tension to the stem of the haemostat and mopped at the blood with cotton. On tip-toe, Doc stretched over the girl to the side-table. He plucked up the needle, the broadest and bluntest in the sax case's collection. He placed it on the patient's chest then lifted his only pair of dissecting forceps from the table. The ligature was fashioned of two strands of braided silk, pre-cut and prepared.

'Keep swabbing,' Doc growled.

Mouse's fingers were like thistledown, soaking away blood.

By contrast, Dock felt clumsy and unprofessional. He experienced a sudden frightful loss of confidence. He hated what he was being forced to do, because it showed up his ineptitude. He didn't lack knowledge, only ability. He thought of summoning one of the Filipinos to assist but tossed out the notion at once. He was better off juggling, better off without some casual idiot hand slabbering about the wound. This wasn't like stitching up a gashed leg or closing a laceration.

Doc worked.

His fingers felt like pork sausages, his thumbs like black puddings. At the back of his mind was worry about the vein, about the possibility of an air embolism being trapped in the system. It would kill the patient faster than a cyanide jag.

Doc's fingers did what they had to do. Passed the hook-tipped needle around the artery, after delicately separating the artery from its sheath. Stripped the artery's contents. Necessary to prevent the first ligature being loosened by the pulse. Fingers and thumb right down close to the vessel. Tighten the silk loop. Couldn't tell by sensation if he had it or not.

'Swab. Swab.'

Peering. Yeah, he had done it. One more and the time pressure would be off, since the jugular vein wasn't pumping heavily after all. Work at it. Fast. Careful. Shit. Careful. Shit. Easy, man, easy. Wish I knew what I was doing, *really* knew what I was doing. That's nice, that's it, though. Holy Moses! Yeah!

The hairfine thread of braided silk seemed to have a life of its own, bending under the emptied vessel, not gripping it or biting into it, just coming under real easy. He placed the second ligature and the third, and anchored the last with a single tiny stitch. He lifted his head.

He had been bent almost double, his nose only an inch from the gaping flesh. Mouse had tucked his sweat-heavy gown back and held it tense with her knee. Sweat beaded his brow and rivered his back. His spine felt as if it would crack with strain. And he had only been in there five minutes or so. He straightened. Groaned. Turned his head. Coughed. Wiped his brow and cheeks with his wrist, daubing blood on himself.

Bad part was over, though Time pressure off.

Still had to ligature the jugular. Recommended procedure in all cases of repair to the common carotid. Could do it now.

Squinting, he dabbed up the last of the braided silk strands.

Patient's pallor and respiration? Breathing steady but shallow. No evidence of great distress. No waxen, sweaty tint that indicated serious trouble. Come on, man, the guy *is* in serious trouble. But he's holding his own. Most you can say. He isn't ready to meet his ancestors yet. More work. More fumbling uncertainty. Shit. Get to it.

Doc leaked the last of the Pentothal into the elbow vein.

He dried his face once more, bent his head.

Mouse grabbed a handful of clean dry cotton. Swabbed.

A quarter of an hour later it was done. Doc closed the long

wound and applied a light dressing. He made a final series of checks on the patient, searching for signs of surgical shock and for adverse motor responses that might indicate an embolism, that deadly little air-lock.

The Chinaman's pulse was weak but steady. Doc was astonished at the guy's resilience. He dismantled the vein-seeker and put it aside with the other instruments to sterilise. He was exhausted now, trembling. But he would go on, do all the chores that had to be done, see the VIP snug into bed. What's more, he would nurse him personally for the next twenty-four hours. Mouse and he.

He stepped back at last. Everything clean and neat before him. Mouse uncurled herself, did not stand but squatted like a real native girl, her knees stuck out. Resting. Her eyes were huge with fatigue.

Doc put a hand on her shoulder. 'Hot stuff, Mouse,' he said.

In Malayan, the girl asked, 'Have you saved his life?'

'Maybe,' said Doc.

But he didn't think so. He really didn't think so.

The medic might have answered *yes* in the flush of optimism that came after surgery. But the soldier in Greenwood was more cynical. And from here on in, Greenwood reckoned, it was the soldier's instinct he would have to obey.

He called for hot water and, peeling down his blood-stained gown, washed his hands wearily while Arunja, from the doorway, watched his every move.

An hour before dawn Deacon roused the team. The men required little rousing, for they had spent an uncomfortable night under a scanty shelter of leaves which did little to hold out the incessant rain. Supper had been dished out from a ration can, and breakfast too, a sickly concoction of cooked oatmeal and honey from a bronze-coloured can, bad enough when warm but quite disgusting when cold. It was the best that could be managed under the circumstances. Deacon would not risk lighting a fire or even the little camp stove that he carried for emergencies. They washed the sticky porridge down with rainwater flavoured with a dash of Gordon's gin from the bottle in Deacon's pack.

They had 'camped', if that was the word, a mile south of the creek, travelling in total darkness away from the site of the bloody incident, led by the Dyak.

The encounter with the Indo patrol had been unexpected. It might have been disastrous. Goddard had examined the corpses, searching for personal papers. He had found nothing to give a clue as to the patrol's destination so far from the beaten track. In fact he had found precious little. It seemed that the soldiers had been 'censored' before leaving base. Apart from soft-metal dog-tags that had recently become standard among members of the RPKAD which, Goddard explained, was the Indos' élite Commando group, the young Tigers bore no identification.

The dog-tags added another dimension to the mystery. If the patrol had been mustered from the RPKAD then it hadn't behaved like an élite unit. Nor did the soldiers have that look about them. They were young and not particularly muscular specimens. They toted no special arms, just the familiar Russian carbines and a couple of BARs. No surprises in that department. Deacon had hoped to find a radio among the Indo packs but the patrol had obviously had ample opportunity to secrete their bergens. Umgah would undoubtedly have located them if there had been light enough and time. But twilight had thickened into night by then. Goddard's examination of the corpses suggested, however, that the soldiers had not been long in the jungle. He estimated three or four days at most.

While Dingo went diving to retrieve the remains of the radio, Goddard and Deacon weighted the corpses with such rocks as they could find and dragged them to the creek, heaved them down into the dense brown water. It was an improvised 'clean-up' but the best they could do under the circumstances. Dingo, meanwhile, had brought out the bergen. The radio was, of course, shattered beyond repair. But the Australian salvaged a number of items from side-pockets and stowed them in his belt.

Deacon held a bried council with Goddard. The policeman was of the opinion that the Indos had been on an exercise in the country that bearded the swamps and had become lost. He tended to dismiss the encounter as pure coincidence, 'hard cheese' for all concerned. Deacon was less certain. He had half a mind to track the movements of the Indo patrol through the jungle; easy work for Umgah. He was curious as to where they had come from, and by what method of entry – canoe or parachute or on the hoof. He was also curious to discover if the patrol had any connection with the installation of the howitzers in the hills above the timber towns, but Goddard scotched that notion, pointing out that they were a full thirty jungle miles from the border and even more from the location of the Indo emplacement.

'Push on, old man. Push on,' was Goddard's advice.

Deacon agreed; there was no other feasible option.

It was just barely daylight when they reached the river, the Tabuli, coming at it, had they known it, by the same narrow path that Greenwood and the Mouse had used just thirty-six hours before. No canoe waited by the mooring post on the north shore, and even the stave that had served that purpose had vanished with river's rise.

Mist clung obstinately to the water's surface and banded the tree tops. The sky was leaden, low and threatening. Rain fell straight and steady. The jungle all around seemed devoid of life of any sort, bird, beast or insect. The village, what was left of it, was equally deserted. Deacon lowered himself to his knees by the trunk of the last tree. Below him the bank sloped down a runnel to the river, to a crossing point. There was enough steam already in the swollen current to have loosed deadfall from the shoals up river and to draw it down, like bizarre and misshapen corpses, past the poles and piles of the blitzed community.

'Jesus, what happened here?' Dingo whispered.

'Grenades,' said Goddard.

'Cannon shells,' Deacon said. 'Fire too, by the look of it.'

Goddard stuck the empty cigarette holder into his mouth and sucked on it wetly, his face screwed up in distaste. 'But who would raze a Bajau river village? I mean, dammit, *we* wouldn't do it, would we?'

'What? An air attack?' said Deacon. 'Absolutely not. It's *verboten*. Not our style.'

'Who, then?'

The whispered conversation was rendered safe by the drizzle of rain and the fluctuating gurgle of the river.

'The Indo patrol?' Dingo shrugged.

'For loot?' said Goddard. 'No, no. I doubt it. The IBT are reasonably well-disciplined. They might do this to a native village across the border. Would do it, in fact. But they aren't that clueless. This is "their people", their territory.'

'Have you no ideas, Goddard?' said the Deke.

Boyd Goddard rattled the holder in his teeth, removed it and spat, turning his head politely to one side first. He sighed. 'Well. One.'

'What?'

'Pirates.'

'Pirates!' said Dingo Harper scornfully. 'Get off! Pirates don't have cannon.'

'Go on, Goddard,' Deacon said.

'The police forces of the East Residency have more trouble with pirates and smugglers than they do with guerrillas,' said Goddard. 'Surely you're aware of their activities?'

'I'm not arguing the matter,' said Deacon. 'But I am bothered by their appearance this far up river. In Indonesia.'

'I've no explanation,' said Goddard.

'Is there a link with the guns that are being hauled into the Seven Rivers?' said Dingo.

'Some pirate captains will work "on contract". Naturally, we don't deal with criminals. But Sukarno might. The CCO certainly would, provided they could keep some sort of control over the pirates' activity.

'What sort of contracts?' Dingo asked.

'To run arms. To attack bases. General disruption of trade and commerce.'

'Sukarno might hire bandits,' said Deacon, 'to keep his nose clean politically.'

Dingo nodded across the Tabuli. 'Why blast a dump like this? An Indo dump at that.'

'Really, I've no idea.'

'We aren't going to find answers sitting on our tails, boss.'

'True,' said Deacon.

'Question is, how do we cross?' said Goddard.

'Reft,' put in Umgah. 'Build reft.'

'How long will that take?' Dingo asked.

Umgah answered, 'Two ers.'

'We could log-swim,' said Dingo. 'It would save time.'

'Looks pretty fast for that,' Deacon said.

'There's bound to be a boat somewhere over there,' said Goddard.

'And maybe a bunch of terrorists staked out round it,' said Harper. 'Anyway, log-swimming's the answer. I'll do it. No point in committing the team.'

'All right, Dingo,' said Deacon, without hesitation. 'But not just here. Upstream, drift down. We'll keep a line on you, of course.'

One by one the men crept back from the river bank and tracked a quarter of a mile northwards, returning to the shore in due course. There was a sand shoal, all but swept over by the frothy brown waters. And there was a log, nine or ten feet long, ironwood, branches still attached to it. Where it had come from, only God would know; yet it bore the bites of an axe plainly and had been hewn, not torn, from its stand.

Dingo was a strong swimmer, product of Australian beaches and the show-off competitiveness of his race. He had no fear of the river and, unlike Deacon, no irrational fear of the presence of crocodiles or kraits. It wasn't croc country or croc weather and he would take his chance with river snakes. He wasted no time at all. Stripped to his undershorts, he strapped a webbing belt about his waist, sheathed a bayonet and a knife separately over each hip bone, a blade for either hand. He fixed the light manilla rope that had ridden on the top of Goddard's pack to his webbing belt. River was fifty, maybe sixty yards across at this point and the line was two hundred feet long. He had some free run, but not much.

He studied the opposite bank. An arthritic palm tree hung over the water, its roots awash, ragged leaves carving the chocolate-brown surface. He would aim for the palm. He dragged the ironwood log off the ribbon of soft sand-silt into deep water and felt the current take it. He didn't need the log for buoyancy. He could probably have kept himself afloat well enough. But he needed its weight, its mass to keep him from being carried too fast and too far downstream. He turned, gave Goddard the thumbs-up and, downstream of the log, thrust himself into the Tabuli.

The water was colder than he had anticipated. Nothing really. He had swum on beaches off Scottish islands where the temperature would have frozen a polar bear. He liked the texture of the river, the density of it. He was exhilarated, not frightened. He had practised the technique of river-crossing: log-swimming. He did not ride with the log, though, but thrust against it, scissoring his strong legs so that he was steering the length of ironwood and not being dragged by it. The mass of branches just below the surface made a great sheet-anchor, gave him time to manoeuvre. Even at that, he was stirred about by the turbulence in the channel and came whirling out on the dart of an invisible rapid, missing a cluster of big rocks by inches. He heard the tree branches crunch and crackle. The log rolled and wallowed, spun away towards the far bank with more directional thrust than he could have managed to impart.

In a couple of hours, Dingo realised, rain would render the Tabuli impassable. They'd never have made it across by raft. It would be perfect for a canoe, though, provided it didn't rise more than another couple of feet and there weren't any rocky passages further down. Spectators to his crossing, civilians ill-versed in the customs of the Special Forces, would have blanched at the sight of the swimmer. But Dingo Harper was relaxed and the effort of navigating the log was not strenuous.

He parted from the log fifteen yards upstream from the crooked palm, dipping and ducking underwater to make sure that the line did not foul the roots. He drove with his legs like a frog, then turned and broke into a few beats of overarm crawl, a stroke that dragged him inshore from the edge of the current. He reared up, reached and caught the leaves of the palm with both hands, hugging the mass to his chest.

The line came taut, springing from the river. Goddard pranced down to the edge of the water to yield the extra yards that Dingo required to clamber, sleek and dripping, from the river. The Australian secured the manilla line to the tree, then, naked as a native, padded into the rain-drowned forest out of sight.

Minutes later he was at the rear of the village of Palan, peering through tall grasses at the weirdest sight he had ever seen.

'Jesus!' Dingo murmured.

The expression was not inappropriate nor quite as profane as usual.

Only yards away, in a clearing behind the burned stumps of the dwellings, the folk of the Bajau Mandelaut, led by a crippled chieftain, were in process of burying their dead.

Fascinated, Dingo leaned on his elbows and laid his belly to the grass, parting the stalks with his fingertips. It was towards the end of the ceremony, he guessed, for young bucks were spading earth back into oblong holes. Eleven holes patterned the knoll between the roots of trees. Eleven holes: eleven dead. Somebody had done a job on this place, fair dinkum. Dingo started slightly as the women opened up with a banshee wailing, a dreadful, heart-torn sound that covered the hunter's approach.

First Dingo knew of the hunter's presence was the graze of a spear-blade against his neck and a voice barking, '*Takitoh. Takitoh. Takitoh*,' which Dingo, wrongly as it happened, took to mean 'surrender'.

Cautiously, very cautiously, Captain Harper spread his hands above his head as a monumental silence clamped down on the mourners and the solemn funeral rite ground to a halt.

'*Takitoh*.'

'Right, mate,' said Dingo, and pushed himself on to his knees.

4 Clouded Leopard

Greenwood was fast asleep when the rain began. It came sweeping over the lagoon from the north-west, a blue-grey curtain that quickly blotted out the evening sky and changed the tint of the water from pale to slate. It was preceded by a stiff rustling breeze that tossed the lakeshore trees and rattled the palm-thatch and caused the troops of assorted units to don slickers and ponchos and to seek shelter from the ideleness that had kept them lounging in the open all day long. Not all the men at the Ukiti training camp had been idle, however.

On the deck of the *Clouded Leopard*, at the instigation of Lieutenant Chun, the crew of Indonesian marines did not relax their vigilance. Of all the odds and sods accumulated at Ukiti, they were the only ones that remained unsettled, aware that all was not well with their corner of the war. The others, including the small handful of regular army officers and NCOs, were only too happy to take a holiday and enjoy the pleasures doled out by the pirate captain, Arunja, a person who, in Lieutenant Chun's opinion, was no better than a Black Devil and quite, quite mad.

Lieutenant Chun would not permit Arunja to board the *Leopard*. It might be that he would later suffer from his discourtesy to a nominal ally. But he could not bring himself to trust the Chinese or the ill-conceived campaign which had thrown him into the pot with Communists and criminals. It should not have been Lieutenant Chun's responsibility. But his captain was dead and he had consequently inherited command. For three days he had hardly closed an eyelid and had expended much energy hopping from the deck rails to the radio cabin where his appointed (Communist) operator was supposedly in touch with the generals at operational HQ at Tarakan, the island base.

It was from Tarakan that the *Clouded Leopard* had set out on its mission, first to convey Chinese Commander Hsing Kao to an assembly camp at Ukiti, then, with a complement of ‘fighters’ (which Chun now understood to mean pirates), to slip from the mouth of the Tabuli into the mouth of the Jaumpong and make a run into Sabah to capture the timber town of Balimbuka. In theory, the plan was sound. Lieutenant Chun had not been informed of the details but his captain had told him that the plan stemmed from the Defence Minister and had been approved by the President. Commando forces and a detachment of artillery had been despatched overland to command the hills behind Balimbuka and forestall attempts by the British Special Forces or the Sabah Scouts to counter-attack. The People’s Republic of China had made a generous contribution, through Commander Hsing Kao, a warrior that Chun had learned to respect even on short acquaintance, by loaning the latest fast-strike craft to roll from the stocks of the Shanghai yards: *Clouded Leopard*.

The Star-class gunboat had been bait for Arunja, who for many years had tormented British officers of law and order by pillaging the North Borneo coastline, wreaking havoc on the fleets of *kumpits* and *padangkangs*, trading craft that plied a legal trade among the islands. Nobody could doubt that Arunja was a butcher. But he gave an appearance of political commitment and, with the rise of the Malaysian Federation, concentrated his activities against ‘the enemy’ and avoided conflict with Chinese and Indonesian vessels. He declared himself to be totally opposed to Federation and, on many occasions, supplied valuable intelligence to Indonesian Naval commanders through the shore base at Nunukan Timor. Currying favour.

Behind the decision to mount a major combined operation against Balimbuka and claim possession of the Jaumpong river lay the incomplete success of an attack on Kalabakan carried out the previous year. A group of IBT, bolstered by river pirates, had defeated an outpost of the Royal Malay Regiment and, for a few glorious days, had held the important timber centre to ransom. The fact that the raiders had been obliterated by a counter-thrust from the Gurkhas was minimised, attributed to the fact that the IBT had lacked firepower and organised back-up. It was to remedy that omission that the Combined Assault Group had been mustered and the complicated plan evolved. The switch from west to east coast and an increasing need to shore up the frontiers at Long Pa Sia and Pensiangan, however, had meant a shortage of trained personnel. Recruitment had taken time, cost money, and the results were not, to Lieutenant Chun's way of thinking, satisfactory. Exactly how unsatisfactory had not emerged until the *Leopard* had left the sea for the Tabuli and, to the astonishment of her crew, had come under attack from a (Malaysian?) commando group who had been hidden in the swamp seven miles from Ubiki. The attack had come suddenly, at dusk. It had consisted of fierce volleys of rifle fire. The captain of the *Leopard* had been killed, together with five marines. Commander Hsing Kao had been badly wounded. Only the timely arrival of the Star-class gunboat bristling with Arunja's cutthroats had beaten off the ambushers, though none had been killed or taken prisoner. The Star had led the *Leopard* safely back to the lagoon.

Arunja had been distressed to discover that Commander Hsing Keo had been on board. (Did the Black Devil imagine that he would have things all his own way?) Arunja, however, had adamantly refused to allow Lieutenant Chun to make a fast run down the Tabuli in search of medical assistance for the CCO commander. That Hsing Kao was also his benefactor, liaison officer with Mainland China and a Very Important Person, did not seem to penetrate Arunja's obstinate skull.

It was at that juncture that Lieutenant Chun decided to take over the *Leopard*. It was *his* vessel now, he informed an angry Arunja. Whatever corrupting influence the Chinese pirate had exercised on the other officers and men gathered at Ukiti, Lieutenant Chun would not be prey to it.

Lieutenant Chun's problem was that he could not unravel Arunja's motive. Did the pirate wish to lead the raid on Blimbuka by himself? Did he hunger for glory or simply profit? He wanted the *Leopard*, of that Chun was certain, for the rest – the young lieutenant was confused. Why, for example, had Arunja gone up river in the gunboat? Was it really to forage for supplies? He had returned with a Britisher, a doctor. Was that coincidence or had Arunja Known there would be a British doctor up river? Chun had been invited ashore to meet the British doctor. He had refused. Not for one moment would he be lured from the *Leopard*.

Arunja had boasted that the British doctor would cure Commander Hsing Kao. But the lieutenant had seen the extent of the neck wound and doubted if any doctor, British or Chinese, could save the commander. What, in any case, would be the advantage from Arunja's point of view? If the pirate did intend to take over the *Leopard* it would only be embarrassing to have Commander Hsing Kao around, during and afterward. Was it merely a gesture, a sop to the handful of CCO guerrillas who were at Ukiti? That, Chun eventually decided, must be it. Such a convoluted but rather stupid move would be typical of Arunja.

Pigs, rice, and dragon-jars brimming with *tapai*, a potent brew made out of tapioca, had been brought back from the forage. And it was raining. Yes, the rain would make much difference. The Tabuli would rise swiftly, as would the level of the lagoon. He, Lieutenant Chun, might be able to run the *Leopard* out of the swamps and back to the open sea, to shake himself free of Arunja and his evil crew. One unit of Commandos had already sneaked away, heading inland.Perhaps it was to seek out the deserters that Arunja had gone up river. If so, had he found them? Had he slaughtered them and let the jungle take their bones? Lieutenant Chun was a prisoner on board the vessel, beseiged by suspicion and fear of what Arunja might do to gain possession of the *Leopard*.

When he asked Operational HQ for orders he received no satisfactory reply. His own signaller had been killed, shot in the head. The man who operated the ship's radio now was a Communist. Was the man lying to him? Had messages been sent out at all?

And if Arunja did intend to possess the *Leopard* . . .

Questions, questions without answers. Lieutenant Chun ran from stem to stern and back again, driven by neurotic agitation and a presentiment that the Black Devil, Arunja, would eventually try to kill him.

Lieutenant Chun was right.

It happened an hour after dark, in the rain, without sound or warning.

Greenwood opened his eyes. He was groggy and dazed and his neck felt as if he had been garrotted. He sat up. The Mouse lay by him, curled into a foetal ball, thumb to her lips, biting the nail. It wasn't a nursery trick, a comforter, but remnant of a pagan belief in warding off evil spirits.

It had grown cool in the bungalow. There was no light, except that which came through the windows and via the curtained doorway.

Softly Greenwood got himself on to his knees.

He still couldn't be sure what had wakened him. God knows, there was noise enough, a hellish racket outside; chanting, like a bleedin' Freemasons' outing spilling from the Ganton Arms at closing-time. Booze, the native variety, and women? Yeah, it sounded like the wind-up phase of an all-night bash. He tried to put the plight of the native girls out of mind, to think instead of the patient in the next room.

At the doorway, just outside, were guards. He squinted. Armed.

Mouse touched him, gestured. He nodded and, with the girl by his side, crawled across the room to the window. Somebody had lowered the shutters but he could force a slat, could look out over the lagoon.

It was pitch-dark in the jungle and raining worse than it ever did in Manchester. The large boat had lights rigged on its deck, incongruous splashes of whitish colour, contrasting starkly with fire-glare. There were several fires, the kind you light in oil drums. They were protected by canvas awnings which trapped the glow and spread it. He could smell meat, pork, roasting. The discipline which he had noticed that morning as the Star slid into the jetty was gone. It was a tribal gathering, a reversion.

Mouse prised the slats open a little wider and stuck her nose out.

If there were no guards on the verandah, then he might even

get the hell out of here now. Those pirates were bad eggs; at least the big bugger was, and he had no reason to suppose that the rest of the gang was much better. He might have expected more order from an Indo training camp – if it hadn't been for the pirates. He wondered how many men Arunja had with him, how many of the gang were criminals, recruited from Indonesian jails.

He cupped his hand over Mouse's dainty lug. 'Guards?'

She wormed one arm through the shutter and enlarged the gap, got her head out.

Then she screamed.

The scream and the *splat* of a rifle butt on flesh occurred simultaneously. For an instant, Mouse was trapped. Dazed by the blow, she could not drag her head and arm through the gap in the shutter. Greenwood reached, folded her shoulder down and pulled back into the room. Just outside, he heard somebody laughing, a squeaky, jeering sound, saw the shadow-shape of one of the Indos, jungle cap stuck raffishly on his black hair, his face split by a monstrous grin. No soldier, a pirate.

Cackling, the bastard stooped, jabbed at the shutter with the rifle barrel. Doc was sorely tempted to take a fistful of the barrel, yank the guy into the room and beat the shit out of him. But he would never have made it. Never. He wondered if the guy was already half-pissed, had already made his visit to the dragon-jar, hand his 'ration' from one of the poor native girls.

Mouse uttered not a sound. Females of the Bajau Maruda were either hysterical or ultra-stoical; seemed to be no middle way. Tenderly, Doc took her chin between his finger and thumb and turned her head to the light. The wound was bad, contused and already swelling under the right eye. He reckoned the cheekbone was crushed or, at best, fractured. Pain would shoot through the initial numbness and into the sinuses. In half an hour or less, Mouse would be in agony. He would give her a shot of morphine from the sax case, if he had an ampoule left. He hoped there was no structural damage to the eye itself. Mouse yielded and he drew her into the crook of his arm, rocking her gently and crooning to her while he continued to examine the extent of the injury.

They were caught like that, in a picturesque embrace, when the curtain whipped to one side and a storm lantern was pushed into the room. There was a little man on the end of the lantern; towering over him – Arunja.

The pirate captain had changed out of California-style beach gear and into something like guerrilla uniform. He wore baggy jungle-green pants and a quilted flak-vest crossed by cartridge belts. Hooked to his fancy leather belt were four round 'Clementine' grenades. In his left hand he toted a big Mauser machine-pistol. The blocky, old-fashioned weapon suited Arunja's image to a T.

From outside came shots to which Arunja paid not the slightest attention. There was, too, a chorus of shouts, gleeful cheering.

'Get up,' said the pirate.

'She's hurt.'

'Get up.'

'Holy Moses! What'd he have to do that for?'

Still on the threshold, Arunja lowered his left arm until the machine-pistol was pointing at Mouse.

'You will come with me.'

'Not without her.'

Arunja smiled. He might appear to be calm and in control but he was bubbling and boiling inside, like fermenting *tapai.* You wouldn't know how bad it was, how potent, until you tried it. Doc Greenwood had no intention of trying it.

'Bring her,' said Arunja.

Doc helped Mouse to her feet, supported her. 'Okay, kiddo, okay,' he murmured and moved to the door.

The little guy with the lantern was a pirate. He appeared fairly ordinary, in T-shirt and duck pants, like a million guys in the bazaars of the East. Crowded into the hallway of the bungalow were four other men, tricked out in the same sort of manner as the captain, armed with submachine-guns. Doc and Mouse were pushed into the larger room. The fans had stopped and the wan electric lights were out, replaced by three lanterns. What had happened to the juice, the generator? Doc had no opportunity to speculate. He was pushed forward with a gun in his back towards the bed. Doc's bravado, his boast, came back to haunt him like a hollow echo. The patient upon whom he had laboured long and hard was dead. The smirking Filipinos flanked the bed. The sheet had been turned down to the patient's belly, baring the upper part of his body. The dressing was intact. The wound hadn't bled.

'Examine.'

Doc let out a little groan and stepped forward. He pushed one of the Filipinos aside and lifted the dead man's arm, felt for the pulse. He bent, listened for a heartbeat, a flicker. No dice. The guy was gone. Doc wasn't entirely surprised; it had been a very long shot indeed that he would survive.

He turned, shrugged. 'Sorry. He's dead.'

'Ah! You have killed him.'

'*Eh?*'

'He has died because of your stupidity.'

'Get fuckin' knotted, man. He was as good as bleedin' dead when—'

Arunja snapped his fingers. The little guy with the lantern, who had been hovering behind his master, produced a piece of paper, a single sheet of typing quarto. There were words on it, printed out in Malayan and, beneath, a block of Chinese characters. There was also a ballpoint pen. Arunja transferred paper and pen into Doc's uncertain fingers.

'Hey, what is this?' Doc said.

'You will make your name.'

'Not on your bleedin' life, man,' Doc retorted.

Arunja's fist was a blur. He caught Mouse by the breast and, with an effortless gesture, tormented her, dragging a great scream from her lips. Doc jumped, but one of the Filipinos had him, an arm about the throat, a knee dug into his spine.

'Make you name, Englishman. It is only to certificate the manner of dying.'

'What . . . what does it say . . . what bleedin' lies—'

Greenwood choked. The Filipino held him. Somebody, maybe Arunja, rammed a fist into his groin. He would have jack-knifed with pain, that searing, breath-robbing agony, if the Filipino had not continued to hold him. Dim impingements of sound, screaming, came through Doc's absorption with his groin and the incandescent fire that vented from it into his belly and chest.

At some point he was released. He fell, retching, to the floor by the side of the bed. The poor bastard in the bed had been marked from the moment he encountered Arunja. For all Doc could tell, it wasn't the neck wound or an embolism or post-operative anything that had done him in. Most likely bet was a pillow held over the mouth and nose. It wouldn't take much pressure or very long to smother a guy in that condition.

Doc bent his head, held his hands against his inflamed scrotum and tried to breathe deeply, to regain his composure. It wasn't easy. After the first rapier-like pains came nausea. He retched again.

Arunja laughed.

Doc lifted his head.

Mouse was kneeling before him, on all fours, her breasts bare. Arunja kicked her as if she was a bitch and not a person, his boot driving accurately bewteen her thighs. She pitched forward into Doc and rolled over beneath him, both of them close to the clean, smooth fall of the bedsheet.

Bending from the waist, Arunja laid paper and pen on the wooden flooring close to Doc's hand.

Doc Greenwood had an overwhelming impulse to rip the paper into a thousand pieces. He resisted. He was too weak. Not morally or anything. Physically. The blow to his groin had sapped him, short-circuited his reactions. Even in the pink, he was no match for the monstrous pirate backed by a gang of bully-boys.

Doc let his elbow sag. He steadied the flimsy sheet of paper with his left hand and, shakily, tracked the letters of his name across the bottom of the page. He did not put his rank. He guessed that Arunja would want it there but the bastard would have to ask for it.

Arunja asked for it.

Obediently, Doc filled in the recognised abbreviation for lance-corporal.

Odd, odd; he had been lectured to about brain-washing and the war on the mind, had read several serious studies on the subject and had imagined himself in situations of confinement, subjected to subtle tortures, to hunger and cold and sensory deprivation. He had tried, as best he could, to prepare himself for the possibility that one unthinkable day he might have to face up to it. He wasn't conceited enough to assume that foreknowledge would make him immune. But the big bleedin' giggle was that he had buckled to the oldest torture-dodge in the world; a brisk kick in the balls.

By the light of the lantern Arunja studied the paper, then grunted in satisfaction.

'Take them away,' said the pirate.

Mouse was dragged to her feet amd, almost insensible with pain, was hauled before Doc out of the room.

Greenwood was left to the Filipinos, those sneering boys, who manhandled him towards the door.

Gathering his strength, Doc Greenwood resisted, turned his head, shouted, 'What good'll it do you, Arunja? What good's a piece of paper signed by a bleedin' British lance-jack?'

'It says I did not kill him,' Arunja replied.

Mad as a fuckin' hatter, no doubt about it.

'It is my signal to take command,' Arunja added.

Crazy, yeah, like a fox.

They took Greenwood out of the bungalow and down the steps and flung him, with Mouse, into a narrow bamboo compound close to the back of the building.

There was nothing and nobody in the cage, not even a bucket. It had no roof and the heavy tropical rain poured down upon the couple.

Greenwood covered the girl as best he could, arms propped and hands in the brown mud, his chest making a shelter for her body.

'It's okay, Mouse,' he reassured her. 'That's it. He's got what he wanted. It's over, the worst is over.'

But the worst wasn't over: for Barry Greenwood and the native girl the worst was yet to come.

*

It was like one of those nightmares, Dingo thought, the kind you get when you've been guzzling Fosters and have dropped off, not pissed exactly, but well on the way, and waken in the wee small hours in a kind of semi-conscious state. Some guys dreamed they were riding in the old Harbour trolley-car filled with sheilas in tennis dresses, and they were ballock-naked and in knee-squeezing, foot-hopping discomfort from a full bladder, and the girls wouldn't let them off to do their business. He hadn't had that particular dream, but he had suffered others like it.

Standing in front of a bunch of Borneo tribesmen in your Y-fronts with your hands raised above your head was pretty fair on for a nightmare. Especially since they wore ritual trig and had been burying bodies in the earth of the hill. Nobody liked having their funeral rites interrupted by an alien bozo in soaking-wet underpants.

Most of his mates would have kept their traps shut. But Dingo wasn't like that. He was a notorious yapper. He started yapping as soon as he saw the cripple with the crutch, the headman, and kept right on yapping as he approached the tableau, prodded by the bloke with the spear who had caught him out so thoroughly.

'Sorry about this, mate. But me and my—' He thought better of it. 'I've gone and gotten lost. Looking for a mate, a friend. Friend.' He tried a cheesy smile, all teeth. 'Sorry to intrude at a time like this. I had to swim your river. Much rain. Much water.'

They were gawping at him. He wanted to believe that they were transfixed by his physical beauty, thought him some kind of god. Bullshit! They just didn't know what to do with him.

Dingo rabbited on. 'If you can spare some fresh water, perhaps a mouthful of food . . . No, I understand. You've had trouble here. Nothing to do with me. What sort of trouble? Somebody shoot – boom, boom – from the river?' He didn't wait for an answer. 'The bloke I'm looking for – white, like me. White man. Doctor. Wouldn't happen to have seen him? Passing through, maybe?'

He had come to a halt. There didn't seem to be too much

pressure on him. The young buck lowered the spear in astonishment. Dingo had a wild thought that he might be able to keep jawing long enough for the Deke to find a way across the river and sneak to his rescue. Then the bloke with the twisted hip crabbed forward, scowling.

He was small, gnarled, ugly, not young. If he was the big chief in this community then he must have something going for him, something not obvious to an outside observer.

'Doktor?' the bloke muttered.

Dingo raise his eyebrows, lowered his hands. The scrape of the spear in his back soon had them up again. He bent his head to look down at the chieftain.

The old bloke spoke in a patois, mostly Malay.

Dingo's memory whirred like the slots in a fruit machine.

He cocked his head. 'Come again?'

Politely the old bloke repeated himself.

Dingo smiled. 'You say – am I friend of white doctor? Yip, me friend of white doctor.'

This wasn't a nightmare; it was a farce. Bob Hope and Bing Crosby might come sauntering out of the bush any minute. But the half-baked, pidgin English made communication possible. At least he had established that Greenwood *had* been here. Wielding his stethoscope. Playing at being a doctor, no doubt.

The tribesmen hadn't tried to take away the blades that were prominent in Dingo's belt, to disarm him.

The chief took another hobbling pace towards him. The interment ceremony seemed to have been completely forgotten. He made no signal but from the rim of the crowd by the graves came forth a *pawang*, one of those strange itinerant jokers you found scattered throughout the East, especially in Malaysian communities. This one wasn't sporting his Wizard of Oz outfit, paint, feathers and bones, He looked almost human. In his right hand he carried an ancient, mildewed Bible, in his left an umbrella, a ragged black thing with bent spokes and a shaped cane handle. Hospitably the *pawang* held the brolly over Dingo's head.

The *pawang* spoke passable English in a plummy accent.

'Vengeance is Mine, Yew know.'

''Course it is,' said Dingo.

'That's whet the Lord seys.'

'In the Bible,' said Dingo, nodding.

The old chieftain looked impressed. His head clocked first one way and the the other as the *pawang* and the white man conversed.

'Yew religious?'

'Baptised Christian,' said Dingo diplomatically.

'Only wen God in t'jungle.'

It was like catechism. Dingo didn't risk a response. He held his tongue.

Droplets of water dripped from the brolly, trickling down his backbone. He steeled himself not to shiver. How long would Deacon give him before tackling a second crossing of the Tabuli? He hoped that the major would not be too impetuous, since he seemed to be making headway with the natives. The bloke with the spear, though, had been joined by three other young men, all with spears. At least there were no blowpipes in evidence. Dingo considered blowpipes spooky.

The *pawang* said, 'Bed men come here, do this terrible thing.'

'Soldiers?' said Dingo. 'Bad soldiers did this?'

'No soldiers. Only wen soldier. Friend of Usop and his people.'

Jesus, Dingo thought, what line do I pursue? Can I trust this lot to skin us alive, and to give us a boat?

He said, 'The doctor?'

The *pawang* wasn't that full of Christian charity. He didn't like competition, wouldn't admit that the white man who'd helped the villagers was a doctor at all. The *pawang* had a haughty sort of face, long, chin pulled down, and a thin, stiff neck. He would have made an excellent RSM in the Border Scouts.

The *pawang* said, 'Yew hev come to bring vengeance for the doktor?'

Dingo frowned. 'Does he . . . doctor . . . my friend . . . does he need vengeance? I mean, is he dead?'

The Australian glanced at the graves marked with short

stout posts from which fluttered pennants of cotton and nylon material. Prayer flags. Goddard would know about the funeral rites and understand the significance of the pennants. Goddard would also be able to talk directly to the chieftain, which would save all this verbal pussyfooting with the evangelical witch-doctor.

'Not killed here,' said the *pawang*. 'Take eway down t'river in t'boat with the big gens.'

'When?'

'Wen dey ago.'

Dingo cleared his throat, then said, 'Listen, I've got friends of the doctor with me. Have you got such a thing as a boat, a canoe, we could borrow?'

The old chieftain's eyes lit up. 'Ermy?'

Dingo didn't split hairs. He nodded. 'Army.'

'Vengeance is Mine,' said the *pawang*, smugly, as if the naked white man had popped up in answer to his prayers. 'Where err they?'

'Across the river,' said Dingo.

And the whole bloody tribe broke, chattering, for the river bank, leaving the dead, rituals unfinished, in limbo.

Barry Greenwood did not know that he had been tracked into Kalimantan by two SAS officers, a copper and a Dyak. It did not occur to him that he might expect help from 'outside'. Self-reliance took on a new shade of meaning for the young medic during the course of that hideous night; a high price to pay for the freedom he had sought. He had been prepared to die in the steamy jungles and quaking brown swamps of Borneo. He had come to terms with all the possibilities – snake-bit, fever, bullet, spear or poisoned dart, even a booby-trap. But he had not been prepared to encounter the plain face of evil which was shown to him at Ukiti.

Old sweats from the war against the Nazis, veteran soldiers who had seen what had been done to innocent villagers during the early years of the Emergency in Malaya, might have instructed the young medic in the forms of wickedness that a soldier was liable to encounter. But it wasn't the sort of instruction that fell within the scope of training officers. Some things you had to discover for yourself; the limits of endurance, base levels of courage, whether your beliefs, whatever they might be, would stand up in isolation, beyond horror seen and experienced. In the rain, in semi-darkness, in the closet-sized compound with the injured girl, Greenwood found himself thus challenged. His beliefs, such as they were, seemed to have been lost with his saxophone case. All the good in his life was contained within the vials, bottles and tubes which were packed into its stained velvet compartments. If he had had the case he might have been able to do something for Mouse for a start. From the Californian hipster children he thought that he had learned 'respect' for life, even in its smallest, most irritating parts. To confront the abominable fact that life had no value at all, Barry Greenwood had journeyed far. Crouched in the rain, in a wooden cage behind a bungalow by a swamp lagoon, he had found the truth.

He didn't know what was going on.

He didn't care.

Greenwood's brain swirled with fear and hatred as he bridged the slender native girl.

It wasn't sufficient excuse that the rabble on the lakeshore were the crossbred scum of gaols and stews from five or six nations, from Sumatra or Singapore, Luzon or Mindanao, Hanoi, Canton or Kunming. Chink, Filipino, Indo or Malay, they were all contaminated by the urge to destroy.

In the shape of the Chinese captain, Greenwood had glimpsed the shadow of a dozen men of his acquaintance. Recognition frightened him more than anything. Choose the trade of conquest and you choose the way of destruction. Was that the whole of the law? In penance for what he had brought her to, Greenwood made a shelter for the girl with his body, knelt on all fours with the rain strapping his back and his arms trembling, to keep her from suffering. But the gesture was futile. She suffered anyway.

Madmen touch off madness. In the hour after sunset the troops at Ukiti went mad. He could hear shrieks, yelling, the stutter of gunfire, see flames, smell the stench of roasting meat.

Perhaps the demise of the Chinese VIP had been the signal that Arunja had been waiting for, backed, of course, by the certificate of death which, so the pirate naively believed, would excuse his mutinous take-over of the *Clouded Leopard*.

By 2030 hours the vessel was in Arunja's possession.

The honourable Lieutenant Chun – throat slit – together with six marines foolish enough to resist, was dead. Their corpses were removed by canoe to the west of the lagoon to be thrown, like herring to seals, to the crocodiles that dwelt along the shore.

If he had applied reason, Greenwood might have deduced what was taking place. But the SAS medic was absorbed in misery, drowned in a sense of abject failure. The first he knew of Arunja's coup was when he was rudely awakened from sleep, huddled in a corner of the compound with Mouse in his arms. He had just enough savvy to check his wristwatch which, oddly, had not been stolen from him. It was twenty minutes to midnight.

Rain had stopped. Heat had returned, and swarms of mosquitoes.

Greenwood felt sick. His head buzzed. His mouth was dry as soda. Stirred by a rifle butt, though, he scrambled to his feet. Mouse stayed where she was, curled up, her face badly swollen, one eye closed. How much damage the pirate's vicious kick had done, Greenwood could not tell. Gently he stooped and lifted her shoulders from the sticky mud.

The soldier-pirate – who could say which trade the guy followed? – was impatient. He had orders from the great Arunja and was anxious to obey. He prodded Doc's legs with the carbine until Doc whirled, snarling like an animal, then backed off a pace.

Anger stimulated Doc. The buzzing in his head ceased. He lifted the girl to her feet. She smiled at him, a grimace of contused flesh. He needed clean cold water, dressings, TCP, and a sedative to give her relief. Mouse required rest and nursing. She had given him everything he had ever asked for. Given it unstintingly. Now, when she had need of him, he could do nothing.

The pirate jabbered.

Mouse managed to move her mouth. 'We . . . go . . . with him.'

'Ask him where.'

The pirate jabbered some more.

'To the big boat.'

'Who's on the big boat?' Greenwood asked, speaking Malay.

The pirate laughed and performed a gleeful, hip-shaking dance, childish yet obscene. 'Arunja, Arunja, Arunja.'

'That figures,' Doc said.

Unsteadily supporting Mouse, Greenwood went out of the cage. He was nudged and steered round the south side of the bungalow, across beaten ground among the tents towards the incongruously trim shape of the strike craft moored by the wooden jetty. One level down from the hangover of the wildest army bash he had ever been at, the human wreckage that strewed the shore at Ukitil reeked of corruption, indulgence beyond pleasure.

Tow boys lay by a smouldering fire, gorged stiff on pig ribs, bones scattered about them. One boy still had his face embedded in a mess of fat. The other, pants shucked to mid-thigh, drowsily fouled himself. Beyond the boys, four men in brown uniforms hunkered by an oil-drim stove. Numbed by alcohol, they scratched in the dirt between their knees, mumbling and sniggering while the naked body of a native girl, sprinkled with filth and apparently dead, lay only inches away. Closer to the jetty, groups of men clustered like vultures around captive girls, using them still, three and four at a time, on the ground amid fruit skins and hacked cans or stretched across logs under awnings, the bellied canvas lit by torches. Afraid of what he might discern in the shadows, Greenwood squinted at the bloodied corpses of dissenters sprawled where they had been knifed or shot, their clothing torn. Looters and murderers were holding a sort of auction, with much laughter, on the steps of the smaller dwelling. If they had been sober the terrorists might have fallen on Mouse there and then, on Doc too. But they were too far gone to do more than make a *yallering* sound, tongue against the upper lip. Greenwood pushed on, holding Mouse tight against him.

At the jetty were four men with submachine-guns. They were sober and alert. Behind them, where the short plank ran on to the deck, were two more guards, each with a shotgun. On the deck itself were another pair of guards armed with *kris* blades. They had a cooked chicken on a leaf-tray and were eating it with enjoyment but no haste. Once on board, the Indo pushed Greenwood down a metal stair, Mouse following. The cramped, claustrophobic quarters below deck smelled of the sea, not of swamp, the universal tang of diesel fuel and salt. There was the soft, somnolent creaking of a ship, though the surface of the lagoon hardly rippled in the breathless night air.

Greenwood didn't know where they were. For'ard, he thought, stepping through a bulkhead door into a wardroom.

A table with stout metal legs was bolted to the floor. There was a hatch with a padlocked steel cover, a couple of swivel chairs and a bay with an upholstered leather couch inset. Two bullet-shaped fittings over the bay provided light. A metal-shaped lamp was clamped to the table. On the wall hung a metal-framed photograph in glorious and gaudy technicolour: Dr Sukarno, smiling.

Arunja was alone in the room. Relaxing after his exertions, he sprawled on the couch like a potentate. He was naked except for a terry-towel jock-strap and a coy loincloth of the same material. On the couch by his side was a bowl of fruit and an almost empty glass pitcher. In Arunja's hand was a tumbler half filled with a colourless liquid. Vodka, Doc guessed, or sake.

Arunja raised the glass in mock salute.

'Welcome to my ship.'

The bastard seeemd to be in a great mood.

The pirate spoke again and the Indo left, slamming the bulkhead door behind him.

Greenwood felt a slow, cold wriggle of fear in his gut.

Arunja was unprotected, as defenceless as any guy of his size and strength could be.

The pirate's piggy eyes observed Greenwood shrewdly. The

medic realised that the guy *expected* him to make a move. He did nothing. There was no weapon in the room, except maybe the table lamp. And the Mouse was in no condition to back him up. She swayed against the table.

Purring, Arunja drank.

'Do you see?' He gestured to the photograph. 'My master. I am working for the government. I have been given a ship of my own.'

'Congratulations,' said Greenwood.

'It is the way in the King's Navy too, no?' said Arunja. Greenwood didn't correct him, tell him that a Queen ruled Britain and the Commonwealth. 'In the British Navy, when one lord goes, there is one more to take his place.'

'That's the way it is,' said Greenwood.

'My ship.' He waved the glass. 'Two ships, I have now. I will take many ports and towns, with my two fast ships.'

It was out before he could help himself. He blamed fatigue and fear. 'Starting with Balimbuka?' Greenwood snapped.

Arunja's grin was huge.

He purred and laughed. 'What do you know of Balimbuka?'

'Timber town,' Greenwood shrugged. 'That's all.'

'Why are you in Kalimantan?'

'I told you already, man. I got lost.'

The grin was all over the guy's face. He put down the glass, perching it on top of the fruit in the bowl.

The chain had been placed there in advance. It wouldn't have mattered much what Greenwood let slip, what he said. The bastard was just looking for an excuse to begin. He had been prepared.

The short length of stainless steel chain had been worked into a double loop and fastened with a big padlock. A key was in the padlock. Given an inch to the left, it would have gouged out Doc'd eyeball. The pirate moved fast in spite of his bulk. He grabbed the chain from its hiding-place under a cushion. He swung it before Greenwood could raise a hand to protect himself. Even Mouse, a couple of steps before him, barely had time to duck. The chain sighed in the air. Scything, it smashed Greenwood across the neck and jaw. The protruding key tore away a piece of his earlobe, causing a gush of blood. Doc slapped his hand to the spot, wincing. The blow dazzled his sense. Arunja was on him, bearing him backward, expertly encircling his forearms, hauling him down. Seconds later, Greenwood was manacled by the wrists to the table leg.

Hands braced on thighs, Arunja stooped. 'Why are you in my country? To search for me?'

Blood trickled across Greenwood's cheek and into his mouth. He tasted it, spat, then answered, 'I got lost, man, that's all. I was sent for . . . to attend to a guy . . . and I came too far across the bleedin' border.'

'The English soldiers sent you to find me, to spy on me?'

'Christ, I never even heard of you before.'

'You have heard of Balimbuka?'

'Yeah, yeah, sure.'

'Do they wait for me there?'

'How do I know? I'm only a medic.'

Arunja suddenly seemed to lose interest in the interrogation. Maybe it didn't matter to him what Malaysian and British forces had in store up the Jaumpong. He wasn't concerned with finding out what Greenwood knew. He was making sport in his own fashion – sadistically.

Doc had begun to drag and rattle on the chain even before the Chink touched her. The table leg was bolted to a circular plate which was in turn bolted to the deck. Solid as rock. He could plunge up and down, slither his wrists from top to bottom of the shaft, but he could not gain one extra inch of movement away from the prescribed circle of the table. He thudded his shoulder against the table, curled his knees and heaved against it, was under and over the table top, in many positions, each more contorted and each more futile than the last. But he kept struggling. He paused only to search for the key which Arunja had plucked out of the padlock and tossed into a corner of the wardroom. He couldn't reach it. He tore at the chains in despair.

Mouse was dappled with dried mud, her face swollen. Her appearance did not matter to Arunja. She was young and sweet. her vulnerability had fanned his appetite. He had been ready to use her, Doc realised, from the moment she had been pushed into the room. There were no preliminaries. Arunja ripped the sarong from her body. His fists closed over her breasts. She cried out. He tweaked the cord of his clothing, bared himself, bulled and bored against her. The violence of entry drove her forward, riding on his gross belly. Her brow struck the coping of the bay, then Arunja bent her like a bow and stabbed her face down into the leather cushions.

Muffled, the girl's cries weakened into shrill little grunts as the rape progressed. Doc could smell the slavering sweat that slicked the Chink. Head turned and eyes averted, he saw Mouse's feet quivering. He bloodied his forearms against the chain. He would have chopped off a hand to gain release if he had had a blade to do it. Anything. Anything to liberate himself, to halt the filthy pounding. But it went on and on and on and on. Greenwood, too, panted, panted and shouted, kneading the chains against his flesh, shouting at the implacable back and buttocks of the monstrous Chinese.

The girl's legs became limp, shaken only by the thrusting of the rider. And Doc knew that Arunja had broken her neck.

When at length he slithered from her body, Arunja discarded her as he might have tossed away a used rubber.

Huddled by the table leg, Doc sat motionless and silent, arms slack in the chains. He looked at Mouse sadly, without hope, stared into dark, moist, lifeless eyes canted round and upwards, her spine contorted, her face crushed by the leather cushions.

Arunja slid to the floor. His fat thighs were obscenely splayed. Sweat dripped from his brow, eyelids heavy, drugged by sexual effort.

At length the pirate got to his feet. He lifted the empty pitcher and sniffed at it, put it down again. He did not so much as glance at the girl, not out of shame but from indifference. He came to Greenwood, stood directly before him.

'Do they wait for me at Balimbuka?'

Geenwood didn't answer for a long time.

The pirate was patient.

Greenwood said, 'Yeah. They wait for you.'

'Good. That is good to be told. Who waits?'

'Gurkhas, Border Scouts and the SAS.'

'SAS?'

'My outfit, my unit.'

'English?'

'Yeah.'

'Why did you come into Kalimantan?'

'To look for you, to find you.'

Arunja was delighted. He gave a throaty roar of conceit. 'Aaahhh! It is true. I am important.'

'Yeah, man, you're important.'

Arunja touched him on the hair. Greenwood closed his eyes and shuddered . He kept his eyes closed until Arunja moved away then he stirred himself, shifted position.

The pirate was at the door.

'Are you leaving me here?' Greenwood said.

'You cannot escape. It is a safe place on my ship.'

'Arunja?'

'Hm?'

'Put out the light, please.'

For the first time the Chink glanced at the dead girl. He hesitated then twisted the switch by the door and plunged the wardroom into darkness, shutting the young soldier off.

The canoes of the Bajau Mandelaut – *gobangs* – were not to be compared to the finely-made and painted boats of the sea-fishermen of the Simporna. They were nothing more than dug-outs, logs hollowed by fire and blade, heavy, broad-beamed, wallowing things designed neither for speed nor stability but easy enough to make.

The Bajau sub-clan did not fish when the river was high, nor when the river was low. The canoes stayed ashore, upturned on a grass sward above the village. Two were kept tethered by the fishing poles but one of these had been blown apart by a direct hit from the pirates' gun and the other, on a frayed vine vable, had broken away with the impetus of the flood current and had gone swirling off into oblivion.

There was no fear of the Tabuli evident among the menfolk

of Usop's *luma* in the village of Panan. But they were incredulous that, given its condition, the warrior *puti* should consider riding down its broad brown back in search of the White Doktor. As far as the Bajau were concerned, the White Doktor had gone into the same sort of oblivion as the old dug-out, lost in the mysterious region that they classified as 'the sea-swamp'.

But luck was with Deacon's team, an uncontrived stroke of good fortune. The Indo Tiger, complete with splinted leg, had not been blasted to kingdom-come. He had been covered by a heap of rattan on the occasion of the first explosion. In his semi-doped state he had lain there, scratched and bruised but otherwise uninjured, during the progress of the pirates' raid and subsequent looting. He, of all the folk in Palan, had an inkling of what was going on and who the perpetrator of the attack might be. He had been one of the commando groups who, disliking the set-up at Ukiti, had taken to the jungle in search of escape. He had been abandoned close to Palan while his companions tried to find the track that would lead then circuitously back to an official army base or, and this was more in their minds, to the gun-trail to the hills above Balimbuka.

The Indo Tiger was grateful to the White Doktor. The Ingo Tiger was recovering nicely from the fever that had racked him and, in the hours between the raid and the arrival of the new, half-naked soldier, he had climbed into convalescence. He had also decided that he would bury his uniform, put on a loincloth and reclaim a place in his grand-uncle's *luma*, reckoning that war was not for him, no matter how many dollars it paid.

The patient was quite a garrulous little devil, as it happened. Goddard extracted much information from him. Egged on by Usop, who was understandably riled at the pirates' invasion, the Indo soldier told all that he knew. Deacon oiled the wheels of his memory with a couple of stingers from the gun flask and kept the chieftain happy in a similarly hospitable manner. The whole process took the best part of the morning, including a parley which ended with four reluctant natives dragging two *gobangs* from the sward to the river's edge.

One unexpected ally was the *pawang*, a God-fearing,

dollar-bill-loving chap who had been padding after Arunja's crew for weeks offering a kind of spiritual back-up service in the razed villages along the Tabuli. The *pawang* did not approve of banditry. He furnished a complete and colourful portrait of Arunja in Old Testament terms, spiced with references to various demons, devils and djinns.

It struck Goddard as strange that the *pawang* did not resent Greenwood's presence in the area. Like all magicians, the *pawang* considered himself a doctor nonpareil. Apparently the chap had spent much time in Brunei, kicking around the seminar. He had learned the value of the white doctor's medicine, enough to admit its efficacy as a method of first aid. Between them, the Indo Tiger and the *pawang* unravelled much of the mystery and gave the SAS team direction. For his part, Usop provided canoes and paddlers for the dangerous trip down river.

Deacon wasted no time in mustering the men. With rain still falling and the Tabuli still rising it was essential to be on the way as soon as possible.

Goddard said, 'If this pirate chap brought a gunboat up, we can be sure the river is navigable. No rapids.'

Deacon said, 'Do you believe the story about a lagoon and a much larger boat?'

'Fellow's been there. I doubt if he has the wit to lie.'

'Hard to swallow, though,' said Dingo. 'Bloody pirates ruling the roost.'

'Bed hets,' said Umgah, shaking his head.

'Oh, that's unquestioned,' said Goddard. 'A law unto themselves. Anachronisms. But customs and police patrols have never managed to control piratical activity.'

'Have you heard of Arunja? Is that the name?'

'That's the name,' said Boyd Goddard. 'Yes, I've heard of him. Haven't personally encountered him, alas. But he's notorious to the north of my beat. Used to haunt the waters off Kudat, down to Jesselton. Gave my predecessor what-ho for a number of years.'

'What's he doing working with the IBT?' said Dingo.

'And the CCO,' said Deacon.

'Gone into another branch of the piracy business, I suppose,' said Goddard. 'Contract killer.'

Deacon said, 'Moving with the times?'

Goddard said, 'We'll have to feed this information back to Dalinart.'

Deacon said, 'The Wessex is our best bet. First, however, we must see what's to be seen, locate the site and pinpoint it exactly.'

'The helicopter isn't due to make its run across the Tabuli until tomorrow,' said Goddard.

'Will the weather stay closed in?' said Dingo.

'It's entirely possible,' said Boyd Goddard.

'One step at a time, then, boss,' Dingo said.

'Absolutely,' Deacon agreed.

Twenty minutes later the team pushed off in two *gobangs* down the swollen river, heading for the swamp lagoon at Ukiti.

Deacon was fully aware of the hazards of river running. He had considered hiding himself and the others in the bottom of the boats, prone under palm leaves. But he was no more sure about the Tabuli than the native paddlers seemed to be and finally elected to be bold, to keep Dingo and Goddard upright, armed and alert.

Though the Indonesian soldier, Greenwood's grateful patient, had provided a general guide to the whereabouts of the camp on the lagoon, jungle was jungle, and there were few obvious landmarks by which to navigate. With a loaded Armalite in his hands, Deacon took the bow position. He sat cross-legged, knees braced against the thick wooden sides of the *gobang*. Even at that it was a rough ride, the canoe leaping in the currents, nodding and bobbing and shipping water.

For the first three miles the fishermen of Palan were familiar with the river route and what lay on either shore but as the village dropped away and other miniature communities fled past – some, Deacon noticed, had also been fired – the paddlers became less assured and nosed and slewed the craft to keep as close to the southern shore as possible.

Normally the Tabuli was placid along its swamp-lined

emergence from the foothills. Sediment and the action of floods had broken down its rocks and the main danger came from shoals of silt and from canoe-gutting debris embedded in them. The Bajau Mandelaut were skilled at reading the river, though, adroit at skirting the darting rippled places where mud and dross collected into whale-shaped banks.

There was little to interest the major, practically nothing to see. The tiny fishing communities whipped past and, after twenty minutes or so, Deacon had become confused as to which direction the Tabuli was taking. He was bamboozled by its broad bends and snaking curves. He began to understand why villagers who lived deep in the jungle acknowledged only two directions. There were only to ways that mattered – upstream and down. Deacon was more concerned with trying to gauge the speed of the canoes, to calculate miles travelled from the watch. This, too, proved impossible. There was no doubt, however, that the great smooth undercurrent which powered the Tabuli was carrying them along with incredible speed.

Deacon had no wish to overshoot the lagoon, to wind up on the seaward side of it. If there was Indo activity – patrols, supply columns, whatever – it would probably be east of the lagoon. There was no saying where the gunboat would be. It was probably powerful enough to snout upstream against the present level of water and might be lurking round the very next bend, hawking the thoroughfare. Whether the base was commanded by Communists or Indonesians or by pirates made no matter. They were unlikely to have the area patrolled. Being thirty-three-or-four miles across the border, they would feel secure.

Ingress and exit would be by the sea at the river's mouth, sheltered – so Goddard said – by a couple of small islands. The islands were mere clumps of palm and mangrove which lay in the strait off the larger and more important islands of Sebatik and Nunukan Timur. It was on one of those tiny islands that the SBS would endeavour to land, to make a pick-up rendezvous if it became necessary. More important than getting out, however, was the business of ensuring that the Royal Navy and

Special Branch set an effective blockade on the mouth of the Jaumpong to prevent Arunja from raiding Balimbuka. In a European setting, there would have been a pristine clarity about the operation by now. But tropical wilderness, the paucity of troops and the lack of the ability to communicate with Dalinart made Deacon anxious in the extreme. He must play it, as he had done so often in the past, entirely by ear.

Throughout the hours of the canoe journey, rain fell ceaselessly. There was no respite on the river. The trough of the canoe was awash, as much with the accumulations of rain as with shipped river water. After half an hour, Deacon's back and knees stiffened and became horribly uncomfortable but he changed position as seldom as possible, only when stiffness developed into painful cramp. Then he would kneel in the water slopping about his cods. God knows what was happening to the stuff in the bergens piled at the stern.

At length Deacon instructed the paddlers, through Umgah, to find a suitable place to land. He was hopeful that they had come far enough. The truth was that he could no longer endure the river and oppressive, crowding trees, the paranoid feeling that the pirates' gunboat was lying in wait around the very next bend.

Chattering, the paddlers wasted no time in ruddering the canoes inshore. Running the bows diagonally across the current, they embedded them neatly on a bank of soggy brown moss above which was a thin ribbob of yellow mud. Deacon stepped over the bow and tentatively planted on foot in the moss. He went in to the knee, found a spongy footing for his boot and lifted the other leg from the canoe. He floundered to the mud, a frail, slippery cliff the height of a tennis net. He bellied over it.

Umgah followed him.

No trail or bridle-path was apparent in the immediate vicinity of the river. The forest was dense, low and flat like all inland swamp country. Almost, Deacon might have said, impenetrable. He spoke with the Dyak. Umgah was cheerful and exuded a confidence that encouraged Deacon. Returning to the canoes, the major ordered the packs to be unloaded. He wanted off the river and under cover.

Whether the lagoon was near or far, they would begin their final trek to Ukiti from here.

Goddard took Deacon to one side: 'Have you asked the paddlers to wait?'

'I have.'

'They won't, you know.'

'Where will they go? They can hardly haul themselves back to Palan, not until the river drops.'

'They'll find a way,' said Goddard. 'Fish out of water. Scared, I suppose.'

'Let them go,' said Deacon, with a shrug.

Goddard pursed his lips round the cigarette holder.

Deacon said, 'What's wrong?'

Goddard said, 'It . . . it goes against the grain, old man. Being quite so deep. No excuse for being nabbed here.'

Deacon could not quite believe his ears. 'If we're caught now, Goddard, diplomacy won't save us.'

'But you still intend to push on?'

'Absolutely.'

'It'll be impossible to get out again, don't you know?'

'Nothing,' Deacon said, 'is impossible.'

'An SAS motto?'

'My motto,' said Deacon, grimly.

Greenwood needed darkness to give him strength to do what had to be done. In one way, of course, it would have been easier to carry out his plan in the glare of lamplight. But he had a daft sort of reluctance to sit there in sight of Mouse. Even if she was dead. He was squeamish about her nakedness, of having to stare at her corpse, its neck twisted and thigh bloody and bruised. Anyhow, it would surely give him an edge to have the wardroom in darkness when Arunja returned.

As soon as the door closed – Greenwood heard a bolt-lever clang into position – he hugged his knees to his chest to give as much play to the chain as possible. It wasn't much.

Blood was everywhere about him. From his torn ear-lobe, from his flayed forearms. The ear didn't hurt much but the arms stung. Close to the table, he manipulated the chain with gentle dipping motions of his elbows. Down. Up. Right. Left. He felt himself to be in control. In reality he was mad with grief and hatred. Hatred made things simple, kept things neat. All he had to do was get himself free of the chain. Didn't have to figure it out beyond that. Get himself out of the chain, stand behind the door. And strangle the first Chink bastard that came through it.

No miraculous Houdini-like escape was possible.

He had to get the key to the padlock.

He had marked exactly where the key had fallen. The round edge of the wardroom table gave him a direction. The round edge of the table pointed to where the key lay. Out of reach. Maybe eight feet away.

Hunkered down, knees on either side of the table leg, Doc dropped his hands until the chain grounded with a silvery noise against the metal plate that clamped table to deck. He cocked his pelvis to give himself extra mobility and removed his canvas boots and socks. He could smell his feet rank and rotting. He waggled his fingertips, pushed the boots behind the table leg out of the way. With his cheek he rubbed the table's edge, fixed a direction in his mind then lowered his body until he was belly-down upon the floor.

Trembling, he rested. Breathed deeply, diaphragm pressing against the deck. Closed his eyes. Suppressed rage throttled his sensitivity. He needed to be sensitive. Aware. Zen aware. Like a crazy Zen exercise, this. Breathing, he murmured, 'Okay, kiddo, okay.' It wouldn't have surprised him to hear Mouse's petulant sing-song ordering him to get on with it.

Think long, man. Think tall.

Stretch.

Chain bit into the grazed flesh of his wrists. Chain rode an inch over his bones and crushed the base of each thumb. Chain would yield no more.

Stretch, man, stretch.

He had a standing jump of twenty-two inches. Was an inch

short of six feet tall. Deduct six inches for loss of hand span. Christ. Maximum of eighty-two inches. Too short. Don't dwell on it. Forget the bleedin' arithmetic. Stretch. Stretch, for Sweet Jesus' sake. *Stretch.*

Ligaments, tendons, joints cracked. Constipated squeaking in his throat. He was short, must be short. He held himself taut as a bow-string, pressed the centre of his forehead, the old pineal eye, on to the metal base of the table leg and walked his toes across the floor. Far, far, far from him. Away from himself. Crabs. Separate. Began to feel. Yeah, *feel.* If he hadn't been short it would have worked, man. Doubt shrunk him. He cast it aside. *Feel*, fuck you, Greenwood. *Feel.*

Touch?

He breathed.

Touch? Metal? Don't knock it aside. Stop. Still now. Empty lungs for one inch more. All air out. Touch again a tiny, flat, free-moving metal object. A key.

With his right foot arched so he couls barely stand the cramp in the muscles of his calf, Greenwood toe-fingered the padlock key inward, drawing it an inch, two inched closer. Must not lose it. Twitch. Jerk. Lost it. Rest the kneecap on the deck. Side of the foot. Instep.

He lost it.

Panic burst into his lungs. He sobbed. Quivering. Sagged.

It was there, though. Not flicked away. Not out of reach.

Rest. Relax. Breath.

Bunion-pad? The inside of the big toe joint? Roll the fuckin' ankle.

Yeah, got it again. A touch. Draw in another inch. Lost it.

Doc paused to work it out. Something wrong. Something kinetically wrong. Think it out anatomically, you medical idiot. When you bend the knee you raise the foot, raise the foot and lose contact. Have to use the whole body, pelvic and abdominal muscles to make the movement. They aren't sensitive enough. Especially in the dark. Right? You got it, man. How far in have you reeled the bleedin' thing? Three or four inches. Fine, great. It's enough. *So do it the other way, nitwit.*

Cautiously Greenwood separated his feet from the line

along which the key lay, regulating the angle by twists upon the chain. When he was sure he was clear, he drew himself into a dog-like position under the edge of the table. The padlock impeded him. He got his teeth to it, held it firm and jiggled his elbows to unfurl the links of the chain. He had lost all feeling in his hands, had cut off the circulation. He tasted salty blood from the padlock. Then he was set once more. In position to begin again.

Cautiously, Greenwood rolled his arms behind his head, scraping the chain up the metal stalk. He could visualise the sequence of movements perfectly, like choreographer can a dance. He felt better. Liberated from doubt. He rolled on to his right thigh, on to the hip bone. His spinal column crackled. Lesions snapped like new elastic in the upper vertebrae. If he slipped he would either break his neck or throttle himself. *So don't slip, man.* He heard chain-links click like balls falling into slots. He wriggled down until he was full-length on his back, then began to grope with his heel for the key.

The rest was comparatively easy. He dabbed his heel on to the key and bent his knee, bringing the object across the floor and up close to his buttock. Another series of contortions and he had the key in his fingers. It was a small key, solid though. If he dropped it now it would bounce away from him. *So don't drop it.* He jerked the chain up the table leg, got the padlock in his teeth, brought his face to his fist and finally slotted the key into place. He turned it.

And the padlock sprang open.

The whole process seemed to have taken hours.

Shaking free of the chains took seconds.

Greenwood got to his feet, swayed dizzily, then found balance. He massaged his neck and shoulders. Forearms were rubbed raw. Would have to do something in case infection took hold. He held the chain in his left hand, groped about by the table until he found a turn-switch for the shaded lamp. He had already decided to risk putting on the lamp. He needed to sort out the wardroom before he settled down for what might be a long wait.

It didn't happen that way, though.

Hardly had he switched on the lamp when he heard the lever-bolt of the bulkhead clang. He hit the lamp switch and darted into position.

The door opened. He could see a wedge of gelid light from the corridor, see a hand on the main turn-switch. The overhead light went on.

Greenwood blinked as the guy stepped over the threshold into the wardroom. Greenwood struck the door with his hip and, in continuous motion, raised the chain and snapped it over the guard's head, bedded it in his thin neck. It wasn't Arunja.

It was the soldier-pirate, the one who'd brought him to the *Leopard* from the compound. Greenwood would have preferred it to be the Chink. There would be time enough for the Chink. One step at a time, kiddo, huh?

Greenwood had been taught how to strangle a man, how to break a human neck. Theory was one thing, practice another. He fumbled, heard the Ingo cry out, fisted the chain deeper into the larynx and swung his backside against the door to close it. If there were other guards in the corridor he didn't want to know, not until the killing was done.

The killing was swift.

Expert or not, Greenwood was charged with hatred. It kept him cold, made him efficient. *No panic, man, no sweat.* Cheek by cheek, he listened to the guy dying, saw the eyes bulging, tongue protruding, the rictus of the lips as they peeled back over yellow teeth. On tiptoe, the guy was still hanging on to the gun, trying to strike out with it. If the bleedin' gun goes off, Greenwood thought, I'm cooked. But the soldier-pirate gave a last dry gurgle. Slumped.

Greenwood dragged back a couple of paces and lowered the body to the deck. He grabbed the gun and dived to the door, peered out, The corridor was deserted. He listened. Heard only a flush of plumbing from some part of the boat. Nothing else. No alarms.

He closed the door.

Mouse hadn't moved.

Greenwood was no hard-arsed pragmatist. He was a

dreamer. Had kind of hoped she might still be alive. He brought her off the couch. Her neck rolled and waggled. Her eyes remained open, staring. He closed the lids with his fingertips and laid her gently on the floor. He flung open a locker, found linen there, a tablecloth. Puffed it out and laid it over the dead girl. He got down on his knees beside her, kissed her brow then slid the cloth over her face. He didn't say anything. No last rites or words of parting. As far as Doc was concerned, Mouse was still with him.

Spirit of the jungle, right? What he was going to do now, he would do for her.

He put out the light, opened the door.

Empty corridor. Silent deck.

He stole along the passageway and climbed the ladder. He craned his neck, surveyed the deck. He had been wrong. The wardroom was aft, not for'ard. Dummy funnel was behind him, the bridge beyond that. Three guards by the gangway, one standing, two seated. He could just make them out. They wouldn't be able to see him unless they strained their eyes. There was only a single lantern on a gibbet at the stern. Where the fuck was Arunja? On the bridge? Bunked in a cabin below deck? Gone ashore?

It didn't occur to Greenwood to seek out the ship's radio, obliterate the operator and use the transmitter. In other circumstances he would have put loyalty to Major Dalinart before all else. Not any more. He was on his own, all on his own.

He came quietly up the ladder and around the chain-post on to the deck. On the port side there was nothing but the dark lagoon and a hinterland of jungle and swamp. No guards. The flank of the funnel was smooth. He paused, realised that he was barefoot. He had left his boots below. He wore nothing but a stained army vest and baggy pants. He looked out over the black water for a moment, breathing the humid night air. Moths and other insects clouded the lantern glow by the side of the bridge. Doc's movement did not disturb them. He squatted by the edge of an empty metal-fret cradle which, he guessed, was a fixture for torpedo launchers. He swung his legs over the side and sat there, then turned and gripped the cradle and lowered himself into the lagoon.

The water parted like silk with hardly a ripple.

Doc pushed himself away from the *Leopard*. He stroked like a frog, nose and mouth just above the water level. After a couple of minutes he let go of the gun. At this stage it was only an impediment and he hadn't the strength to swim with it. He headed for the oily darkness away from the shore lights. towards the channel in the *lalang* beyond which lay the river.

He wasn't running away, though.

Not me, kiddo.

He swam slowly for a while then turned towards the shore. He required two things. He must search until he found them – the saxophone case and the armoury.

And after I find them, Mouse, I'll come back to kill some more.

East and north-east of Ukiti, a half-mile across the breath of the lagoon, there was no shore to speak of. The lake accumulated out of the ribs of mud and vegetable mush and only a band of thorn and scrub bamboo indicated where the forest ended and the swamp began.

The lake at Ukiti was in reality no more than a shifting clearing in the swamp, slanted against the channel of the Tabuli, its one obvious line of demarcation. It was not like any other place in Borneo that Boyd Goddard had visited. It had all the fundamental features but in a confusion which, in glimmering moonlight, puzzled the Special Branch officer and made him uncertain. He had no sense of distance, no consciousness of the nearness of the lake. If it hadn't been for Umgah, Boyd Goddard would have trudged out of soupy shallows and into deep water, following nothing more concrete than a glint of moonlight through the scrub bamboo.

'Bess. Bess.'

The Dyak barred the SB man's progress with the shaft of his spear.

Goddard stopped. In fact, he had been three parts asleep.

'What is it?'

'Big wetter.'

The Dyak's hand on his shoulder was as light as a withered leaf. Goddard allowed himself to be directed two paces to the left. There, through a lattice of sapling branches and snaking creepers, he saw the lake. Even with cloud covering the moon, the lake would have been sharply defined. Lights on the far shore were vivid enough to add dimension.

Calf-deep, boots sinking into base mud, Goddard stopped again, the Dyak's fingers still holding him. 'Big wetter' it most certainly was. Ukiti, no doubt about it.

Major Deacon and the Australian splashed softly up to Goddard and, in line, the four men gazed out across the lagoon.

'Dear God!' Deacon whispered.

'Fair old set-up,' said Harper. 'What the hell've they got there, boss?'

'The smaller boat's a Star,' Goddard answered. 'Same type as Special Police use for patrol duties.'

'The other,' said Deacon, 'appears to be an MTB.'

'Can we get closer?' said Goddard.

'Crackadills near,' Umgah warned.

Goddard nodded. He should have recognised crocodile country. Place would be swarming with them, particularly if the Indo camp had been established for a while and discharged its garbage into the lake. On the other hand, perhaps the Indos had had a croc-shoot. If he'd been in charge of the base it's what he would have done.

'A tree then, Umgah,' said Deacon. 'Find us a stout tree. I want to make a recce.'

The Dyak left them. He was only gone for a minute. On his return he took Deacon by the hand and led the major and the others in a zig-zag through the shallows among the thickets. They skirted a bank of sandy mud upon which Goddard imagined he could make out the shapes of reptiles. The tree was poised on the verge of the water, a squat-boled thing, some kind of mangrove. Its roots were twined with wiry flower stems, the flowers closed like pus-filled fingers.

Gofdurd was tense. He disliked crocs and could still – just –

make out the sandbank and the shapes upon it. Borneo crocodiles were usually savage and would not hesitate to attack a man. Goddard fished for his cigarette holder and sucked on it to soothe himself, while Deacon and Harper climbed into the tree. The SB officer followed, leaving pack and rifle at the base. Umgah would stand guard.

The view across the lagoon was unimpaired now. Deacon had binoculars. The major wrapped an arm around a mass of branches to give himself a stance. Goddard was just below him, Harper around the trunk, all three close enough to converse.

'Training camp,' said Deacon. 'More probably an assembly base.'

'Is this the point that the howitzers start from?' Harper asked.

'It's hardly relevant,' said Deacon.

'What can you see, old chap?' Goddard said.

Obligingly Deacon handed down the binoculars. Goddard pressed himself against the spiky branches, brought the glasses to his eyes, took focus. He scanned the distant shore from left to right and studied the two craft carefully for a couple of minutes then returned the glasses without comment.

Even at a distance of a half-mile, through the powerful lenses Goddard had made out enough to realise that both vessels were bristling with guns. Loaded with guerrillas, they would pose a major threat to a remote community like Balimbuka. With big guns in the hills and the two fast boats on the Jaumpong and teams of guerrillas, of whatever shade, in the timber, the defences at the lumber town would soon be overwhelmed. All the scraps of Intelligence that he had gathered so far began to coalesce. Pirates and Communists together. Skill and rapaciousness. Discipline and ruthlessness. Principles and sheer greed. A damned lethal mixture.

If the encampment had been closer to the border it would have been possible to trek back to one of the friendly villages to summon assistance, even an air strike. But it would be too much of 'an infringement' of the insane rules of the conflict to bomb a site so far into Indonesian territory. He could just imagine the sort of capital that Sukarno's ministers would make out of an act of so-called aggression, how photographs of dead native children would be flashed about the desks of the world's Press and on to the conference tables of the United Nations. The problem with limited wars, campaigns of protection, was that nobody understood them very well except the men who fought them.

In terms of strength of numbers, there wasn't much to see. But the presence of the strike craft, spanking-new by the look of them, confirmed Goddard's worst fears.

Goddard climbed to the ground, followed in due course by Harper and, finally, Deacon.

'Well?' said Goddard. 'We may not have found the Greenwood chap but we have confirmed Dalinart's suspicions. We must get news of this back at once.'

Deacon did not answer.

Harper said, 'I reckon we could do it, boss.'

Goddard said, 'Do what?'

'Paste the camp,' said Harper.

'Three of us? Don't be utterly ridiculous,' said Goddard. 'Direct action is out of the question.'

'What about it, boss?' Harper said. 'Shouldn't be too difficult.'

Deacon spoke slowly, weighing each word. 'The boats are the key, aren't they?'

'Yip,' said Harper. 'No boats; no show.'

Goddard protested, 'There are two or three hundred—'

Deacon said, 'Without the boats the Indos won't be able to work a large force across country to coordinate an attack on Balimbuka. The howitzers already in place can be taken out by a pinpoint air strike. Quite legitimately. Removed from Malaysian territory.'

'What do you mean . . . without the boats?'

'Goddard,' said Deacon, 'can you pilot an MTB?'

'No. It's too large and too quick. You need a trained crew to handle that sort of power output.'

'What about the Star?' said Harper. 'You said it was a standard patrol-type craft.'

Goddard paused. He licked his dry lips. He was no coward but he *was* used to organisation, not impetuosity. The scheme that the SAS officers seemed to be evolving struck him as suicidal.

'I . . . Yes, I can pilot the Star. It isn't difficult.'

'Excellent!' said Deacon.

'Pilot it where?' said Goddard.

'Out of the lagoon and, if necessary, down the Tabuli to the sea.'

'River pilotage,' said Goddard. 'Look, I don't wish to appear sticky, old chap, but an MTB will outrun a Star and, with that load of armament, blast it out of the water. Assuming, that is, that we can somehow commandeer the patrol boat in the first place.'

'Won't be an MTB to outrun us,' said Harper.

'What do you mean?'

'The big 'un will have gone up in smokeski,' said Harper.

'But . . . but how?'

Harper chuckled softly. 'Ask Major Deacon, sir. He'll figure out a method in a minute or two. Won't you, boss?'

'Absolutely,' said Deacon.

'What about . . . what about your soldier? Greenwood? What if he's on board the MTB?'

'Hard cheddar,' said Harper.

'How do you propose to board and capture the Star?'

'Under cover of darkness,' said Deacon.

'You mean immediately? Tonight?'

'By tomorrow they may be on their way to Balimbuka.'

'Not until the river drops a little,' said Goddard.

'How long might that take, assuming no more rain?'

Goddard did not answer. He heard the casual splash of a crocodile launching itself into the lagoon only yards to the right of their position. He was under no illusions now about Deacon's intention. Swimming would be involved. A trek around the lake was out of the question. Oddly, he approved of the SAS major's decisiveness, that quality which lay close to impetuosity.

Goddard said, 'No more rain and the river will be down by

mid-morning, unless storms continue in the hills.'

'I'm not willing to take the chance,' said Deacon. 'Of them leaving, I mean.'

Harper said, 'Remember, we've got surprise on our side. the last thing in the world those buggers will expect is a raid on their boats.'

'Shoot and scoot?' said Goddard. 'Is that the expression?'

'In spades,' said Harper.

The croc had found something edible not far off shore. The rest of the pack were plunging into the water now, thrashing ferociously.

'Four of us in the gunboat,' said Deacon, 'with the MTB scuttled, and we'll be perfectly safe. Run *up* river and wait for the Wessex to lift us out. If that doesn't come off, we can still lose ourselves in the jungle.'

Goddard had already reached a decision. He had little or no choice. He was no feather-merchant. He was a Special Branch officer. He had raided camps before. Four against two hundred, however, did seem like rather heavy odds. He took Deacon's point about possession of the boat. He stared across the lagoon at the sprinkle of lights on the further shore, listening to the snap and roar of the feeding crocodiles.

'What do you want me to do?' Boyd Goddard said.

'Something rather dangerous,' said Deacon.

'What?'

'Capture the Star on your own,' Major Deacon said.

Come daylight, he would be long gone. Anyhow, he didn't have to make long-term plans. Even if he wasn't long gone, he didn't much care what happened to him. He had one purpose. To killArunja. He had left the MTB only to find a sure means of accomplishing that end. He could use himself up. Had nothing to save himself for. He had wormed his way into the situation out of conceit and wilfulness and it had cost a lot of lives. He didn't grieve over the Chinese VIP but it made him mad that he had sweated so hard over the operation when the guy had already been marked for death.

What grieved him, of course, was Mouse. Poor kid. She

should have steered clear of him. Stayed home and played *humpi-humpi* with some nice guy with a quick spear and not too many tattoos. Had children, given to the world – her world – more beautiful, slender girls, dainty as mouse-deer.

Greenwood wept as he swam, his tears lost in the bow-wave that preceded him across the lagoon.

Swimming was soothing. Water warm and milky, like swimming in a mug of Horlicks. If only his forearms didn't hurt so much, distracting him from logical thought. Wasn't much logic in it, though. Bungalow, then armoury. He would carve his way to what he wanted with a bush-knife and a knotted cord.

Doc emerged from the lagoon on his belly, paddling ashore. He was five or six hundred yards north of the last of the camp lights, close to the strip of tall grasses which screened the lagoon from the river. He could hear the rush and belly-gurgle of the Tabuli. The clarity of the sound emphasised how quiet it had become at the encampment. Arunja's freebooters' orgy had burned itself out. Maybe all the girls had died, like Mouse.

Greenwood rested in the silt, head on arms.

After fifteen minutes or so he got up and reconnoitred the scene. There was nothing to see. Embers, lights of the gunboat and the *Leopard*. He would never have known the name of the vessel if Mouse hadn't told him. There were a lot of things he would never have known about if it hadn't been for her.

He moved off the shore into the forest, thin stuff, cleared for furl.

Bare feet were a disadvantage now. He felt the earth for big, loose needle-sharp thorns which might cripple him as he skirted the shrubs and stole towards the dumps left of the bungalow. Grasses and leaves held the rainwater sleckly, As soon as the sun came up, the whole area would vanish into thick mist. And he would vanish within the mist. Provided his task was done. Arunja killed.

Not just killed, man.

Slaughtered.

5 Have his bones

The wonder of it was that you kept going at all. The Deke could have told the boy wonder what was in store for him in fifteen years time. But the Deke wasn't a moaner. Only if you looked closely could you see how the major stiffened after rest, how there was more willpower than free-running exuberance in the tough physical action.

Dingo had no notion of how old Deacon was. Such esoteric questions weren't in his mind as he dipped his hands into the water and sculled the bamboo raft forward. Some bloody raft! Six lengths of bamboo lashed together with rope. None of your SBS sophistication for lubbers like Dingo Harper; wet-suits, inflatables, rope-soled shoes and infra-red lamps. Any muggins could make an attack on a moored craft with all that clobber. Dingo preferred it *au naturel*, though he wouldn't have minded crunching a couple of benzedrine tablets to boost him for action at the end of the half-mile paddle across the lagoon.

The Deke was off to his left. Old Umgah was attached to the Deke by a short line, though the tracker had his own float, as crude and jerry-built as the others. On the line attached to Dingo's shoulder was Boyd Goddard, that cautious representative of law and order. If they had been peeled to the buff and carrying nothing, the journey would have been easy. Bergens were essential, though. Plus weapons, they made sculling bloody exhausting.

Dingo inserted his hands gracefully, turning them open only after they had slipped into the water. Making long, strong, smooth strokes eventually taxed even his strength and caused a dull ache in his shoulders and chest. It was about then that he began to worry about Goddard, who, by Dingo's lights, was no spring chicken. Night attacks across lakes were games for young men.

The mud with which Dingo had plastered his face had washed off. He had no blacking in his kit, cursed himself for not bringing a little tin. Mud was no substitute for a swimmer. Christ, his pale face would be shining whiter than a croc's arse. He kept his head down, showed to the shore only the crown of his khaki-green hat.

Harper had suggested splitting the team. Deke and he would take out the MTB and try to capture the Star, bring it across the lagoon to Goddard. Goddard and Umgah would wait safe in the swamp trees – just in case. Goddard wouldn't wear it. He didn't want to be left out. Scared, maybe, but no coward. Just as well. The hard part would be getting from the MTB to the Star. The wreckers would need some kind of diversion. The Deke had figured it right. Let Goddard nab the gunboat. Boyd Goddard was no slouch as a copper. He had a lot of experience in raiding, though maybe not this kind of stuff.

To Captain Maurice Harper there was nothing outrageous in the plan. Once they had possession of the Star the rest would be, literally, plain sailing. They would even be able to take a leisurely shooting cruise, wreak a fair piece of havoc before chugging through the channel into the Tabuli and heading off into the sunset. The moments of maximum danger would occur before they got out of the lagoon and on to the boat. He questioned if the craft would be well guarded, however. The larger craft, the MTB, would be on a deeper mooring; not a mooring, a berth? Anyhow, the boat was tied to a jetty of solid construction, a short, T-shaped pier. The Star was of shallower draught, so Goddard had informed him. The pier against which it was moored looked to be made of bamboo. It would disintegrate with a couple of grenades or one well-placed shell.

Dingo squinted at the shore. Even through the Deke's powerful binoculars he hadn't quite been able to make out what the hell the Indo pirates were up to. Seemed to be some kind of picnic, a sprawling cook-out. Certainly there were no signs of military discipline or orderliness. All of which confirmed the theory that pirates ruled the roost.

Goddard splashed. The sound seemed very loud. Dingo scowled, head cocked, at the copper, then he fanned his arms and feathered the tiny raft while he peered at the boats again.

Only forty yards away now. Still deserted. The MTB was a

big fish. Eighty feet long, twenty feet in beam. The Star looked a bit like a bath-tub toy by comparison. Thirty feet in length, only nine or so in beam. No problem muscling out of the water on to her deck, in spite of a bulging fender.

There had been some discussion as to how best to carry out the operation. Take the Star and blast the MTB? Sneak on to the MTB, sabotage it and capture the Star in the confusion? The Deke had settled on the latter plan. Prime objective was to render the MTB unfit for service, to make it useless as a fast strike vessel and a transporter of guerrillas, whether regular IBTs or pirates made no matter. Dingo was happy enough to go along with Deacon's judgement.

The Australian trod water, steering the raft gradually to the right, closer to Goddard. He was tempted to whisper a question, ask Goddard if he was okay. But voices would carry across the surface of the still water and he couldn't be sure that all the guerrillas were in a state of torpor. Sure looked like it, though. He could see the buggers sprawled by fires in the dead-away, catatonic attitudes of Scotsmen on January 1st. Blotto. He glanced left. The Deke made a signal, urging him on.

Dingo pulled in a deep breath and sculled forward towards the MTB.

Still nobody visible on the deck. He was practically under the stern now, skirting a patch of brilliant reflection under a stern lantern. The windows of the wheelhouse – did you call it a bridge? Dingo wondered – were without interior light. Shouldn't there be a bloody watch or something? One white lamp on each wing of the bridge gave light, smearing it down the curve of the streamlined little funnel. He could see Chinese characters on the hull and along the bow. Boyd Goddard would probably be able to read them. Chinese vessel, though. Confirmation that the CCO were behind this cooperative assault.

Dragging Goddard after him, Dingo eased against the side of the MTB. The middle-aged copper was gasping, trying to stifle the noise. Badly winded, he looked hellish. Hair slicked his bald dome, his eyes were sunken. Maybe he had been a hotshot in the jungle fighting Japs, but that was twenty years ago. The poor bloke was knackered. Not so knackered that he had lost control, though. Struggling to hold air in his lungs, he sounded like a wart-hog with a head cold.

Dingo brushed the side of the MTB and steadied himself. He gave the line a firm tug and brought Goddard's raft against his own. He hooked a boot toe around it and, with his legs, anchored the bamboo bundle. The rafts would be a problem now. Couldn't just let them drift away. Might be seen, might rouse the curiosity of somebody for'ard or a patrol on the beach. Dingo solved the problem with his knife. He cut the rope that bound the bamboo poles together and let the bloody thing disintegrate around him. He sank into the water. Not deep but not shall enough to touch bottom. With no current, he held position, in spite of the weight of pack and gun. One hand on Goddard's raft. He made a signal. Goddard nodded. Dingo cut the bindings of the second raft. The two men trod water in a mess of bamboo poles.

Dingo looked up. The sweep of the MTB's lines brought the edge of the deck within reach. Long stretch, hauling bergen and Sterling with him. Deacon and the Dyak had come in against the MTB's hull further down, under the wheelhouse lantern. Perspectives were deceptive. Dingo could actually see the bloody Star, brought out by a subtle curve of the lake shore. He moved Boyd Goddard towards it, passing the copper down the side of the MTB, handing him on to Umgah and then to Deacon.

As always, the Dyak appeared perfectly comfortable, even up to his neck in water. Only flying discomfited Umgah. Water was a natural medium. He toted the spear on a rattan strap, bound safe against his shoulders, metal tip bunged with a wad of grass. He gave a wet, wrinkled grin as Goddard floated past him. Christ, Dingo thought, the old bloke looks as if he lived in the lagoon! Goddard was gingerly handed past Deacon. SAS major and SB officer were face to face for a moment, exchanging silent signs like mutes. Goddard nodded, swam out of the cover of the MTB and along the curve of the shore just beyond the range of the lights.

Moment of maximum danger *numero uno*. If one joker raised his blowsy head, if somebody on the boats staggered to the rail to pee . . . Goddard appeared to be hardly moving. Had the copper seized up? Jesus, will you shift it!

The Deke had drawn himself to the bow of the MTB, anxiously watching the SB officer's progress. Dingo was ready to unsheath himself from the lake the very instant that Goddard reached the stern of the gunboat.

Goddard stroked on, ripples reaching to lap the shore.

On shore, somewhere, somebody let out a cackle of laughter. Small noises stirred along the beach. On the deck, overhead, Dingo heard a soft footfall. Somebody on watch after all, some bloody pirate.

Dingo held himself slack, very slack, ready to reach up to the deck's edge. He was watching Goddard, Goddard progressing about as speedily as a waterlogged mealie-sack. The he heard a startled grunt and, looking up, saw an Indonesian directly above him, a carbine in his hands.

Bergen, Sterling and all, Harper was out of the water like a kraken. He grabbed the guard by the ankles and yanked, thrusting himself backwards as he did so, sinking with an almighty splash. He still had a grip on the Indo, who came over with him and plunged over Dingo's head. The Australian was after him like an otter. He touched bottom, five or six feet down, rolled on the pack, came up at the guard from below, put the blade below the breastbone and thrust upwards. When he wallowed over, the blade sank into the hilt. Dingo pulled it out, broke connection.

Mouth open, blood poured out. The lake water blurred the Indo's features. Naked arms were weed-like as the man rolled and, with a peculiar bobbing motion, sank. Two or three feet below surface Dingo held himself, watching. Spurts of blood, like octopus ink, pumped out of the wound, and Dingo knew that the bloke was dead. He pushed the corpse to send it below, then, on a rush of bubbles, came up for air. Not just for air. Came up for engagement. Came up to fight. The odds were stacked against them. Goddard probably hadn't made it to the stern of the Star. The Deke and the Dyak were still trapped in the water.

Dingo glanced left and right. No sign of the major or the Dyak. Even more surprising, the pirates hadn't hammered to the rail or flocked to the waterline to repulse the attack. What in God's name *had* the bastards been drinking? Then a series of explosions ripped through the bungalows, and Dingo, protected by the hull of the MTB, realised that there had been previous detonations while he'd been occupied sub-surface. It was one hell of a bang too, a fair old ripper. It would have caused confusion in the best disciplined barracks. Here in Ukiti it caused chaos.

On his back, Dingo stroked round the stern of the MTB, dangerously near the props, and took a swatch at the happenings on shore. Jesus, what a fireworks display! Both bungalows had been blasted and petrol fires were spreading like a blue plague across the compound. Chunks of burning debris hissed into the water around him. Bloody Indos and Chinks hared every way which, scrabbling for carbines and to man stations to which they had been allotted but the memory of which was vague in their fuddled brains. Two Chinks, naked as jays, sprinted into the lake. On shore, an NCO in shorts and combat jacket screamed at them to come back.

Dynamite had done for the bungalows. Not shells, certainly not grenades. Dynamite.

Christ, there was hardly any standing wreckage, just stump-posts to show where the buildings had been, flat beds of flame and a pond of petrol-blue fire with a dragon's tail flicking across the compound while soldiers and pirates leapt from its advance. Classic sabotage. Neatly set up from materials on hand. Diesel oil, gasoline, dynamite and fuses. Somebody had done a real trim job.

But who?

Dingo didn't wait for an answer.

He had gotten himself over the prop-housing and on to the deck of the MTB. He didn't have much worry about being spotted. On deck, the Chinks were otherwise occupied. And bloody how! Somebody was giving them purple murder with an SMG. Sounded like a Sten, a genuine British chatterjack.

Dingo dropped to one knee and stripped the oilskin wrapper from his Sterling. He had practised the movement a thousand times and the wrapper peeled away, leaving the weapon and two clips bone-dry. He slotted the sheet-metal box magazine into the side fitting, jerked out the butt-stock and locked it on the lugs in the receiver cap. He had twenty-eight inches of lethal metal in his mitts now, thirty-four rounds in the mag, and the drop on the ginks by the rail.

The SMG was whopping out. He could see it over to his left in a kind of foxhole in the sand of the upper crescent of the beach. You couldn't really call it a beach, that flattening of earth and silt by the compound. Burning fuel gave light. Some smart NCO had mustered a squad. The Tigers were dragging their hangovers to a point on Dingo's right, up where darkness gathered. He thought he could see a shack of sorts, maybe just a canvas-cloaked frame over food stores. The compound was already littered with bodies, not all of them dead.

Report, Captain Harper?

A fucking shambles, sir.

Maybe there *were* two hundred so-called trained guerrillas out there, though it didn't look like it. Only a handful appeared fit and willing to fight. Plus the bunch on the MTB. And he really had the drop on them.

The Deke and the slap-happy Dyak tracker had come on board by the wing of the wheelhouse and, like Dingo, had weapons ready to fire.

By now Dingo had realised that the bloke who'd blown the bloody works and had the MTB under fire could only be Greenwood. Unless crafty old Dalinart had wormed in an SBS team without informing Deke of his intention? Nope, Harper decided, it's Greenwood. His image of the milksop medic altered radically at that instant. But he had no leisure for further speculation. Greenwood's act of sabotage had come at precisely the right second and it was up to them, up to him, to sustain the impetus and advantage of surprise.

He took out six pirates with his first burst.

You didn't get medals for that sort of shooting. Not under the circumstances. If you missed, you should have your arse kicked. The targets were lined up on the port rail, plugging away with their carbines. A division of Marines could have swarmed over the starboard rail without catching their attention. But as they went down, writhing and torn by the 9mm parabellum cartridges, Dingo had run up his flag and became focus for retaliation. He didn't hang around. He went left, along the narrow strip of deck that hugged the rail. There was hardly room for his feet against a heavy metal-fret cradle. There were two pirates ahead of him. They wore Levis and gaudy shirts. One had a handgun, a big brute. The other brandished a carbine. They were pinned down on the forward section of the deck, under the window of the wheelhouse.

Dingo was tempted to shout out to Deacon. But he bit his lip and leaned his shoulder against the cradle. It gave excellent support. He thumbed the selector on the Sterling and pumped a burst of automatic fire across the foredeck, taking out the couple who'd gone for the cannon. He couldn't see the other cannon from where he was. For a split second he was hung-up on what to do next.

Bullets spat and spanged off the frame. Still unfortunately saddled with the bergen, Dingo dove towards the wall of the wheelhouse. Then a very tall, very angular Chink folded over the edge of the wheelhouse roof and dropped on his conk about three feet from Dingo. His hand had closed on the trigger-guard of the SMG and he fell on it. The T-stock buckled under his chest, crushing ribs. The bloke was a gonner, though, drilled through the chest. He splatted to the deck and didn't move. Dingo crabbed back, shucking out of the bergen and dropping it beside the cradle.

The MTB had seemed bloody large when he was sculling towards it across the lake, but now he was on it, and bullets were buzzing, it seemed as cramped as a dog-kennel.

Dingo wasn't a boat freak, had never been a member of the Sydney yacht club or any of its provincial imitators. Sea-training wasn't part of the course. Truth was that the total competence expected of SAS officers had its limits. Dingo just hoped that Goddard knew what he was doing and that the Special Branch officer had made it on to the Star. What *he* had to do, and you didn't have to be a bloody jolly Jack Tar to figure it out, was to set the MTB adrift, get it the hell away from the jetty. After that he could start to worry about how to blow the thing up.

Dingo went around the stern again, the Sterling at the ready. Three blokes were against the rail, fighting off fire from the bow section. The Deke had not been idle. Without hesitation, Dingo dragged the Sterling across the three, saw them slither. He hesitated by a hatch leading down into the nether regions of the boat, pivoted and delivered a burst of fire down the ladder into the face of another Chinese pirate. The bloke slumped to the steps. Dingo fired again, though he couldn't see anybody else down there. That done, he bounded across the deck to the stern rope and saw that it wasn't rope at all, but cable.

'DINGO.'

Deacon was standing by the open door of the wheelhouse.

'CAST OFF,' the Deke bellowed.

Simple: so bloody simple it hadn't occurred to him. He knelt by the eyebolt to which the cable was secured and lifted the cable loop. Carrying it in lubberly fashion in his arms, he dumped it over the port side.

Withering fire from the gun up by the jungle fringe continued, though its position appeared to have altered. Retaliation, led by Indo NCOs, was scattered because of the angle. Dingo couldn't comprehend what was going on out there. All he knew was that somebody was making the job very much easier than it should have been; an accidental, coincidental two-prong attack had materialised. Glancing left, he glimpsed Umgah at the head cable, detaching it too.

Then, abruptly, Dingo had no time to think of anything except his own survival.

The Chink was frigging enormous. He wore denim shorts and a flak vest. He had been caught below, obviously without weapons. He moved like a judo champion on the balls of his feet, arms stretched out. For once, Dingo was out-classed for speed of reaction. He had no time to swing the Sten, to squeeze the trigger. The big yellow bastard was out of the hatch, coming up from below, trampling over the corpse, and on him.

Dingo felt the Sterling being plucked from his grasp as if he was five years old and the bugger was stealing his lollipop. Dingo tried to step back. He tripped on the eyebolt and fell.

The Chink's heel slammed down on the deck only an inch from his head. Dingo rolled. Toes curled into a deadly into a deadly sort of fist, the foot whacked him on the side of the skull. Stars, rockets and Catherine wheels exploded in Dingo's brain.

Whack.

He felt as if his teeth would fall out.

Instinctively Dingo jabbed out a hand and grabbed the ankle as the foot sliced in for the kill. It was like catching a buffalo by a horn. Dingo was yanked from the deck and shaken. He had a blurred impression of muscle sheath, hairless flesh, then the deck tilting under him. The Chink flailed with the Sterling and swayed. The pounding in Dingo's skull was intensified by the sudden thrashing roar of the MTB's props. The Chink fell, Dingo hanging on to his leg like a hound to a ham-bone, as Deacon managed to start the powerful diesels.

Later the Deke would claim that it was luck that he had hit the right buttons. Luck for Dingo okay. Otherwise the Chinese giant would have stomped him into hamburger. When the big bugger was cut to size, however, Dingo found that he could cope. It wasn't even a question of devising a plan. He did what any animal would do. He went straight for the groin.

He was still rattling, headwise. But somewhere west of the ankle was a kneecap and above that a thigh, above that again, genitals. Not even a monster from Shanghai or wherever had armour-plated ballocks. Dingo released the ankle, locked his fists deep into the crotch of the denim shorts and lifted. He had enough residue of sense to keep his head tucked in, chin buried in his chest, so the victim couldn't tear his noddle off. As if he was hauling up a log, Dingo rose, lifting the chink by the balls.

The bloody deck was vibrating like the rim of a brass cymbal. Churn of brown spray was thrown up from the props. Dingo had no knowledge of what was happening elsewhere. He focused his waning strength on his arms and fingers. Hooked deep, he did not dare release a hand to grope for his knife. If he could've got the knife, though, he would have gutted the joker like a gaffed pike.

The struggle fused while the MTB punched away from the jetty and, effectively out of control, carved into the lagoon. Another fifteen seconds and the vessel would have been clear of the shore and Dingo would have been safe enough in the deep, dark, mysterious waters, with nothing to worry about except staying afloat until the Star picked him up. None of that, of course, entered Harper's thinking. He hadn't a clue what sort of mess the Deke had gotten into in the wheelhouse.

The fist broke Dingo Harper's collar-bone. Pain syphoned into his fuddled brain, gave him brief clarity. He shouted aloud, bulldogging the big bloke's ballocks. He felt the fist come again. His upper arm went numb. He was still yelling. The Chink was yelling. The struggle was no longer combat but a variety of defeat for both participants. Both sensed that the boat was out of control, over-powered, and carving away in a wild oval from the jetty. Both men sensed that the other was in too much pain to inflict further harm. It was the Chink who yielded, though, who stopped trying to rain blows upon the attacker. Suddenly he tore himself away.

The MTB had swung upon herself, hull scraping the slope of the shore, teeth-on-edge tearing along the jetty posts. An SMG was going *bam-bam-bam-bam* like a demon heartbeat, very close. Dingo was already losing consciousness through pain. The Chink was before him, contact broken. Dingo Harper throught, *If he hits me now, I'm a bloody gonner.* But the Chink didn't. He too had had enough. He vaulted, turning, and was gone out of sight.

Dingo fell to his knees.

He would have tried to flatten himself on the deck if he'd known what was about to happen. The sudden mule-kick of the port-side prop on the jetty caught him out. It was like being swatted by an invisible fist. He staggered, tried to brace himself with his left hand. But the left arm was useless. He caught his belly on the rail and clasped vainly at the chain.

Stern props chewed into the jetty and the MTB bolted.

The violent forward thrust somersaulted Captain Maurice

Harper over the rail and down into the shallow water which fringed the lagoon, only yards from the Indo shore.

Doc's tally of kills was high even before he laid his mitts on the SMGs. Not Russian rubbish either, but Chinese-made M.38s, which were almost identical copies of the British Mark II Sten, a weapon he had been trained to use. He could, in fact, have had his choice of guns. But the M.38s were jim-dandy and would suit his purpose fine. Backed by grenades, of course. What really tickled him was his discovery of a quantity of dynamite and Cordex fuse. He reckoned he could handle stuff that simple without blowing himself sky-high. He had already 'removed' – a nice, painless word – five terrorists, including one of the smirking, English-speaking Filipinos who had been in on the operation.

The surgical operation seemed to belong to another era, to have been performed by another person altogether. Somebody not quite as sane as the guy who stole into the bungalow from the edge of the jungle and 'took out' – another nice phrase – the solitary guard. For an experienced medic, one who could expose the arteries in a man's neck, strangulation and the cutting of throats were simple exercises of craft.

Doc didn't run wild in the bungalow. He killed only two men. There must have been six or eight guys dossed out in there. Privileged types. Officers and big-wheel pirates. He didn't want to stir up trouble, though. Not yet. All he wanted was the saxophone case – which he found lying by the wall in the room where he'd operated, by the shrouded bundle on the bed. God knows what Arunja intended to do with the VIP's corpse. Have it embalmed, maybe, wrapped in vine leaves, decorated with flowers and sent back to Shanghai or Peking for a state funeral, the forged death certificate pinned to it like a delivery note.

Once he had the saxophone case, Doc felt a whole lot better.

He went out back of the bungalow through the unshuttered window by which he had entered, into the jungle. He opened the case and spread out the contents, peering, not risking a light. He could tell by feel what he had. He found a metal tin which contained a clutch of pep pills. He picked one of the oval ones, its main constituent being caffeine, not benzedrine. He had never been one for bennies. He popped the pill, letting it dissolve under his tongue while he checked over the items in the case like a miser going over his hoard. To waste time was irrational, especially with two dead guys in the bungalow liable to be discovered at any moment. But Doc wasn't concerned. Objective Number One had been achieved. With the terrorists lying about the compound like fall-out victims, he didn't feel pressed. In due course he was ready and, dragging the case with him, went in search of Objective Number Two. The armoury.

The second of the pair of bungalows which dominated the north section of the encampment contained the weapons. It was no more difficult to enter than the first bungalow had been, though it was guarded by two uniforms, both of whom were awake.

Doc spied out the verandah from the cover of the leaves then turned his attention to the rear of the building. There were windows there, looking out into the jungle. But they had been boarded over with sheets of plyboard; or so he thought. Fingering the board, however, he realised that the plyboard was in fact a crate. Boxed ammo was stacked up inside the building.

The pep pill was hitting him by that time. He was lit up like a neon tube. He lifted the saxophone case and crept to the gable of the bungalow where the verandah ran down four shallow steps on to a muddy pad. Kneeling in the mud, the case propped on the steps, he opened it and carefully extracted a scalpel from the surgical kit, a thin sharp blade, better for the work than the *kris* in his left and went softly up the steps to the corner. He was doing fine, just fine, and didn't want to blow it now. Off to his left he could make out the embers of cooking fires but he couldn't see a soul.

There was a lantern on a hook by the door of the bungalow. It shed straws of light along the verandah. Against the rays, Doc could see the shadows of the guards. He waited, breathing shallowly, the knives held upright. If they settled together by the door, he would have problems. If they went indoors, he would have to be wary. But his luck was running. Mouse was with him, a spirit of good fortune, 'cause the guards split, one going indoors and the other coming to the gable. *Tramp-thump, tramp-thump* of rubber-soled boots.

Doc didn't even bother to press himself against the wall. He just stood there until the guy was an arm's length away. Then Doc stepped right. The guy turned. Doc inserted the scalpel cleanly into the back of his neck and, at the same time, drew the blade of the *kris* across the gullet.

The guy gurgled and dropped his rifle with a clatter.

Doc kicked the rifle over the end of the verandah, bear-hugged the guy, turned him behind the gable and laid him – dead as pork – down.

The second armed guard came out of the bungalow.

He was small, with tiny hands. He had taken off his bush-shirt and wore a white crew-neck undervest. He had a bottle in his hand. Beer. The rifle was trailing in his left hand and looked too heavy for his skinny arms.

The guy said something; a name, a question.

Doc waited. He hadn't a chance to extract the scalpel which remained buried in the first guy's spine. He had the *kris*, though. That would be enough. When the little guard put his head round the corner, Greenwood took him neatly, pulling his head down into his chest and zig-zagging the heavy blade across the nape of his neck. Doc had no notion of just how juiced-up he was until he saw how he had nearly severed head from shoulders. He lowered the second guard to the boards and pulled him, too, round the corner, leaving a smear of blood like a slug trail in his wake.

Into the bungalow. Close the lightweight door. Take in the lantern.

Inside, nothing but guns, guns racked, guns packed. Three hundred pieces. Rifles and SMGs for the most part, Russian and Chink. Ammo too. And dynamite. Plain, honest-to-God dynamite. Not locked away. Not even stashed properly. In a British unit, even a guerrilla group, somebody would have been on the carpet for such gross negligence.

The rest of it was easy. Incredibly, unbelievably easy.

Doc Greenwood moved between the bungalows unchallenged, had all the time he needed. Kept the head, didn't rush. Used the rear windows of both buildings. Dynamite wrapped in Cordex fuse.

It took twenty minutes to set four bundles in the 'hospital' bungalow, another ten to place charges inside the arms depot. Before he fired the nubby fuse-ends, though, he carefully selected the personal weapons he would require. SMGs, clips galore, a basket of grenades packed in straw like avocados. He sheltered in the dirty strip of jungle that backed the encampment. All was done, everything ready; Doc took a breather. He popped another pep pill. When he came down out of it, he would be jangled, nerves twitching. But what the bleedin' hell would that matter? He had work to do now. Time to rest up later. He still hadn't given any thought as to how he would escape from the encampment. Slip quietly into the bush? Maybe. Maybe not. Perhaps he would just keep at them, picking the bastards off, notching up kill after kill until Mouse had been avenged, her life paid for, plus interest; a whole lot of fucking' interest, man.

Last thing Doc did, before lighting the fuses in each of the bungalows, was to stash the sax case where he could find it again. He had already selected the best fire position, one that would give him maximum cover and range. One that would the the *Leopard* into his sights. Yeah, he was not unmindful of the need to keep the *Leopard* in view. It was the *Clouded Leopard* that Arunja would come to meet his death on the end of a stream of bullets.

No matter what it took, Arunja would not survive.

Greenwood lit the fuses.

He has set them for three-minute separation. It wasn't enough. He got caught out, only just into the jungle. The first blast from the 'hospital' bungalow bowled him arse-over-tip. He shouted, the explosions covering the bellow of triumph that escaped his lips. He scrambled to his feet and raced for the guns, grabbed one into his hands and began firing.

Below, in the compound, guerrillas scattered, stumbling out

of boozy slumber, dazed and addle-brained and, Doc suddenly realised, caught for the most part unarmed.

Yeah, there might be a couple of hundred soldiers in Ukiti but whoever had been in command had seen to it that there weren't many weapons floating free. That was the clincher, the beautiful, unexpected factor that made what followed possible. The guys just didn't have firepower. The weapons stored in the bungalow would be issued daily for training. There would be knives and maybe bayonets out there but not a concentration of slugs. Perhaps the pirates and appointed guards had been issued with weapons. That was sure how it looked.

Two Chinese terrorists, bare-arsed naked, plunged in fear into the lagoon, ignoring the NCO who ordered them to return.

Surprise night attacks were terrifying experiences. Doc had been through a couple. You didn't know how many hands were against you or where they were. You didn't know nothin', man. Except that somebody was trying to plug you.

And those explosions, those deafening thunderclap detonations; boy, they would scare the pants off anyone, Indo or Chink, soldier or pirate. It would have been like this for the poor buggers up at the timber town, Balimbuka, if he hadn't got here, if Mouse hadn't sacrificed herself. Doc experienced fierce gladness in his heart, a sense of having done the right thing, of having become a warrior at last.

It was only when he saw spray fly up from the MTB's propellors and the boat begin to move that he recognised the situation of the men on its deck.

They weren't bloody Indos. They were Brits. Major Dalinart hadn't left him to rot. The SAS were everywhere they should be. Naturally.

He was not, after all, alone.

Boyd Goddard was afraid. He was not used to the emotion, to the uncertainty and physical tension that accompanied it. Jungle didn't frighten him, nor snakes, nor scorpions, nor belligerent natives, nor fear-crazed bandits with swords. He couldn't recall being afraid of the Japanese, not much at any rate. By God, though, he was afraid of the SAS officer nicknamed the Deke; Major Jeffrey Alexander Deacon.

Behind that particular foible lay a basic fear of failure. It was years, Boyd Goddard suddenly realised, since he had put himself into a simple win-loss situation, with his life positively on the line.

Unlike Deacon and Harper, Boyd Goddard did not revel in danger. He wanted to have the thing done, to be away, away home to Tawau again. But that wasn't possible. He remained in the waters of the lagoon surrounded by hostiles. As silently as he could, he stroked towards the Star. The Indonesian Navy had vessels like this in service but he hadn't encountered one with a pirate crew, thank God. Sulu junks and *padangkangs* were bad enough, being very slippery in the hands of a good crew. If Special Branch and Customs had had to contend with craft the equal of their own, however, crime along the coast would boom.

Boyd Goddard trod water.

He was not by nature a 'rusher', didn't hurry. He surveyed the deserted deck of the Star. It seemed squat compared with the raffish lines of the MTB behind him. He kicked gently with his legs, stroke-floating towards the stern. No doubt Major Deacon would be silently bellowing at him to get on with it. But to each his own, method-wise. Being methodical was ingrained in his nature. He could not change now.

Goddard was still some twenty yards short of the Star when the bungalows exploded and the shooting started.

He was startled, of course, but did not panic. He dipped his head beneath the surface and swam with strong strokes underwater until he reached the stern of the Star. He came up hard against its fender, the oak rim which ran around the hull of most river craft, dividing the deck from the plates. He could tell now that the Star had not been long in service. Boats in Borneo quickly collected a greenish slime which was as difficult to clean off as barnacles had been on the old men-o'-war. The hull of the Star was hardly discoloured at all. Goddard made this passing observation while the dynamite charges were thundering and bullets flying and debris whistling around like an air raid. Greenwood, of course. It couldn't be anybody other than the renegade SAS corporal who had blown up the bungalows and who was strafing the compound.

Treading water, nudging the fender with his shoulder, Goddard glanced behind him, just in time to see Deacon and the tracker clamber over the side of the *Leopard.*

Goddard grinned and shook his head. He felt less apprehensive now, fairly calm in fact. He paddled his legs while he dug the handgun in its oilskin pouch from his shirt. Using his teeth, he tugged off the rubber bands and unwrapped the Colt .45 Government Model automatic. He had preloaded four magazines and inserted one now into the butt. The other three he rewrapped in the oilskin and returned to his shirt. Holding the Colt out of the water, Goddard elbowed his head and shoulders over the edge of the fender.

Pirates were in charge. He could see two of them on the foredeck. They had rifles. One wore a traditional silk bandana around his brow and the other – ye Gods! – actually sported an eyepatch. Tough-looking customers, not too youthful. Whether there were other pirates in the tiny upright wheelhouse amidships, Goddard could not be sure.

Fortunately Eyepatch and his companion were distracted by the furore on shore. They probably supposed that they were under attack from raiders situated in the jungle to the east. They were skipping about on the deck trying to fix on a target. When they found one, Goddard assumed, they would man the cannon. In the meantime, however, the pair were confused. Goddard accepted the risk, dragged himself from the lake. His objective was the wheelhouse. But he must make sure that the boat was 'clean' of the enemy before he steered away from the shore to pick up the others. It was imperative now that he gain possession of the gunboat. With the guerrillas on the warpath the only certain means of escape from Ukiti would be by the Star.

Dripping wet, the policeman found cover in the nick of time. Three more pirates appeared from the wheelhouse. They were less colourful in sweatshirts and chino trousers, and were not, so far, armed. Star-class gunboats were not built to accommodate large crews. As far as Goddard could recall, sleeping accommodation was limited to eight berths. With the party or celebration on shore, Goddard doubted if there would be many men on board. Crouched by the ventilator cowl, Goddard already had five of the enemy in plain sight. Come to think of it, they weren't soldiers of a foreign power. They were criminals, the sort of fellows he had fought against for the last decade: Sulu pirates, Chinese bandits. What the devil was he waiting for?

Kneeling, Goddard grasped his right wrist in his left hand.

Aimed.

Fired.

Exceedingly methodical, he went for Eyepatch and Bandana first: they were armed. He shot both men, stayed on his knee, swung his arms, picked off two others. The third pirate went overboard in a kangaroo leap. Pausing only to cast off the stern rope, Goddard hastened for the wheelhouse, changed his mind, scuttled to the bow and cast off there too. When he turned back towards the wheelhouse, he found his way blocked by a sixth pirate.

The man was grizzled and squat, wore shorts. His legs were bowed. His complexion indicated that he was of Chinese origin. He bore a short, sickle-like boathook in one hand and a hank of rope in the other. Out of the corner of his eye Goddard caught the flash of an SMG from the compound and heard a clamour of shooting. Rifles singing high whining notes. Rivers of spilled fuel, burning thinly, hissed across the shore.

The Colt .45 held seven rounds. Goddard had fired five – or was it six? The Chinaman charged, slashing with the rope. Though he hadn't engaged in hand-to-hand combat for years, Goddard felt amazingly cool. He had one shot, possibly two. He kept his right hand tucked, elbow braced against his inner thigh. He swayed as the hank of rope *swooshed* within inches of his forehead. The pirate chap was enraged, actually had froth at the corners of his mouth. Goddard wondered if he had been snorting a drug or tippling raw alcohol. Feet splayed, the fellow pranced furiously on the spot, then darted in and chopped with the hook. With his forearm, Goddard parried the blow, deflecting it. He felt rather pleased with himself. Full of guile. He caught the pirate's shorts at the waist, yanked him on to the snout of the Colt and squeezed the trigger.

The muffled report sounded inadequate.

Goddard shoved the pirate. Arms raised, rope dropping and hook falling, the man slumped against the port rail. The entry would was comparatively small. But Goddard knew from experience that the chap's innards would have been blown out through his spine by such a close-range shot. He caught the man's calf and hoisted the corpse overboard, then sprinted for the wheelhouse as rifle shots from snipers somewhere on shore sought him out.

Inside the wheelhouse, Goddard fitted a fresh clip into the Colt then turned his attention to the controls. He had piloted in coastal waters on several occasions. He was not an expert seaman but the huge 'bicycle' wheel and throttle switch were obvious. Once he had the engines warmed and roaring and the propellors turning he would find the rest of it easy enough.

Two minutes later Boyd Goddard pulled the Star away from the jetty out into the lagoon.

It was not that he would go down without a fight. He was, after all, a man honoured for his courage and determination. He had come to Ukiti with the blessing of the Minister of Defence, a great gentleman who had personally sanctioned the raid upon the Jaumpong. But Arunja – who had no other name and hardly remembered his birthplace or his mother through a fog of appetites – had become a captain without a ship and without a crew. He was not dismayed. All along, in dim recesses of reason, he had known that he had reached high into the thorn tree, and risked a fall. He had not supposed, though, that he would be thwarted before he had an opportunity to demonstrate his strength, to make his mark upon the page of history.

Once, long long ago, he had been taken by the hand by Colonel Setusko into the captured port of Hong Sen and had seen there how even the Colonel bowed to a man they had called Mindanao, a pirate whose junks had taken the port for the Colonel. In the Post Office and Shipping House black-haired Mindanao had installed himself like an emperor, surrounded by all the booty that the port had given up. Even a boy like Arunja could understand that all of it belonged to the man called Mindanao who was named after the place from whence he'd come, as some famous pirates were called by the name of the sea or the wind. Colonel Setusko had given him over to Mindanao who smiled and offered his canned fruit and sweet drinks in bottles, while the soldiers deferred to the pirates and portered the port's treasures to spread before the great man. From that day forth Arunja had hungered to be the emperor of a town.

Spawned in a dry paddi by a native girl, fathered by a fisherman who had gone on his way under swift sail, conquest would atone for his origins. Arunja had little intelligence, only power and strength and a matchless inclination to violence, qualities which Mindanao recognised and valued.

Five years later Arunja had a ship of his own. And the impatience of a man possessed of a dream but no brains, only guile, lust and impetuosity. He was as fickle and as dangerous, even to himself, as the offshore winds of the Moro Gulf. He sought profit where he found it, not easily but rapidly, snatching chance without discernment – until he heard of the ransom of Kalabakan, the soldiers' camp at Ukiti and the navigability of the Jaumpong. He had peddled the concept – the dream – to the Indonesians at once. But once more he had been turned aside, as he had been so often in the past. He had never taken a town to sit in and be a tyrant, pampered in every whim, only villages and hamlets. He had seen the Chinese colonel as a threat, had got rid of him with an ambush and a piece of paper. Important men put store in pieces of paper. He had the boats to call his own, fast craft, well armed. He put *his* store in *them*, not in the future. He put store in his physical strength and in the force of random ambition. Yet it was random ambition which caused Arunja to run from Ukiti without a fight; to leap from the deck of the *Clouded Leopard* as the boat sucked out of reach.

Most of his crew had been wiped out by the soldiers. Arunja

was only dimly aware that they were British soldiers. He had sunk into a state of fretful urgency. The notion that one of those soldiers might seek to destroy him did not occur to the pirate captain. He had no drop of desire for revenge within him, only a desire to be free again, to begin again anew.

Arunja swam as Greenwood had done, along the line of the shore, fifteen or twenty yards out. He did not realise that the gunner in the jungle, the dynamiter of his dreams, was the skinny, sickly doctor. Greenwood had not been missed. To the pirate, the attack was a piratical attack, carried by weight of numbers. If he had lingered, observed, learned that there were but four men against him, plus the puny English doctor, he would not have bolted.

What Arunja observed, however, confirmed his initial impulse.

He was not in the least surprised to see the Star draw off from the jetty, and the *Clouded Leopard* shoot away at full throttle and turn and falter. He had lost possession, had been dispossessed.

But he had been clever enough to escape.

He reached the store and, dripping and unarmed, set off into the neck of the swamp, heading, inevitably, for the sea.

For Barry Greenwood the whole bloody caper had become almost too much to bear. He was hopping mad at the SAS – he was sure it *was* the Regiment: who else would be daft enough to make a raid thirty-five miles into Indonesia? – when he realised that they had stolen victory from him.

True enough, Major Dalinart wasn't to know he had his mind set on disembowelling a big Chink bastard, that he didn't give shit about the rest of the Indo assault group.

Doc held position in the shallow foxhole between the bungalows for as long as he could. When he glimpsed Arunja in the water, though, he nearly went crazy with frustration.

What tore Doc Greenwood apart was the fact that decency demanded that he stay put.

It would have been so easy to hop through the trees, wait for Arunja, pump him full of lead as he emerged from the lagoon.

So bloody easy, man. But there was a guy down there in the water, alive but injured. And the boats, obviously in the hands of SAS team members, were cavorting about and couldn't reach him. And the Indos, those who hadn't crawled off into the jungle or sprinted into the lake, had finally mustered a counter-attack.

The guy who'd come over the side of the MTB was flapping and splashing by the piles of the jetty. The MTB had thrashed away. Even as Greenwood hesitated, the Star chugged slowly from the shore. Sure, that was it. Nobble the boats. Once the boats were nobbled the rest was a bust. The surprise attack on Balimbuka was kicked on the head. It would take the CCO or the IBT, or whoever, months to set it up again. They sure as heck wouldn't trust pirates next time. They would have to devise a plan of their own, less daring and foolhardy, to sack the timber town and plug the Jaumpong river.

Greenwood felt no satisfaction. He was hardly aware that he had contributed towards the 'success' of the SAS operation, unaware that he had been the cause of it. He was wrapped up in killing, in the appeasement of a virulent sense of failure.

Missing the Mouse, missing the assurance, the innocence that had gone from him in the last dozen hours, Doc Greenwood was suspended in a vacuum of hatred.

Out of two hundred assorted Tigers, there were bound to be some who wouldn't snap a white flag to the mast-head, who weren't going to run-rabbit and scoot home. Some of these guys were professionals. Like professional soldiers the world over, they would be stirred into retaliation. What they lacked, thanks to the fact that the armoury had gone up in smoke, were weapons. Apparently, though, they had enough to mount a counter-thrust. Somebody at the far end of the compound had retained an ability to think clearly – girls and booze notwithstanding – and had gotten together the rifles and SMGs and had split the available manpower. They were pretty far away from Greenwood, but instinct and experience told him that they would be zoning in, that commando-type tactics might result in his being nabbed from behind.

Also, he had to take account of the guy by the jetty, a

hundred yards away. He was alone, wounded by the look of it, in sore need of aid; the one and only British uniform Greenwood had clearly identified. But he could see Arunja too. Arunja in the lake, a sheen of reflected light, the V-ripple around him.

The MTB was staggering out of control. The Star, which had been moving sedately towards the river, began a big curving sweep.

There was no fucking way Arunja could make a fast getaway. The big yellow bastard didn't have a chopper hidden in the bush. Greenwood snarled. He beat the butt of the SMG on the earth. He reached, snatched up the magazines and crammed them into his pocket, cursing, kicking, spitting-mad. Mad at himself. Mad at the reflex that made him behave like some shining lickspittle from the lower ranks. Fuck honour. Fuck loyalty. He wanted that Chink. Nothing else would do. Yet he couldn't abandon the SAS guy by the jetty, leave him to be riddled by bullets from the Indo guns.

Greenwood got to his feet. Behind him, flanking him, were the spluttering remains of the bungalows. All around, debris. Twisted weapons, shattered lengths of bamboo and strews of thatch. The corpses were further off, separated from the foxhole by pale ribbons of spilled fuel from the drums that Doc hadn't even known were there.

He took everything. Stuffing reels and grenades into his vest, rounds of live ammo into his trouser pockets. He slung one SMG over his shoulder and hoisted the other, standing now, standing in the scrape-pit that he had hidden in for the last ten minutes and that must be a focus for the Indos.

Bullets snapped and stammered around him, pocking the sand.

One last glance at the shape in the lagoon, the seal-head, the ripple.

Doc's eyes narrowed. He glared at the jetty.

'*Bastard*. BASTARD.'

Firing the weapon, Lance-corporal Greenwood ran to aid a stricken comrade, a man he had never met. And risked letting the Chink get away.

Dingo didn't feel too chirpy. He had a fair notion of what was wrong with his shoulder It wasn't the first time he had damaged a collar-bone. But what scared him was the fact that his bloody fin was useless. The big bloke had broken it and it was not only agonising but immobilised.

The shock of hitting the water robbed him of consciousness for a second or two. When he came out of the swoon he found himself lying on his side under the jetty, his lugs full of mud and his left arm trailing. When he tried to move, though, pain radiated into his neck.

Not on, Dingo, me old mate. You're not going to wrestle your way out of this 'un.

Rolling, he watched the MTB. It wasn't out of range yet. Hale and hearty, he would perhaps have pursued it. He could see Umgah on the deck, scanning the water. Umgah would tell the Deke where he was and the Deke would come back for him. But the MTB was dancing about like a dodgem. Major Jeffrey Alexander Deacon had finally lost it. Fast, powerful craft weren't thing s you could master in a minute. Skill, not will, had given out.

Rain-plops on the water an arm's length away. Rain-plops? Bullets! Some bright Tiger had his number, knew he wasn't dead. Dingo drew himself closer under the jetty.

What got him, really got him, was the fear that the massive Chink was also lurking in the drink, ready to drag him down and drown him. Wouldn't be too much he could do about it, not with one arm out of comission. He supposed he could just about fire a pistol, maybe a Sterling, if he could fiddle it into his right hand. But not while splashing about in brown liquid. Brown liquid was right. He was up to his neck in it in more ways than one.

Dingo didn't see Greenwood's charge across the open expanse of beach. Dingo was optimistically awaiting the return of the MTB. Maybe even the Star if Goddard had miraculously got control of the smaller vessel. Perspectives weren't so dusty at water level. The exertions of the past days crowded upon him in the wake of that period of blackout. To his chagrin he found that all he could do was hold on to the piles and waggle his legs a little.

He was still there when Greenwood reached him.

He heard the bloke's feet on the jetty then a Yorkshire accent, overlaid with a bizarre American drawl, bawling at him to come out.

Dingo cricked his neck, stared at the planks over his head.

'Greenwood?'

'Can't reach you in there, man.'

Dingo nudged himself away from the piles.

Lance-corporal Greenwood wasn't what he expected. For starters, he was pared to skin and bone. But it wasn't his physique or the straggling whiskers on his face that startled Dingo. It was the sheer naked ferocity that blazed in the young man's eyes.

'You wounded?'

Dingo found himself reluctant to yield up that piece of information to a stranger, even if the stranger was a member of 'K' Squadron. It would sound like whining, and Dingo Harper detested whiners.

'Talk to me, man.'

Greenwood was belly-down on the jetty.

Dingo realised that the promontory of logwood and bamboo was under fire.

Paddling, Dingo moved in-shore. His feet brushed sand. Obviously the beach shelved steeply here. He paddled hard, handing himself of with a fist to the posts, then standing, head, chest, belly above water. He squinted across the compound.

LIght in the air now, a coiling ectoplasmic mist in the forest. He could smell a sickly odour, like burning flesh. He sneezed, sneezed again. Every time he did, it felt as if somebody was ripping his arm out by the root. He caught his left wrist, dragged the arm down and held it stiff. Pain nearly conked him out again.

Greenwood was too busy to notice. Kneeling, the lance-jack was returning fire. And bloody how! He tossed the hot SMG to one side, jerked the second SMG from around his body, plugged in a magazine and whipped the distant reaches of the beach. Indos clustered like flies round dung about two hundred yeards away, tucked down by a couple of shacks, like privies. Dingo had no doubt that somebody among them would have sent out flankers. Greenwood couldn't hold them for long. The only way out of this fucking mess was by boat.

Backing, Greenwood kicked the first SMG towards Dingo.

Dingo took it in his right hand. The muzzle was almost too hot to handle. He stuck the muzzle under his left armpit and fumbled on the floor of the jetty for the magazine that Greenwood had disgorged from his clothing. Fitted it. Felt decidedly better.

'Get off of there, Greenwood,' Captain Harper shouted.

'Wha'?'

'Come in by me.'

'Bugger off! You badly wounded, man?'

Greenwood was off his rocker.

'*Get down here*,' Dingo yelled. '*Hear me, soldier*.'

Greenwood backed and lowered himself over the edge of the jetty. They were in crotch-deep water with the tail of the jetty to lean on. Dingo rested the SMG on the woodwork, cocked it and experimentally squeezed the trigger. Shots went off, wild as oats. He felt as if he had been electrocuted. It was so fucking unfair, a simple busted shoulder having this effect on him. A belly wound or a head wound, maybe. But to suffer incapacity because of a simple busted. . .

'Shoulder's gone,' Dingo shouted. 'Can you do something about it?'

'Are you kiddin'?' Greenwood shouted back.

Officer and lance-corporal glanced at each other.

Greenwood wasn't amused.

Then both MTB and Star entered the frame. Dingo had the unearthly feeling that the Deke, too, had gone loco and intended to grind him into the mushy dirt of Ukiti beach. The strangest thing of all was that he had felt no threat from the fifty or so armed guerrillas at the far end of the area. But he *was* fearful of the looming hull, sheer bows and thrashing props of the strike craft, and the Star's blunt prow, as the craft converged on the jetty.

'Jesus! Look behind you,' Dingo shouted.

'Yeah, yeah!' Greenwood answered at the top of his voice. 'They're comin' in for us, man. But they're not gonna get me.'

A splatter of fire over the boards of the jetty forced Dingo to duck. He stood there like a hunchback, trying to keep tension on the left arm, a procedure which seemed to reduce pain to a manageable trobbing, the SMG resting above him on the jetty. He swivelled and watched in horror as the torpedo-boat carved towards them.

Carved wasn't the right word for its motion. It came at an odd angle, one third broadside. And it came fast, though Deacon had finally cut the engines.

The Star glided down on them too but further off. Anyhow, who the hell was going to worry about the Star when the MTB was aimed at you, dead at you, approaching on a bow-wave strong enough to demolish a wall? This might be the all-timer, ultimate, super-de-luxe 'own goal'; not just an accidental, over-hasty slug in the gut on a dark night, but crushing a brother officer and a medical corporal to pulp with a hijacked torpedo-boat. Wait until that tale got around.

The bow-wave lofted over Dingo and the hull was right on top of him. He didn't have a chance to grab at the SMG. He flung himself on Greenwood, catching the young man around the throat and hauling, pulling and hauling, dragging and mashing his way through the shallows, away from the boat, Greenwood spluttering and yelling in the crook of his good arm. Isn't it absolutely amazing, old chappie, how suddenly you aren't suffering any pain at all, just one fat, indigestible lump of utter, all-out panic?

Dingo and Greenwood were swamped. Borne backwards, they were crushed against the sand slope on the volume of water cast forth by the MTB. Registration numerals and weird Chinese characters looked huge, like a hoarding, on the grey-painted metal sheets. Plates, rivets and welded joints were graphic in close-up. Then Dingo was on his back, flapping his arms, even the one in which he had no flexion. For a minute or so he didn't know whether he was drowning or dying of shock or what the bloody hell was happening to him.

The sweeping bows and keel shuddered into the jetty and ploughed on, snapping the piles, cracking posts and planking and bamboo infill, sending it in a crushed mass, like straw stalks, into the sand-silt. Shuddering, the *Clouded Leopard* ran around with more than enough momentum to scour through the jetty, destroying it totally, and ride her bow high over the debris before she came to a halt. After a pause, she listed steeply, settling on her plates, the lagoon lapping over the deck rail starboard and aft.

Vomiting lake water, Dingo surfaced. His eyes were teared with pain, bleary with sediment. He groped with his right hand and touched. . .what? He kneaded his eyes with his knuckles. Stared. Touched the bloody boat. Touched the hanging rim of deck and hull. Thirty inches and he would have been stamped beneath it, squashed like a mosquito. Dingo crabbed backwards, dragging his legs away from the monster lest it settle again, heel right over. Back scraped on the beach. He kicked. He came on to his bum, sitting up. He felt as if his face was encased in ice, frozen in an expression of terror and disbelief. And then the Deke was at the rail, only six or eight feet away, leaning against the angle of the deck, shouting.

'Are you all right, Dingo? Dingo, are you wounded?'

'I. . .'

The Dyak came over the side, a step, no more, and waded to him. Dingo felt the old man's hands on him. They still managed to be as light as leaves even in that moment. Dingo left himself go, let Umgah direct him, support him over the edge of the deck. It was ramped at an angle of about fifty degrees. Finally he got his good arm locked around the stanchion of the LMG and hauled himself upright, partly protected now by the *Leopard's* superstructure. Gunfire from the south end of the compound seemed remote.

'Is it serious?' Deacon crouched by him, gripping the gun's upright too.

'Shoulder, that's all.'

'Fit enough to help?'

'Help. . .do. . .do what, boss?'

'Send out a radio message.'

'I. . .'

'Good.'

'I. . .'

'Then we'll blow up this beast.'

'Blow. . .how. . .?'

'Grenades in the engine room. Anything and everything we can scrounge to create damage. Are you capable?'

'I'm capable.'

'I want this boat rendered totally unseaworthy.'

'And the radio message, boss?'

'Ask for a chopper pick-up on the Tabuli. Noon today.'

'Got you, boss,' Dingo Harper said. 'Listen, Greenwood was with me a couple of minutes ago.'

'I'll find Greenwood, never fear.'

But Deacon did not find Greenwood, not in the lake nor on shore.

There was no trace of the medic to be found. Doc had vanished once more.

Greenwood didn't give a good goddamn whether he was court-martialled or not. He could always claim that he was concussed, struck by the *Leopard* as it was grounded by the officer. He wasn't confused, of course. Not in the least. He'd never been less confused. He knew where he was going. After Arunja.

Mist gave excellent cover. It was a whisper before dawn and rain followed by humidity brought mist creeping from the swamp and across the bosom of the lake. It didn't come in a bank like fog but just suddenly seemed to be there, standing on the surface of the water. In the trees it clung dankly to leaves. In the underbrush it rolled stealthily towards the *lalang*, into the broad mists of the Tabuli. Lagoon and river, forest and swamp were linked by mists which swiftly consumed all sight of the boats and made the gunfire woolly and eventually smothered it.

Greenwood had dived deep when the *Leopard* grounded; away from the jetty. He had done what he could for the Australian officer. It was a desperate situation, anyhow. Either the boat was going to get him or it wasn't. Either way there was nothing Greenwood could do about it.

He had to look out for himself. Had to get away.

After Arunja.

He'd surfaced about twenty yards from the jetty. Nobody was on the scout for him, not at that moment. Every eye in Ukiti was drawn to the sight of the MTB battering into the jetty like a bloody torpedo.

Mist layered the shore line, thin for a yard or two, soon shrouding. In twenty minutes or so the entire lagoon would be invisible. Since Doc had no weapon – like Dingo, he'd jettisoned the SMG – he went first to the place in the trees where he'd stowed the saxophone case. He knelt beside it. Opened it. Hesitated. Maybe he could take it with him, that 'friend', that talisman, that long-time companion. He'd never travelled in the Borneo jungle without it, though it was an awkward shape and cumbersome. He smoothed the torn surface of the case with his hand, then, biting his lip, quickly selected items from it. He took the caffeine-based pep pills.

And he took the knives.

Shiny, flexible, surgical knives. Two of them.

Everything else he left behind.

Closing the case he pushed it under a stunted fern. Never can tell, Barry, perhaps you'll come back for it some day.

From the lagoon, now drowned in mist, came the sound of cannon; the *Leopard*'s guns firing. Some bright spark in the SAS team obviously knew more about armaments than he did about driving an MTB. The remnants of the Indonesian assault group would have no chance of mounting an attack against the boats, even if they had the will and some hard-nosed NCOs spurring them on. With the machine-guns on the Star and cannon on the *Leopard*, a handful of SAS guys could hold off the hordes of Attila, never mind a bunch of hung-over Indonesian pirates.

At that moment, only for a moment, a question entered Greenwood's troubled mind – why were the SAS here at all? His earlier assumption that they had come to 'rescue' him no longer seemed valid. Had they known of the encampment, of the Chinaman's idiotic plan to invade the timber towns of the Jaumpong? Forty miles into Indonesia, they were risking the escalation of an 'incident'. But, yeah, it was a typical hairy manoeuvre, one of those discreet, small-scale operations that SAS teams are occasionally encouraged to attempt and which would receive no publicity at all.

But not for him. Nope, they hadn't come in for one lousy, conceited medic who had gone rogue.

They wouldn't mind if he buggered off.

After Arunja.

Greenwood knew exactly what he was doing. His motives might be downright crazy but his method was sound. No way would the SAS team – however large, however small – be able to come after him now. It would be Shoot-and-Scoot with a vengeance. They would destroy the boats and retreat towards a rendezvous with a chopper up-river somewhere.

Greenwood didn't fear for the safety of his comrades back at Ukiti.

The slamming of the 20mm gun was the last positive sound he heard as he struck into the forest, north-east for the Tabuli and the sea.

After Arunja.

Boyd Goddard was enjoying himself at last. His apprehension had waned with the beginning of proper action. Now that he was at the helm of the Star and everything was running comparatively smoothly, his methodical temperament shone. He had been jolly glad to see the MTB run aground. It made him feel insecure to watch it buzzing around the lagoon.

The episode would bring the cold-eyed major down to earth with a bump, puncture his arrogance a little. Goddard felt slightly smug at the contrast between his own ability to handle a sea-going craft and Major Jeffrey Alexander Deacon's ham-fistedness.

Once the *Clouded Leopard* was thoroughly beached, however, the rest of the procedure soon fell into place.

The enemy were hardly worth their salt. Lord knows what had been going on the previous night. For men who were supposed to be trained in jungle warfare the denizens of the encampment at Ukiti were hopeless. Quite, quite hopeless.

Boyd Goddard touched the controls lightly.

The Star was a sweet-running little boat, almost identical to one of a pair that patrolled the beat from Kudat to Tawau. Inshore craft. With a bit of sprint speed, but not rapid. He had been on several hauls with Special Branch. Interceptions of Bajau fishing craft suspected of smuggling arms. Made a couple of fat captures too, both without bloodshed. The sight of the guns was usually enough to put the wind up the wily Bajau.

In the little wheelhouse, Boyd Goddard was completely at home. He found a packet of cigarettes in the bridge locker and stuck on in his holder and lighted it. All the comforts. The fag was of Indo manufacture and tasted terrible. But beggars can't be choosers.

Methodically, Goddard held the Star in position fifty or sixty yards offshore to the rear of the grounded MTB. He had an excellent view of the proceedings, rather gratifying proceedings at that, with Indo resistance pinned down and Mad Major Deacon manning the cannon. Something the major did with considerable expertise, Goddard noted.

It did not take Deacon long to do what he had to do.

As mist coagulated in the palms and claimed the nether region of the lagoon, Goddard heard the first explosions in the grounded craft; deep inside the hull, tinny, but of sufficient force to shift the *Leopard* upon the sand. Deacon would not be able to render the MTB totally unserviceable, not, that is, until he had pulled himself and the men under his command off. The guns on the Star would finish the job from a safe distance.

Minutes later, Goddard saw the Dyak upon the aft deck, waving his arms: a signal.

Grinning, the SB officer rolled the wheel between his fists, levered more power through the gunboat's engines and brought the vessel closer to the *Leopard*. Bands of white mist stretched along the shore, mingling with cauliflower clouds of smoke and debris that the cannon sent up. The scene reminded Goddard of ancient battles, skirmishes against Japanese-held positions when the use of light artillery had been enough to turn a victory.

Goddard took the holder from his mouth, tapped out the

cigarette and trod on it. He nosed the Star alongside the stern of the *Leopard*, barely holding off. There would be lots of water to support a shallow-draught craft. He scanned the deck. The Dyak came first, still brandishing his infernal spear.

Umgah hesitated. Goddard nudged the Star closer still. The old tracker clamboured directly from one boat to the other.

The for'ard cannon on the *Leopard* boomed.

The Australian came next. He was soaked and wounded, held his left arm with his right hand. The expression on his face told Goddard that he was in intense pain. Through the open window of the wheelhouse Goddard shouted to the Dyak to help Harper. But Harper needed no assistance. He must be running on raw nerve by now, Goddard thought, as the Australian swarmed over the stern and jumped on to the Star. Goddard had no need to issue instructions. Captain Harper was well aware of what he must do before he collapsed – cover the Deke's retreat from the *Leopard*. Australian and Dyak manned the gun in the Star's bow. Seconds later, Goddard's eardrums were blasted with its unholy chatter.

The Indos had no chance to make a last-minute bid to storm the boat.

Of Arunja there was no sign. Of the emergence of another leader among the pirates – nothing.

The Dyak acted as loader, the Australian as marksman. The twin-stocks of the LMG were under his arms, and he steadied it with his body. God knows what the vibration was doing to his injured arm. But that was Dingo Harper, Goddard supposed, a sterling example of the 'new breed' of Special Force soldier, men who would not shirk their duty no matter the cost in personal suffering.

Bare-headed, white hair like a coxcomb, face gaunt with fatigue, Deacon ran from the cover of the *Leopard*'s deck-house. He carried a shotgun but nothing else. He vaulted the stern on to the foredeck of the Star, under the muzzle of Harper's gun. The officers conversed in shouts and gestures, then Deacon turned and signalled to the wheelhouse.

Goddard didn't loiter. He slammed power through the gunboat, added another deafening note to the racket outside.

He trolled the craft along the shore and backed her round. Dipping his knees, he peered through the glass at the washed grey-white trees receding into the enveloping mist.

It *had* been a bloody battle. He hadn't realised quite how much damage the SAS officers had inflicted in the course of the brief raid. Dead and wounded strewed the beach. The compound was pock-marked with craters. Drifting brown smoke from the stumps of the bungalows and tongues of jetted fuel stirred into the mist. And, dominating all else, the *Leopard* lay stranded on the beach amid wreckage of the jetty like a gigantic shark, smoke seeping from her ports and through the fin-like vent on her deck. Undoubtedly it was beyond the ability of the Indo crew, those that had survived, to make the craft seaworthy again.

Four shells soared out of the 20mm cannon and completed the destruction of the *Clouded Leopard*. Each of them was dead on target. It was Deacon who had sighted, who had taken range, who had fired the weapon.

Harper sagged from the mounted machine-gun, hung on it, watching. The expression on his face was one of pleasure, hardly warped by the pain of his injury.

Borneo – Indonesia – jungle; in ten minutes the mist would claim this isolated pocket of swampland, would swallow Ukiti up. Before the Star had nosed out of the lagoon, the inimitable, primitive effusions of land and climate would obliterate the carnage, claim another bloody secret for its own.

Deacon pushed open the wheelhouse door.

The major was drenched with sweat, his clothing saturated.

'Harper put out a radio message.'

'Was it received?' Goddard asked.

'Yes,' said Deacon. 'Dalinart has promised a chopper.'

'When?'

'Noon today.'

'That's only five hours from now. Where?'

'In the area of Palan.'

'The pilot should be able to pick us up on the river,' said Goddard. 'He's a very good pilot. What's wrong with Harper?'

'Collar-bone. Painful but not too serious. Are you all right?'

'Never better, old man. Never better.'

'All right,' Deacon snapped, still tight with excitement. 'It's up to you get us out of here. Find the exit into the Tabuli and head up river.

'What about the medic: Greenwood?'

Deacon paused. 'I don't know about Greenwood. I assume he's dead.'

'Aren't you sure?'

'No.'

'In that case,' said Goddard, 'couldn't we risk—?'

Deacon shook his head. 'So far, Goddard, we've been incredibly lucky.'

'Indeed, indeed.'

'We daren't push our luck too far.'

'Of course not,' Goddard said. 'Job done?'

'Job done,' Deacon said. 'Now. Out.'

'Aye-aye, sir,' Goddard muttered, and coaxed the Star towards the strip of *lalang* where the channel lay, and the start of the long haul home.

Greenwood moved fast. He was reasonably confident that there would be no Tigers or pirates – Holy Moses, didn't it sound like a kids' game, one of those airy-fairy games little folk in silly novels play? – none of the enemy in that quarter of the jungle. The soldiers would have been driven south, away from the Tabuli, by the burning bungalows and the rest of it, would reckon that that's where the task force was positioned. Task force. Some bleedin' task force. One skinny no-hoper of a medic.

If Mouse had been with him, been alive in body as well as spirit, he would have been chuffed to fuck about it all. Would have been crowing and exultant right now. Would have relished the chase. She would have an' all, the Mouse. She liked a bit of excitement, a bit of danger. You'd think a girl born in a jungle hut would prefer comfort to danger. Not Mouse. Not her. He had been closer to Mouse than to anyone. Chittering and chattering in that made-up, polyglot language.

Their language. Christ, it had been a naïve relationship.

Talk about games? Doctors and nurses. Tarzan and Jane. Cowboys and bleedin' Indians. He had loved every minute of it. But it had all been pretend. Mind you, man, he reckoned some hard-arsed bastards in the Regiment were up to the gills in fuckin' games too. Tough-guy games. Do-or-die. Rockfist Rogan, John Wayne and Burt Lancaster given a lick of reality by tradition and the need for war. Chubby wee Barbara Badillo, over there in the sunshine of America's West Coast, what sort of games did she play? Dreaming of peace and good fellowship and love, ready to drop her panties to prove the point, snorting coke or whatever to hold truth and harsh reality at bay.

Doc Greenwood halted, his shoulder against a sapling.

The tree was young enough to be graceful, out of place in the rough, rotting timber of the *belukhar*. Clean. Like the mist was clean. New every morning, man. Used to hear that on the wireless, lying in bed waiting for the old man to shout to him that his cornflakes were getting soggy. Soggy cornflakes and New Every Morning and the canvas bags full of cat-tray litter.

Doc Greenwood put another pep pill in his mouth.

It tasted bitter.

Bitter as sin. Bitter as his need for revenge.

You could worm your way into a helluva lot of trouble when you started to monkey with revenge.

Tigers and Pirates and the Mouse.

I don't know what I'm doing here now, pretending to be a man.

Chinks and tigers and pirates. Rape and murder and war. Yeah, yeah, man! I never had the right kind of innocence to begin with. But take what there was away and I've nothing left. Only revenge.

Doc Greenwood moved on, slipping through the trees on his bare feet, vest and trousers clinging to him like snakeskin. All his senses – if not his reason – were tuned into the jungle.

Mist boiled off the surface of the Tabuli. The *lalang* stood in water. Water up to the tip of his penis. Water alive with leeches ready to suck his blood. They were welcome. He stopped, upright as a squirrel, listening.

The gunboat's engine was unmistakable, beating slow, slow and steady and methodical. One of the super-competents of the SAS raiding party would be navigating it through the channel.

He couldn't have done it, couldn't have handled a fast gunboat, not even in a lake. Could have found the channel for them, though. Could have stood in the bow and called instructions about the flow. Let's face it, Barry, any recruit could do that.

He listened.

The boat couldn't have been more than fifty, sixty yards to his left, nosing through the channel's blonde grasses and mist-wreathed undergrowth.

He waited, motionless.

He didn't want *them* to rumble him, either.

They had done their work. They would be on their way back to Tawau, back to base. He, Lance-corporal Barry Greenwood, still had his work to do.

Squatting, he took out the surgical knives and laid them on his knees. They looked flimsy; one was short, with a broadish sort of blade, the other only slightly longer. He had used both in the operation on the Chinese VIP. They were used to blood. Used to slicing through tissue. Hunters in Mouse's village had talked to their spears, coaxing them with ancient spells to seek out the fattest bucks and plumpest does. They talked to the dogs, too. Making extravagant promises.

The gunboat was gone, wrapped in the silence.

Greenwood put the knives back in his pocket and pushed on. He had this strange feeling that he wasn't the only one in this neck of the woods who'd heard the engines receding into silence.

It was weird in the forest, swamp country with hunched mangroves and thorn and fever trees and stubby gargoyle-like palms. Only towards the bank of the Tabuli, where there were shoals of earth, did trees grow taller, soaring towards the sky. But the mist cut everything down to size. Mist webbing the shrubs. Mist entangled in the leaves. Mist across the bosom of the water.

Doc Greenwood hadn't expected to pick up a trail. Hadn't even been looking for one. An hour out of Ukiti, on a kind of broken path on the southern bank of the Tabuli, however, he stumbled across a sign, an unmistakable mark. It proved, that roll of warm human excrement, that Arunja did not know he was being followed. Not even Arunja would be that careless.

How come Doc knew it was Arunja? Because the guys at Ukiti had scoured out the natives. No tribesmen would be hunting this close – couple of miles – to the encampment, not with word coming down river about razed villages, enslaved girls and looting.

This was dead country, dead for miles.

The column of human excrement had been dumped fresh by the side of the path.

Greenwood trembled.

Until that moment he had merely been pushing on, pushing forward, depending on chance, luck, fate, any of those old standbys, to bring him to Arunja. But now it was up to him. The Chink *was* heading east along the bank of the Tabuli. It would only be a matter of time until he, Doc, caught up with him.

It was sometime around mid-morning. Greenwood had lost account of time. He was torn, his feet bleeding, leeches attached to his body under his pants. He had taken no respite, had pushed on, almost as if Mouse were dragging him by the hand. Around mid-morning he came suddenly on Arunja.

The path had petered out about a half-mile back. Distance was irrelevant. Direction was dictated by the Tabuli, the current forceful after yesterday's rain. Much of the mist had evaporated, for the sun was struggling to become visible through the leaves in waves of steamy heat.

Greenwood had been walking in a kind of trance, tense though. The ingrained habits of the past months were working for him, though he didn't will them to. Shuffle, pick step, part leaves, bend branch. Shuffle, crouch, rubber-kneed, head peering this way and that, like a nervous pheasant.

That's what you look like, Greenwood, Sergeant Stewart had bawled at him, once, *a fuckin' nervous pheasant*. It had raised a laugh. Sergeant Stewart had told him to *straighten up, smarten up, shape up, you 'orrible little reptile.*

But not now. Not here. Here, the best thing to be was a reptile, a crawling, creeping serpent.

Arunja.

The man was to Greenwood's left, fifteen or twenty yards away. If the disposition of the underbrush had been different the lance-corporal would have slipped past, would have missed the quarry completely. He, Doc, could not claim to have tracked the Chinese pirate down. Simply to have stumbled upon him.

Greenwood stopped, stock-still.

Arunja was by the river's edge. He had a raft. He hadn't built the raft. He had found it. Probably he had been on the scout for a canoe or a big log or some means of crossing the fast-flowing, heavy-brown-water Tabuli. Greenwood had no notion of what went on in the head of the tusk-yellow animal, a guy who could humiliate, who could evolve plans that seemed logical and reasoned but which were incredibly stupid at root, a guy who could break the neck of a native girl and make love to a corpse; a guy who could turn tail and flee at the first sign of trouble.

Quivering, holding his breath, Doc Greenwood lowered himself to his knees, then on to his hands, on to his belly. He touched aside the coarse stems of grass. There were ants by his thumb, only a few, stragglers from the nest. Beneath a fern frond was a blood-red slug. Greenwood paid no attention to any of these unpleasant manifestations of profligate Nature.

He concentrated on Arunja.

The pirate was working hard, feverishly, in fact, on repair of the fish-raft. It was one of those practical, primitive tools that abound in Borneo; a useful thing but simple. An oblong of cut bamboo lashed to two cork-tree logs, the whole thing held together by vine-creeper.

God knows, it looked as if it had been in the river for weeks. Soggy, battered, bamboo poles barely adhering to the base logs, all askew as if it had been crushed by elephants. This was what the master of the *Clouded Leopard* was reduced to. Yeah, there was some small satisfaction in the sight of his desperation.

Greenwood thought: when it's all boiled down, you can give the savages high military technology, whether it be diesel-powered MTBs, bazookas or guided missiles, but when the situation gets tough, when the carapace cracks, the bastards will return to what they know, to the spear and the stone axe, the arrow, the fire and the raft.

Letting air glide into his lungs, Greenwood moved closer.

He was strung out now, strung between physical collapse and brilliant clarity of mind. He had found the man who killed Mouse. But the murder of the girl was only part of it. By a fusion of chance and intention, Greenwood felt that he had located the black heart of evil, the Genie of All Mischief that plagued all men, brown, yellow and white; the Genie of neglect and ignorance and greed.

As he watched Arunja fumble to cobble the raft together again, Doc recalled the long *patun* that Mouse sang. He never twitted the kid about her superstitions, her charms and prayers and chants, least of all that one.

He had learned it by rote, and as Mouse crooned and whined through its irregular verses, Doc Greenwood repeated it silently to himself, for himself, that prayer against 'mischiefs', against the force of the evil principle which inhabilts all things.

As he lay above the river, with Arunja below him, Doc's lip moved.

Let my prayer be sharper than steel,
Swifter than lightning,
Fleet as the wind,
My neutralising charm louder than thunder.
May the Upas tree lose its venom.
May the poison lose its venom.
May the sea-snake lose its venom.
May the poison-tree of Sabah lose its venom.
May that venom all be mine, to neutralise the Black Genie,
To fight the Black Genie, with the black spleen,
black liver, black lungs, and a heart of bone.

Deliver me safe from the Black Genie.
Let the venom be gone.

Doc slipped the longer knife into the palm of his right hand and got to his feet.

Broad back flexed, the Chinese pirate tugged at the vine knots, drawing the loose poles together. Across the crown of his shoulder, Doc could make out the weal of the bullet. If only he hadn't missed up there at Palan. But if he hadn't missed, the rest of it wouldn't have followed and the killing wouldn't have counted. Yeah, that was it. It had to count. Black genie or yellow devil, it had to count. There had to be venom in the soul, permeating the spirit.

Greenwood nodded. He was high, high, high. Caffeine, maybe? Killing, yeah! But he understood it. He had found truth.

Arunja stiffened. Not turning. His hands came away from the vine. He sensed a presence in his heart of bone.

Greenwood sprang.

The Chink whirled. In his hands was a length of bamboo. The end formed a wedge where a tribesman's axe had chopped across it, a bevelled chisel-like edge. Jutting upwards. Doc reared in mid-air, dropped on mist-slicked grass and slithered down a mud bank on to the spit where the river lapped.

He had blown it. Fuckin' blown it. Not *enough* venom, maybe. Not *enough* poison.

The bamboo stave ribboned his breast with blood, tearing the vest from his neck. Doubling up his knees, Doc dove under the flail. He was between Arunja's legs when the bamboo struck him again, not like a spear, like a whip. He felt the fierce, hot pain of bone breaking – a rib. But he had knives and knowledge and hatred again. He drew the little blade across the backs of the man's ankles, two savage slashes, severing the Achilles tendons.

He heard the guy shout. Nothing more for an instant. Doc flung himself forward like a lizard, rolled and rose.

The bamboo stabbed into his calf, puncturing the muscle.

Now Greenwood could see his enemy clearly. Arunja looked as if he had been chained to the ground. Twisting and swaying, slashing with the pole, he was striving to keep balance, while blood oozed from the deep, neat cuts above his heels. His body was top-heavy, all muscle. His arms bulged as he fisted the air, trying to hold himself upright. But he fell nonetheless, crashed down, sending mud spattering, back and shoulders on the raft, mouth agape.

The bamboo rod was held across his breast. Instinct told him what to expect next. Doc did not disappoint him. Doc went for the throat, a surgical knife in each fist.

One bayonet, one dagger, a single moment's patient consideration and the medic could have finished the giant by thrusting a stout blade into his belly or chest. But he did not find that moment. The best he could do was straddle the Chink's torso, fight down against the bamboo rod and punch, punch, punch with both fists into Arunja's sides, making the Chink grunt with each scissoring motion.

The raft, inched off the clinging mud by the violence of the struggle, floated free, carrying both men out into the current.

River water slapped over Arunja's face, making him gag. He had enormous strength, however, and exercised it by extending the pole upwards and bringing it down behind Greenwood's neck. Snapping his face into slopping water, Doc was pinned against the pirate's chest. The tautness plunged the raft deeper into the water. It floated, though, of its own volition, whirling heavily, while the two men lay upon it in a deadly embrace.

Crushed, Greenwood's nose began to fill not with water but with blood. His mouth, smeared against flesh, was closed by his lips and the drag of his cheek. He could take in no breath at all. The bone-hard length of bamboo collared him, pressing upon his nape, cutting off the blood to his brain. He sensed the finality of it, how the man would kill him slowly, not breaking his neck casually as he had done to Mouse, but grinding the life out of him inch by inch. Once he lost what vestige of consciousness remained, the Black Genie would have resisted him, defeated him. He would die with venom eating at his soul.

Shit, Barry. Shit! His hands were free. The little stainless steel knives, designed to perform the filigree work of surgery, pressed into his fingers. Razor-sharp. he centred his mind as the raft wallowed and brown water boiled over them both. He could not see Arunja now, but he could smell and taste him, tasting and smelling flesh, the earthy river, the blood that stained the wavelets, pumping from wounds in Arunja's sides. Could not see how Arunja's eyes were closed, mouth pressed shut to keep out the water. Could not see the whiteness of Arunja's knuckles gripping the ends of the pole.

The singing in Greenwood's ears was like a chant, a *patun*, insect-whining, high, high and thin. In his lungs unexpelled air turned leaden.

Skinny, damaged, incomplete, Greenwood spread his arms, pressing by a less than measurable degree the pole away from his neck. Not enough to breathe. Enough to lift his forearms one inch.

The raft rode smoothly on the current, rushing forward.

The motion soothed Greenwood. He was almost gone, nine-tenths dead, but suddenly he was comfortable. He needed a split-second's peace, so that he could do what he had planned in the breathless cell of his brain in blind darkness.

He punched the surgical knives into the sides of Arunja's neck. Deep, deep through the carotid sheath. And with a snapping gesture of the wrist, slashed arteries and internal veins.

The knives slipped from his fingers. The knives dwindled down into the river, spinning like silver fish-lures.

Greenwood lay motionless.

How deep was penetration? How accurate his placement? He needed ten seconds' worth of competence to ensure his survival now.

Arunja twitched.

The pressure of the pole on Greenwood's neck slackened very slightly.

Doc slid his cheek across his teeth, sipped breath, blew out stale air and sipped again. The watery air ached in the cavities of his skull. Then the pressure was gone, the pole released.

The Chink surged orgasmically, quivered, sagged, died.

Greenwood twisted his head, ear against breastbone,

listening. No heartbeat, no sound but emptiness.

Unable to find strength to shift the weight of Arunja's arms, Doc rested, composed now and at peace, while the raft supported him and the tug of the current gathered him and rushed him heedlessly out of the swamp-land towards the open sea.

Fiction

☐	**Options**	Freda Bright	£1.50p
☐	**The Thirty-nine Steps**	John Buchan	£1.50p
☐	**Secret of Blackoaks**	Ashley Carter	£1.50p
☐	**Hercule Poirot's Christmas**	Agatha Christie	£1.50p
☐	**Dupe**	Liza Cody	£1.25p
☐	**Lovers and Gamblers**	Jackie Collins	£2.50p
☐	**Sphinx**	Robin Cook	£1.25p
☐	**Ragtime**	E. L. Doctorow	£1.50p
☐	**My Cousin Rachel**	Daphne du Maurier	£1.95p
☐	**Mr American**	George Macdonald Fraser	£2.25p
☐	**The Moneychangers**	Arthur Hailey	£2.50p
☐	**Secrets**	Unity Hall	£1.75p
☐	**Black Sheep**	Georgette Heyer	£1.75p
☐	**The Eagle Has Landed**	Jack Higgins	£1.95p
☐	**Sins of the Fathers**	Susan Howatch	£3.50p
☐	**The Master Sniper**	Stephen Hunter	£1.50p
☐	**Smiley's People**	John le Carré	£1.95p
☐	**To Kill a Mockingbird**	Harper Lee	£1.95p
☐	**Ghosts**	Ed McBain	£1.75p
☐	**Gone with the Wind**	Margaret Mitchell	£3.50p
☐	**Blood Oath**	David Morrell	£1.75p
☐	**Platinum Logic**	Tony Parsons	£1.75p
☐	**Wilt**	Tom Sharpe	£1.75p
☐	**Rage of Angels**	Sidney Sheldon	£1.95p
☐	**The Unborn**	David Shobin	£1.50p
☐	**A Town Like Alice**	Nevile Shute	£1.75p
☐	**A Falcon Flies**	Wilbur Smith	£2.50p
☐	**The Deep Well at Noon**	Jessica Stirling	£2.50p
☐	**The Ironmaster**	Jean Stubbs	£1.75p
☐	**The Music Makers**	E. V. Thompson	£1.95p

Non-fiction

☐	**Extraterrestrial Civilizations**	Isaac Asimov	£1.50p
☐	**Pregnancy**	Gordon Bourne	£3.50p
☐	**Jogging From Memory**	Rob Buckman	£1.25p
☐	**The 35mm Photographer's Handbook**	Julian Calder and John Garrett	£5.95p
☐	**Travellers' Britain**	Arthur Eperon	£2.95p
☐	**Travellers' Italy**	Arthur Eperon	£2.50p
☐	**The Complete Calorie Counter**	Eileen Fowler	80p